THE MYSTERY OF SORROWS

A Barkow Novel

THE MYSTERY
OF SORROWS

Archie J. Hoagland

To Sarah,
my favorite granddaughter!
Love,
Grandpa
Archie

The Mystery of Sorrows: A Barkow Novel

Published by Wheatmark®
1760 East River Road, Suite 145, Tucson, Arizona 85718 U.S.A.
www.wheatmark.com

ISBN: 978-1-62787-085-6 (paperback)
ISBN: 978-1-62787-084-9 (ebook)
LCCN: 2013955427

To Agnes Jeanette—my soul mate, wife, and best friend

CONTENTS

PART ONE: ASSEMBLAGE

PART TWO: CONVERGENCE

PART THREE: TERMINATION

Part One

ASSEMBLAGE

IN THE BLUE NOTE NIGHTCLUB

APRIL 23, 2012, MONDAY, 10:32 P.M.

GEORGE BENNET BARKOW was referred to as Barkow—just Barkow—never George or GB or Ben or Bennet. His life was one of solitude, tinged with sadness. Women were attracted to him, although he had no desire to form a personal relationship with them. Somewhere in his past, he had built an invisible, boiler-plate shell of protection around himself. His eyes were set beneath a confident brow, giving the impression he was analyzing whomever, or whatever, he had turned his attention upon.

At times a strange, unbidden music ran rampant in his mind. He did not comprehend from where the melancholy melody came or why. When crucial, a sudden pitched sound warned him of impending danger. A high-pitched note had just exploded in his brain.

Barkow slammed the glass down hard. *Ka-rack!* Bourbon and ice splattered across the table as creases of anger slashed between his narrowed eyes. His chair fell over backward as he stood up to glare at Bert, the man tending bar. Two men striding between the regulars talking or laughing quietly among the tables and across the empty dance-floor broke into his line of sight. He stepped away from the table onto the polished wooden floor just as the first man grimly smiled, displaying tobacco-stained teeth as he approached. Behind him, the other thug veered to attack from a different angle. *Divide and conquer* flashed across Barkow's mind.

The first one quickened his pace. "C'mere, piss-ant."

Barkow shifted left and drove a hard right fist into the man's solar plexus. The thug's eyes opened wide as the air swooshed

3

from his chest. A left hook smashed his jaw, breaking bone and loosening teeth. In the next instant, Barkow kicked the other thug's kneecap, inducing a forward lurch. The second kick crushed the man's nose.

Both would-be attackers lay on the dance floor, one sucking air through a damaged mouth, the other whimpering and bleeding profusely from the pulpy remains of his face.

The bartender rushed up. "I called an ambulance and the cops."

Barkow straightened his jacket. "All right, give this to them and point out where I'm sitting." He handed the man his business card, then walked back to his table, righted his chair and sat down. A faint rhythm, like distant background music, accompanied his thoughts as he stared at what remained of his drink. A question hovered in his mind: *Why in hell would anyone slip me a Mickey Finn?*

Across the room, a woman rose from her table with feline gracefulness. Barkow thought of Mary, the love he could not have. The woman walked slowly toward the exit with chin up, shoulders back, arms moving slightly at her sides; innuendo swayed in hips that rolled with each slow, drawn-out step.

A brutish man in a tight suit, his arms too long for the sleeves, followed. As they reached the beaded entrance to the lounge, two uniformed police officers brushed past them, entering. The woman paused a moment and stared at Barkow, who simply gazed back. She slowly raised a finger to her mouth, smoothing away an imaginary smudge of lipstick, her blue eyes fixed on him. With a toss of her head, she pushed the beads aside and stepped through the exit; the brute followed.

"What happened here?" The lead officer said to the barkeep and listened as he explained, pointing first at the two men, then to Barkow. When they tried to question the ruffians, neither was able to speak coherently. Barkow put his thoughts of Mary away. When the police came over, he handed the first one his driver license.

The officer looked at the ID, then at him. "Okay Barkow, what's your story?"

Barkow shrugged. "I never saw either of them before, but they obviously knew who they wanted. They came straight at me."

The second cop said, "What do you mean, they came straight to you?"

"I mean the first guy called me a piss-ant and was looking for a fight."

The cop smiled. "So these two guys came out of nowhere and attacked you?"

"Yeah, that's what I said."

"You sure you've never had any contact with them before?"

"I said that too."

His story matched that of the bartender. After asking a few more questions and returning his ID, the officers turned their attention to the two thugs, who were being helped to an ambulance by paramedics.

"How bad are they hurt?" The first cop said as he fell in step with the medics.

"This one has a broken right jaw. The other one a smashed nose and dislocated knee."

Terry wandered among the customers picking up orders. "Want another drink?" she said when she stopped by Barkow's table. The small, pert waitress had striking green eyes. Her round face, framed by dark red hair, brought renewed thoughts of Mary.

"No booze, just black coffee and ask Laura to play 'The Chains of Love,' low and slow for me."

"One coffee will be right up," Terry said and turned to walk to the piano. There she bent and said in a low, throaty voice, "Barkow, request 'The Chains of Love'."

Laura glanced at the table by the wall and smiled at the brooding man, knowing the song-type he would call for. He had been in every week or two, always asking for the same kind of heart-broken music. She was aware he did not remember meeting her several years ago. He'd been extremely drunk at the time. Laura shook out her long, blonde hair, flexed her hands and began the low, melancholy refrain of his request.

He watched the piano player and sipped acrid coffee, cognizant of an odd feeling that somewhere in his past they had crossed paths. *She is beautiful,* he thought. He respected her musical ability and refused to start a relationship just for sex, knowing his heart was forever bound to Mary, the first and only love in his life. As the song ended, he swallowed the remains of the coffee and stood up, dropped a five dollar tip on the table and walked to the piano. He leaned over the parlor grand and placed a twenty in the brandy-snifter tip jar. "Thanks, Laura."

She looked at him with concern, knowing how dangerous he could be in a fight, or for that matter, in her arms.

He held her gaze for a moment, then turned and strolled across the dance floor to the dark end of the bar where he motioned for Bert.

The bartender came. "What do you want?"

Barkow reached across the bar, grasped the barkeep's tie and yanked him forward. Quietly he said, "I want to know why you slipped a Mickey into my drink."

Bert's tone took on a defensive whine. "Not me, man. I poured that Blanton's straight from a new bottle."

"Here's a word of advice, Bert. You ever do that again, I'll beat your ass so bad you won't be able to walk for a week. Understood?"

"Yes, Mr. Barkow.... I got it."

Barkow released him, turned, made his way to the exit, and walked into the night.

THE STRANGE CASE OF G. B. BARKOW

May 7, 2012, Monday, 7:00 a.m.

Two weeks had passed since the fight in the Blue Note. Barkow's life had become muddled. Strange things seemed to happen in a confused, disordered way. One day, without knowing why, he stepped into the Axelwood Arms, a shabby hotel.

From behind the counter, the seedy desk clerk said "Hey Barkow, here's your room key, 201 second floor."

"How do you happen to know my name?" he said quietly through clenched teeth.

"With a suit like yours, you'd be dammed hard to miss."

Barkow ripped the key from the clerk's hand, turned on his heel and stomped up the creaking stairs. Behind him, the clerk snickered, and that sound integrated with a haunting melody slowly welling up in Barkow's mind.

An unnatural state of amnesia affected his psyche. In his pockets, he found a set of keys, an old ivory handled jackknife and a heavy gold ring. The room displayed cheap quality, with faded wallpaper and a bathroom of 1930 vintage. A leather brief-case lay on a small table. He spun the combination lock and opened it with ease to find business cards and insurance claims.

Barkow looked about the room with distaste, promptly gathered up his things and left the dilapidated hotel. Days passed in confusion. At times an ordinary task, like turning a page or picking up a cup, seemed to flash past, as if he were a character in a movie with the film running through the projector too fast. At other times, the same task might move at a crawl. Thoughts arrived and departed in flashes of quick-slow recollections.

One morning in Phoenix, Arizona he woke up alert and alive in his familiar bedroom. Whatever had caused the strange delusions had worn off. His mind had become perceptive, clear and focused. *Did I just wake up from a bad dream? Was all of that a weird nightmare?* He remained in bed, thinking of his youth, the Army and growing up. The painful years of Mary undeniably not loving him still stung like an ulcer on his heart, but life seemed normal again. Barkow—taciturn, distant, cold and calculating—was his old self and living the familiar routine of processing insurance claims.

He hated his first name, George, and as time passed, he kept that hatred in a mental corner and tried to bury it with the strange music in his mind. He presented an insinuation of sorrow and unhappiness of which most people were distinctly aware. He was pleasant when dealing with clients, but privately Barkow tended to be moody and solemn. His demeanor radiated a particular aura: *I am to be left alone.* Even panhandlers never approached.

IN PHOENIX ARIZONA

H E WAS AT breakfast when the familiar jangle of his cell phone interrupted the morning paper.

"Barkow."

"Hi Barkow, Judy here. Plane tickets and documents are ready for your next assignment if you want to pick them up."

"I'll drop by."

"Okay. They're on my desk in case you arrive while I'm at lunch."

"Thanks Judy."

His coffee didn't have the normal richness. He skimmed the news, finished eating, took a shower and dressed in a black suit. Tired of local claims work, he was glad something had come up to send him on a business trip.

🕑 AT THE SAME time Judy and Barkow were discussing his upcoming case, a conversation pertaining to G. B. Barkow was taking place far away in the exclusive Executive's Restaurant in New York City.

The President of Great Metro Insurance asked, "Then he handled the claim to your satisfaction?"

"Yes indeed. Precision Thrust is most pleased at the way it was handled, with efficiency and understanding of the situation. Your man Barkow is highly knowledgeable and incredibly perceptive."

"How well I know. Whenever we're faced with a delicate set

of circumstances such as yours, Barkow is the man to call in. A while back he saved us four million on a bogus insurance claim."

"We would hire him in a second if the chance became available. By the way, was he an athlete, perhaps pro-football, hockey or such? The man is built like a wedge and must be what, over six feet?"

The president spoke with a smile, his eyes bright and sharp. "Six three I believe. We wouldn't let him get away from us without a long and expensive fight in court."

The CEO of Precision Thrust also smiled. "Understood. You know, I've never seen him in anything other than a black suit, and he accomplishes so much with so little talking. He seems to always have complete control over the situation. Odd though, he seems to shun friendship."

"It's just his way, and we wouldn't change him for anything."

The two men parted, each to his corporate world. In the mind of both lingered thoughts of G. B. Barkow.

A THICKENING PLOT

HIS LATEST MISSION, to settle a damage claim on a boat fire, was in Seattle. He hoped to complete the business and fly out the same day. Barkow landed at Sea-Tac International in the afternoon. He drove to downtown Seattle in a rented car, found Lake Union and located the impaired boat.

"Ahoy, the *Temptress*," he called.

A man appeared at the railing of the flying bridge. "What you want?"

"I'm a Great Metro insurance claims adjuster. May I come aboard?"

"Use the ladder. I'll be in the salon."

Barkow found the Jacobs ladder hanging amidships. *I'd think they could afford a decent boarding-ladder*, he thought as he climbed the rope-and-wood contraption. He gained the deck and entered the salon to find the owner waiting.

The ancient, squat and wrinkled man of Native American heritage mumbled, "I'm the owner of *Temptress*."

"My name is Barkow." They shook hands and he offered the man his card.

"I got the coffee on," the boat owner said as he set two mugs on a railed table and filled them with steaming coffee from a battered old percolator. Barkow picked up a mug and sipped the bitter black brew.

When they finished drinking coffee, he began an examination of the damage to the boat. He looked at a charred bulkhead below a gaping, burned-through hole in the overhead. "What do you think happened?"

"Maybe someone walking on the dock flipped a burning cigarette or cigar up on the deck. It occurred sometime during the night. I'm damn lucky the fire station is close."

Barkow filled in several reports, than completed the business without any problems. "A check will be mailed to you within twenty-four hours."

"That's good," the owner said.

They shook hands and parted company, and Barkow headed for the airport. The sun shone pleasantly and the tangy smell of salt water brought the sudden desire to spend an extra day. He saw a Sheraton Hotel and on impulse pulled into the curving entrance driveway, parked beneath the elaborate portico and checked in.

He enjoyed a seafood meal topped off with a splash of Blanton's on ice. Later, as he was unlocking the door of his room the phone rang. *Not the office... Judy always uses my cell.* He crossed the room and expected it to be the front desk. *Besides, how would they know I was here?* The harsh jangle stopped as he picked up the phone. "Hello?"

The line crackled and popped with static.

"Hello?" he said harshly, and was on the verge of hanging up when someone, who sounded far away, the voice intermingled in interference, said, "Gee-horge? Gee-horge Bain-ate Bah-Kho?"

Anger emerged like a black shadow, blotting out reason. He gripped the phone tightly and snarled, "Who is this?"

In a quavering voice, rising and falling between the layers of static, the person said, "Tay lift they veil o' sorrow. They must come house on Herring Head Drive."

Infuriated, Barkow growled into the mouthpiece, "Who the hell are you?"

With a sizzle of static and a metallic click, the line went dead.

Calming his rage, he replayed the dialogue in his mind.

The odd manner of oral expression, halting and foreign, seemed somewhat familiar although he had no clue why. A call to the front desk brought no further information regarding the strange communication or its source.

Barkow turned on his laptop and opened the Internet. As he searched the name Herring Head, he found a like-named headland projecting into the Pacific on the desolate western coast of the state, located between Kalaloch and the town of Aberdeen.

"Damn crackpot," he muttered. *Who would possibly know my name, not to mention where I am?*

IN SEARCH OF ANSWERS

MAY 7, 2012, MONDAY, 4:05 P.M.

BARKOW MADE A decision, picked up his gear and went to the front desk. "Something has come up; I will not be staying tonight. Can you please tell me where I can find a road map of the State?"

"Certainly Sir. Just across the lobby at the gift shop. I hope your cancellation is not due to an emergency."

"No, just some unfinished business."

After purchasing a map, Barkow drove out of the city, heading southbound on I-5. He cruised through the late afternoon sunlight as he thought of who knew his full name. Nobody came to mind.

As he drove, he called the airlines and canceled his return ticket. He texted the home office: *Taking a few days off. Personal reasons. Will call later. Barkow.*

The day dissolved in a tangerine sunset banded with the narrow, indigo strips of a distant cloud formation. Later they thickened and changed the day to a dark, moonless night. The radio station turned to static and sputtered into silence.

"Damn it," he cursed at the loss of music. He turned north on highway 101, keeping a sharp lookout for any sign of Herring Head. He hummed the doleful "Chains" melody as he drove north.

At 11:30 p.m., he passed the small Native American town of Amanda Park. After midnight, he was surprised to come upon Kalaloch Lodge, located on a bluff above the pounding surf of the Pacific Ocean. He parked in front of the lodge and turned off the headlights.

Somehow, I missed Herring Head. He snapped on the courtesy lamp and rechecked the map. It showed a land mass named Herring Head, projecting into the Pacific, located between Kalaloch and Aberdeen. *Maybe I can ask someone how to find it.* He turned off the courtesy light and rolled down his window. He looked into the deep shadows beneath the steep, overhung roof of a covered walkway to the front door of the lodge.

The surf washed up on the beach, followed by the muffled roar of receding water streaming through gravel back to the sea. He got out of the car, approached and entered the long walkway. When he gained the front entrance to the lodge, he tried the handle, which was locked. A dim nightlight shone inside. The place was deserted.

As he turned to leave, he became aware of someone sitting on a long bench beneath the covered entry. "Hello," he said. "Do you live around here?"

The Indian, an old man, hardly moved as he nodded. He was wearing a plaid shirt and a sleeveless hunter's vest, and he reeked of alcohol. More unconscious than awake, he slipped farther down on the bench.

Barkow bent toward him. "Where is Herring Head?"

Eyes closed, the man mumbled, "South... past lake." The Indian started to lean sideways.

Barkow caught his vest, pulling him around to lie lengthwise, then picked up his feet to place them on the bench. Feeling sorry for the old man, he tucked a twenty-dollar bill into the faded shirt pocket and returned to his car.

He drove south, retracing his route until he arrived at the town of Amanda Park.

The map shows this is close to the shores of Lake Quinault, he thought. He followed the highway across the map with his finger. It cut through a portion of a National Park, where the map indicated the headland.

As he passed Amanda Park, he slowed, vigilant for any sign that might direct him to Herring Head. The headlamps caused the old growth timber to cast weird shadows along the roadside as he looked for a road that headed toward the sea. Barely audibly, he muttered fragments of a haunting melody "Time will come when you are old and bent...."

As the lyrics faded into obscurity, his thoughts returned to his destination: *If the road is named Herring Head Drive, it has to be on that headland protruding into the sea on my right as I drive south.* Since he'd left Kalaloch, the highway had cut inland, away from the coast.

He continued south as a light, cold rain began to fall. The wipers slowly slapping back and forth had a hypnotizing effect on his senses. He rolled the window down so fresh air would keep him from getting drowsy.

Gray fog began to form, and drifting patches settled near the surface of the blacktop. Barkow cut the headlamps to low beam. He almost missed the metal sign standing at an awkward angle to the highway. The rusted name read *Bowes Road* and the road headed west toward the coast. He turned into the narrow, graveled lane. Soon he recognized a battered old pickup truck coming toward him through the fog. He braked to a halt and waved out the window. When the pickup stopped, he called, "Can you tell me how to get to Herring Head?"

The other driver, an old Indian with creased and weathered face, said, "Man, you on the wrong road for that place. There's a way through the back roads, but it's easy to get lost that way. You got to go round by Hoquiam and take the 109."

"I have to get to Herring Head as soon as possible," Barkow said. "I'd be willing to pay you to show me the way."

"No prob! No prob! How about a hundred dollars, an' I get ya over there?"

Barkow looked at the old, rusty truck covered with dents and with one front fender hanging precariously loose from the body. Barkow handed him the money.

The driver pulled ahead and waited for him to turn around. After much forward and reverse effort to turn around on the narrow lane, he followed the battered old pickup down the road.

Almost an hour passed, driving through the mist and foggy darkness, on gravel roads that turned and twisted, taking some turnoffs and bypassing others. Eventually, the Indian pulled over where the gravel road crossed a paved highway.

With a wave of his arm, the truck driver motioned Barkow to turn north and as he did so, he turned south.

He passed through the fog-shrouded hamlet of Iron Springs, which consisted of a few shabby buildings that were dark and appeared deserted. He concentrated on his left side for an entrance to Herring Head until at last he found it in the gathering rain, nailed to the trunk of a tree. The weather-beaten sign, almost faded out, read *Herring Head Drive.*

The fuel gauge showed close to empty as he drove the unused lane. He slowly skirted small bushes leaning into the pathway. Eventually, the lane deteriorated into two muddy tracks with grass in between. About a mile and a half in, the soggy, unused driveway ended at a large iron gate. The hinges were mortared into stone columns on either side. A tangle of green vines crawled over the rusty ornamental designs of the once formal gate.

Grass and twisting creepers grew at the base of the greenish, moss-covered stone walls that extended away in either direction.

Granite support columns stood like soldiers as the diminishing walls disappeared into the foggy darkness of a rain-drenched forest.

THE GATE

BARKOW SWUNG THE car door open, stepped into the rain and walked up close to inspect the gate. A rusty chain with half-inch thick links hung around the uprights of each gate-half, secured with a heavy brass padlock.

He had almost decided he would need a ladder to gain the top of those rough stone walls when he discovered a smaller, vine-covered personnel gate inset into the right side of the main gate. He was about ten feet from his car, which had almost been obscured by the coastal fog, which had thickened while he was inspecting the gate. A melancholy feeling hovered around his thoughts as gray fragments of fog drifted among the trees.

Barkow pulled some of the tangled vines and creepers away from the small gate and found the latch. He lifted the iron latch, then pushed and pulled, tearing away the trailing vines as the rusted hinges squealed in protest. The raised edges of a weed-covered driveway receded into the gray fog.

A low moaning sound drifted through the dripping rain and slowly swirling fog, rising and falling in pitch. It grew louder as it came closer, picking up speed. In a rushing roar and blood curdling screech it exploded in his face.

Barkow froze. Tiny, high-pitched notes of fear worked their way up his spine, and he realized he was holding his breath. He slowly exhaled as he brought his heart-hammering fear under control. *A screech owl... it must have been a goddamned screech owl... must've flown straight at me.*

He picked his way slowly along the overgrown bed of the

driveway, following its curve through a corridor of dripping fir and cedar. The rain slowed and finally stopped, but heavy ground-fog, rolling ashore from the Pacific, kept everything soaked.

Shade by subtle shade, the decreasing darkness of night faded into an iron-gray morning. The driveway straightened, running along an open expanse of flat, grass-covered ground. In the increased light, the low-hanging clouds, heavy with unreleased water, wallowed in a lead-colored sky.

He scanned the surroundings and made out a vague treeline across the meadow-like expanse of wet land, punctuated with hillocks of bunch-grass. Then, all but lost from sight against a gloomy stand of trees, the rain darkened, stone walls of a building rose like an ancient fortress. Long unkempt, the driveway veered into the open ground and faded in a wide curve toward the building.

Barkow stopped. For the first time since he'd checked out of the hotel, a shred of doubt slipped into his conscious mind. *Why in God's name am I tramping around here in the fog?* He stared at the stone mansion, now easily visible as night mushroomed into day, then turned and gazed back on the semi-sunken driveway. *I should be in Phoenix, not out here chasing—* His cell phone rang. He pulled it from the pocket of his coat and flipped the cover open. "Barkow."

"George, you are so close... don't turn back now!" Her voice was crystal clear.

He clenched his teeth. "Who is this?"

Click.

He snapped the phone shut, shoved it into his pocket and started toward the old stone mansion.

THE MANSION

IN THE OMINOUS, gray cemetery-like stillness the only sound was Barkow's shoes swishing through wet grass. The unkempt, overgrown driveway ran in a wide curve toward the mansion. The building had a steep, tiled roof with oxeye dormers. A wide walk of flat, mossy paving stones led from the edge of the driveway to the entrance of the house. He followed the path to a raised landing beneath a gabled extension. The door was made of hand-hewed planks, bound with iron strap hinges. Two hideous gargoyle faces flanked the door.

An iron knocker, forged in the shape of a ram's head, hung at the center of the door. Barkow lifted the knocker and let it drop against its strike plate. The heavy thud of the metal fixture seemed muffled. As he reached to lift it again, the door slowly opened. The interior was darkly shadowed.

Someone whose voice was edged with the thickness of age said, "Yes?"

"I am G. B. Barkow. I believe you are expecting me."

"One moment, Sir."

His footsteps faded away. He returned in a few seconds with a lighted candle held high above his head and murmured, "This way, Sir."

Barkow followed.

The butler was a short man. As he carried the candle above his head, his features were lost in the shadow cast by the base of the candle holder. Behind them, the door swung shut, leaving them in virtual darkness.

The butler led Barkow across a masonry floor and through an arched entryway. Ghostly portraits lined the wall to his left. They passed some large, bulky furniture, perhaps chairs and went through a second wide, arched opening into a room where a fireplace was burning with a low flame.

"Please be seated. Madam will be with you shortly." The man shambled away.

The faint glow from the fire produced enough light to see two massive carved and cushioned chairs, on either side of the fireplace, each with a small side table. A coat of arms adorned with crossed lances hung above the mantel. A thick carpet covered the floor beneath the side chairs. He knelt to touch it and realized it was fur, soft as mink.

As he rose his eyes became accustomed to the fire-lit area. Along one wall receding into darkness hung gigantic portraits, done in oils and featuring warriors clad in armor. The elaborately carved and gilded frames faintly reflected golden highlights. Along the opposite wall were similarly elegant assorted paintings of women. All were exquisite in their exceptional beauty. He returned to the fireplace, chose the chair on the right side of the low-burning fire and waited.

From the shadowed end of the room, the woman seemed to materialize. She had pale white skin, blood red lipstick and high, arched eyebrows. Her lashes fanned from slightly slanted eyes, giving her appearance an Asian cast. Her black, braided hair was coiled into a rose-like mass at the back of her head. Barkow wondered how long it would be if it were hanging free. She was the most alluring and beautiful woman he had ever seen. Her dress, a black hip-hugging sheath reaching below her knees, was slit up the right side to mid-thigh. A plunging neckline revealed a cleft between ample breasts, cradled in drapes of a sleeveless top. She approached the empty chair across from Barkow and settled into the cushions with cat-like grace. In a soft, muted French accent, she said, "Welcome to our home, George. I am glad you chose to visit, rather than leaving empty handed."

"Do not call me by that name!" He spat the words like a harsh oath. "Our home? I have never been here in my life, and I want an explanation for the phone calls and the strange things that have been happening."

She was unperturbed by his angry outburst. "Let us please be civil. We have a delightful fire and I have your favorite drink on the way."

A heavy, squat man in formal attire appeared with a tray that held a glass and goblet. He approached Barkow and offered the tray. "Blantons, Sir, on ice." His face, softened by firelight, was like an ancient mahogany map etched on darkly tanned leather. The black eyes were bright, but sunken. His face, a mass of creases and wrinkles in dusky skin, was shaped somewhat round, full fleshed and vaguely familiar. His hands were large, thick and firm.

"Ladies first," Barkow said and shifted his eyes to the woman.

She smiled as the waiter straightened and turned with the tray toward her. She took the goblet of dark red wine. "*Merci, Jacques.*" She turned to Barkow. "*Je vois que vous n'avez pas oublié vos manières, George.*"

What? When did I learn to understand French? He took the proffered bourbon. "*Merci,*" he muttered, then said, "*Mon français n'est pas très bien parlé. Quel nom puis-je vous appeler?*"

She said, "You may call me Marie, and please speak in English."

"Thank you, Marie. You may call me Barkow."

She smiled. "Of course, Barkow. I understand why you do not like the name of George. Now tell me what you remember of your past."

He frowned. "No, Madam, it is I who shall ask the questions. I am not accustomed to driving up and down the coast in the night or being questioned like a school boy."

Her smile transformed into a compressed line between her lips. Two small furrows of annoyance appeared between her eyes. "Have it your way." She relaxed into the seat cushions. "I would not wish to have you dash away now that we are finally face to face."

"Good!" He picked up his glass of bourbon and drank it in a single swallow.

"First of all, you are never to call me George again. How did you get my hotel and phone number?"

The old man in the formal black suit had returned. "Would the gentleman care for a second drink?"

Barkow glared at the man. "No, I would not." He turned his attention back to the woman.

She smiled. "You should be thanking me instead of making demands."

"What would require my thanks?"

She pouted. "Look at me Barkow. I can and will give you anything a man wants from a woman—anything."

"You can start by answering my questions."

"And, you, Sir, can be civil."

"I *am* civil."

"No, you're tired, Barkow. It's no wonder since you've been through a lot today. I suggest we delay our conversation until breakfast. It will give us a both an opportunity to start with a rested mind."

"I am tired," he admitted.

Without a word, she rose and faded into the shadows.

"Madam has retired. May I show you to your room?" The old man held his hand out as if to show the way.

He stood up and followed Jacques, who was holding a lighted candle high above his head. They walked through the darkness to a massive staircase, where Jacques began the ascent. "Right this way, Sir. Mind your step, please."

THE ROOM

THEY ASCENDED THE staircase, walked down a hallway and stopped at a wooden door. Jacques unlocked and opened the door, then handed Barkow the iron key. "That, Sir, is your personal key to the room. Your clothing is laid out and breakfast shall be served at nine." He gave Barkow the candle, turned and disappeared into the darkness.

Barkow, holding the key in one hand and the candle in the other, stepped inside and elbowed the door shut; then, seeing the candelabra with a dozen tall, thick tapers, he lighted them one at a time.

The light revealed a fireplace and a canopied, four-posted bed with the headboard against a wall. Each post was carved in an intricate ivy design; in the headboard a crest was sculpted deeply into the wood. Small rugs were scattered here and there across the stone floor. There were a few overstuffed chairs, a writing desk, a piano and a hearth.

Opposite the fireplace was another door, a short distance from a shuttered window. It opened to a spacious bathroom.

The bathroom had a recessed, polished marble tub and a matching stall shower. Along one wall was a stone vanity with double basins, a small padded chair beside a side table and a commode. Some clothing, a pair of pajamas and a robe were laid out on a heavy, carved table.

Back in the bedroom, Barkow looked at his watch. It read 7:05 a.m. He lay down on the bed and was asleep before he could gather his thoughts.

🕑 HE BECAME AWARE of an increasing light on his eyelids. His mind sluggish, he tried to place some coherent thought patterns while wanting to go back to sleep. One thought connected to another and then another as the night before came rushing into his brain. His eyes snapped opened and he sat up, blinking and still fully dressed. His wristwatch showed the time to be 8:02. He felt fully rested, though he had slept less than an hour. He frowned. *Impossible.*

His mouth was dry and sunshine filtered through the slats of the wooden shutters. On the way to the bathroom, he glanced at the candelabra. What had been unusually large, heavy candles had burned down to nothing. He realized with a start that he had slept over twenty-four hours.

In the bathroom, he filled a glass with cold water and drank. After removing everything from his pockets, he stripped off his clothing, hung up his suit and tie, tossed the rest into a pile on the floor and stepped into the shower.

Afterward he noticed a mug of shaving soap and a brush on a shelf above the stone basin. He turned on hot water and lathered his face. Without a second thought, he picked up an ivory-handled straight razor and removed his growth of beard, then washed away the remaining traces of soap. He examined the clothing someone had laid out. Trousers, shorts, socks and undershirt, all black, lay next to a dark maroon shirt, with a high, wide collar and bloused, cuffed sleeves and a pair of black half-boots lined with soft red leather.

The clothes fit as if they had been hand-tailored to his exact size. The boots hugged his feet. He thought about the strange turns his life had taken over the past two days.

A startling thought occurred! *There had only been the soap mug and brush on the shelf. When he used it, the straight razor had materialized when he'd needed it.* His thoughts varied from crystal clear to blurred. He checked his watch. It was ten minutes to nine. *The old servant said breakfast was served at nine.*

He went to the door, unlocked it, stepped out into the hallway, relocked it and went in search of the dining room. He walked along the hallway, doors on either side. There were no wall sconces, but from somewhere, a dingy light kept it from being utter darkness. He passed door after door until eventually, with a sense of annoyance, he picked one at random, stopped and knocked. No answer, so he tried the door latch.

It, like all the rest of the doors he had passed, had a heavy, brass, loop handle with a thumb latch at the top. Finding it locked he looked back at the way he had come. *Damn it... maybe I went the wrong way.* He turned to go back, walking briskly. *Every door is exactly the same.*

All the doors had heavy strap hinges that ended at the center panel, and they were staggered, so he passed one on the left, then one on the right. *Why is it taking so long to return to my room?* After a few minutes, he stopped before a door.

THE RIDDLE OF THE ROOM

MAY 8, 2012, TUESDAY, 9:30 A.M.

THE INCESSANT BACKGROUND music in his brain began to swell in volume and the tempo increased. As he tried to ignore the music, he looked at the door. *My knuckles would not make a sound on such heavy wood.* He took the iron key from his pocket and used it to tap a few times on the door. He shrugged. "What the hell... I'll try the damn key." He slipped the key into the keyhole and turned it, then pushed the door open.

"Hello? Anyone here?"

No answer.

Again he called, louder.

No response. The decor and furniture were exact duplicates of that in his room. Then he noticed the candelabra with puddles of wax in the collection bowls. The mind-music climbed to a crescendo. He went to the bathroom and in a pile on the floor were his clothes.

He laughed with sudden relief as the music in his head waned. *Last night when I followed Jacques upstairs, my room door was on the left. So to return the same way, I would have to turn right as I leave this room and that will take me back in the direction we came.*"

Once more he left the room but turned to his right. After a few minutes, he stopped at a door on his right and tried the key. It opened as before. He walked in. To his astonishment, he found the candelabra with melted wax and his clothes.

He stepped across the hall and tried another. It opened with the key and he went in to find the same melted wax and clothes.

His mind reeled. "What the hell is going on?" He picked up his dirty shirt from the bathroom floor and tossed it on the center of the bed. He left the room, but in his haste forgot to lock it. He strode down the hall and picked a door at random, tried the key and heard the lock snap shut.

"Damn it!" he snarled. Turning the key the opposite way, he unlocked the door and went in. The shirt was on the bed.

Barkow walked out of the room, leaving the door open. Out in the hall, all the room doors were open. *All the rooms are my room.* "How in the hell do I leave?" he shouted in the rising volume of the "Chains" melody. No answer came.

Gripping the iron key in his fist, he entered a room with a torrent of music roaring in his head. He laid the room key on an end table, strode to the window and tried to rip the shutters away from the glass. The slats appeared to be thin strips of horizontal wood that could be broken easily. Try as he might, he could not break them or even change their position.

He went to the fireplace and removed one of the ten-foot pikes. At the window he thrust the iron head of the pike at the glass between the slats. It bounced back as if he'd stabbed a steel wall.

Barkow discarded the pike and sat in one of the overstuffed chairs, which all but molded itself to his body. He forced his mind to relax and himself to breathe with composed calm, eyes closed and hands resting in his lap. The cacophonous music slowly receded. *There has to be an end to the hallway.* "If I go far enough, simple logic says the hall must end."

He left the room, leaving the door open, and turned right. He'd gone about twenty feet when the sweet scent of perking coffee came to his nostrils. A single burst of four sharp, treble notes spiked in his brain. Ten feet farther, the aroma grew stronger. He arrived at the head of the curving staircase. *What changed?* He ran back to his room, retracing his steps in his mind. *I tried to break the glass with a pike. It's on the floor and I couldn't rip the shutters away.* Out of nowhere a cascade of harp-like notes, but higher in pitch, exploded in his mind. "The key! I left the damned key in the room when I went out the last time!"

He snatched the intricate iron key and went back into the hall. Every door in the hall was open. He shut his door and all the doors shut. Back inside he tossed the key on the bed, walked out of the room and slammed the door. In both directions was only a short hallway. A few steps to his right and he was back at the stairway with the fragrance of fresh coffee calling him down, as gentle, soft strains of music faded into the background.

SEARCHING FOR MARIE

May 8, 2012, Tuesday, 10:14 a.m.

Barkow walked down the stairs, the coffee aroma growing stronger. *What kind of place is this?* He stepped from the final stair tread to the stone floor. Across the spacious room, an arched entry led into a hall.

The dining room was a narrow, high-vaulted room that would easily seat eighty people. A row of chandeliers hung over the polished wood table. From the foot of the table, Barkow looked along its length to a narrow door in a far corner. On both sides were high-backed chairs and before each, a formal sixteen piece place-setting of china, crystal and silver. He walked with a steady, purposeful gait toward the small door.

He tried the door and it opened easily. Inside were cooking hearths with hanging pots and utensils. A wooden chopping block dominated the room, which was quiet and unoccupied. He sniffed but no longer detected the aroma of coffee. Barkow returned to the room where the stairway began. The scent of fresh brewed coffee filled the air. At one side of the room, he recognized the fireplace with matched chairs where he had met the mysterious Marie. He walked toward the chairs, noting the walls were not square to each other. They slanted in opposite directions, confusing the mind as to which way they actually led.

He walked into another room and the scent of coffee lessened. He crossed to the opposite wall and returned the way he had come. The bouquet of fresh coffee was much stronger. He continued along the wall, peculiar because he never passed the fireplace, although he did pass a row of closed doors. A multipaned set of double-doors, through which sunshine streamed, became visible at the end of the semi-dark room. It had formed at the instant he became aware of the light. He hurried to the French doors, looked through a glass pane and was blinded by sunshine. He squinted and stepped back into the darkness of the room. He waited a bit for his sight to adjust and then slowly approached the sunlit doors again. He grasped a door knob, twisted and pulled it open.

He stepped onto a flagstone patio and walked to a nearby table with four empty chairs beside a breakfast buffet. He filled a cup with coffee and inspected the food.

After he'd finished breakfast, he was considering what to do next when a servant appeared at his side.

"Has the gentleman any further requirements?"

Barkow turned to the man, who was dressed in a white jacket. His familiar face was scarred. "You are Jacques, Right?" Barkow said.

The man returned Barkow's gaze with a dead stare. "Oh no, Sir, my name is Peter." He had a clipped British accent and skin like wrinkled mahogany.

"Tell me Peter, where are the rest of the guests?"

"We have no other guests, Sir. Only you."

"In that case, where may I find Marie?"

"Marie, Sir?"

"Yes, Marie, the lady of the house. Where may I find her?"

"I do not know anyone named Marie. Perhaps if you speak with Mr. Weatherby, he can be of some assistance."

"Good. Where is Weatherby?"

"I am not sure, but if you would care to wait by the hammock, I shall ask if he would speak with you as soon as possible."

"Hammock?" Barkow looked around. A hammock was slung between two small palm trees in a park-like vale. Nearby two chairs of natural rattan were set beside a small table. Sad strains of music began to build in his mind. "Very well, Peter. Please do so and tell him I am in the utmost haste."

"Certainly, Sir. I shall go at once." He quickly walked to the house and entered a side door.

Barkow went to the rattan chairs and sat down. On the table were an ashtray and a wooden block inlaid with wood strips, forming an intricate Celtic pattern. He picked up the block, apparently a conversation piece. The ashtray appeared to be stone.

As time passed, he thought, *Maybe Peter's not coming back.* Four needle-sharp notes exploded in his mind. He quickly stood and began walking toward the house.

Someone said, "I say, did you wish to speak to me?"

Barkow whirled around. There was a man in a black suit and checkered vest beside the chairs. "Is your name Weatherby?"

"Yes, I am Jonathon Weatherby."

"Good, I have a few questions." Barkow returned to the chairs.

"Of course, if I may be of assistance. Please sit down." The man seated himself on one of the cushioned chairs.

Barkow placed the other chair so he was facing Weatherby. He looked like a kindly, older gentleman, with a square jaw and rather deep-set eyes with a wide forehead. His lips were relaxed as he waited for Barkow to speak.

"First of all," Barkow said, "where may I find Marie?"

"Marie is, of course, in the house. Would you care for a cigar?"

Weatherby reached for the inlaid box and pushed a hidden part of the Celtic pattern, which caused the top to open. He offered the open box to Barkow with one hand as he placed a gold lighter before him with the other. Barkow did not smoke, but without thought, he took one from the box. He picked up the lighter and ignited the end of the cigar, drawing hard to get a live coal burning.

The smoke had a warm, comfortable, yet rather astringent taste. When he exhaled, a cloud of pure essence swirled about him. He held the smoldering cigar comfortably as he studied a crest on the side of the lighter. Comparing it to the ring on his hand, he realized they were the same. A low warning chime sounded in the back of his mind. He watched blue smoke curl from the end of the cigar through narrowed eyes. "Do you know me, Weatherby?"

"No, Sir, I do not."

"What are your duties here?"

"I answer questions."

"Very well. Why am I here?"

"You are here, at present, to search for Marie."

"Where will I find her?"

"That, Sir, is an unanswerable question at this time."

"Why do you say it is unanswerable?"

"Because, Sir, I do not know. She is not stationary."

Barkow thought, *Something is amiss... something that, for some bizarre reason, is evil.* The man opposite him seemed composed and serene as he stared back at Barkow. *Why evil?* he thought. *Why would I even think that when I have been treated with the utmost courtesy?*

He set the lighter before Weatherby. "What is the meaning of this crest?"

"It is the crest of Argon, Sir. It signifies the nobility of Argonites."

"Am I from Argon?"

"You wear the ring, Sir; therefore, I assume you're a noble of Argon."

"All right Weatherby, take me to Marie."

"That is not a question, Sir."

"Tell me where Marie is."

"I have already answered the question Sir, which indicates you have no further inquiries at this time. I shall return to my duties now. Enjoy your cigar, Sir."

As quickly as he had arrived, the man vanished in a fragrant cloud of cigar smoke. The gold lighter still lay where Barkow had placed it. He picked it up and at the same time stubbed out his cigar in the ashtray. *I'm amazed.* He gazed at the manicured grass.

There were also palm trees as well as hemlock, oak and redwood, all flawlessly shaped without a leaf or twig beneath them on the ground. The grass was cut specifically. No single blade was different in height. *How odd,* he thought. *How damned, bloody odd. I remember a wild fir and a hemlock forest, but no manicured lawns, no palm trees... only pine needles and dead weeds.* Thrumming low in his mind, mournful music began to well up.

He stood, placed the lighter in his pocket and began to walk toward the mansion, noting a gargoyle perched on each corner. He used his telescopic vision to bring them into clear focus. They were grotesque and appeared almost alive. Realization washed over him like a sudden wave of cold fog. Thoughts tumbled pell-mell over each other, swirling within a garish rendition of the "Chains" melody.

A thought suddenly formed. *Telescopic sight? What in the hell is happening to me? I don't have telescopic sight. I never smoked, not ever. Wait, yes I did when I—*

THE SEARCH FOR MARIE CONTINUES

MAY 8, 2012, TUESDAY, 4:30 P.M.

THE THOUGHT VANISHED as though it had never started to form. He quickened his step beneath the watchful eyes of the repulsive gargoyles, which leered and licked their lips with long, black tongues. Barkow walked along the building beneath enormous mullioned windows set with ledges eight feet above the ground.

He became aware of heart-broken notes of sadness which seemed not in his mind, but to float nearby. He stopped and listened, trying to ascertain where the music was coming from. The lawn led away into a long, upward-sweeping slope. A few groves, consisting of two or three broadleaf maple trees each, dotted the vastness of grassland. The sorrowful, depressing melody compelled him, and Barkow lurched uphill toward the horizon.

The Wagner-like composition seemed just beyond his reach. It swelled and receded in tempo with such emotional harmony that Barkow felt a restriction build in his throat as he rubbed tears away, enthralled by the draw of the music. Something in his mind clicked as a warning cried, *Beware! Beware!* He forced himself, by sheer willpower, to stop although his brain wanted him to keep walking to find the music.

He cupped his hands over his ears and with superhuman effort turned around. Far, far away, at the base of a long downward gradient was the tiny shape of the mansion. It appeared as if he were looking through the wrong end of a telescope. Using all his strength, as if walking in wet, knee-deep cement, he forced his legs to move. The muscles in his calves began to ache with the powerful pull of the material adhering to his legs, feet and ankles, adding layers of drying concrete. Still holding his hands over ears, he began to repeat aloud, over and over. "I will not stop moving! I will not stop moving!"

Suddenly he was walking next to the gray stone mansion again. His breathing was labored and his calves ached as if severely cramped. Cautiously he removed his hands from his ears. As his breathing became normal, the weird melody decreased in volume and the aches gradually diminished. A building anger raged through his mind. He walked steadily and soon came upon a gardener, trimming a bush.

"Hello!" he tried to say in a friendly way.

The gardener continued to chop away. "Good afternoon, Sir."

"Can you advise me of the nearest entrance into the building?"

"Yes indeed, Sir. That would be straight through yonder doorway."

Barkow stared into the old and somewhat familiar face. The pupils were much like those of a bird on a limb as it watches you pass below.

"Which doorway do you mean?"

"Why Sir, I mean that door!" He pointed with his closed hedge trimmers at an entry between two pillars.

Barkow, eyes narrowed looked first over his shoulder, then deep into the jet-black eyes of the worker.

"That door was not there a moment ago!" he spat.

"Of course it was, Sir. Maybe you need to rest a bit. Would you like a drink of water? Perhaps you should sit down."

"I'm okay," he growled in a dangerous voice from where anger smoldered. He turned away and walked toward the door.

Behind him the gardener said, "Quite all right, Sir. Have a nice day."

BACK TO THE MANSION

HE GRIPPED THE knob and twisted. The door was locked. Barkow, unperturbed, removed a ring of keys from his pocket, chose a small brass one, inserted, unlocked, entered and relocked the door. He passed through the small entry room, unaware this was the first time he had ever used the keys which apparently he always carried with him.

He wandered down a wide, carpeted hall and met two people: a young woman was followed by a man with a tray of covered bowls and dishes. His black hair was combed straight back. The woman's tresses were the color of ripe corn, her face pale and her eyes glittering like those of a cat in candle light.

As she passed Barkow, she met his gaze and winked. He stared after her as they moved on, leaving a wake of gardenia-scented perfume. *I know that woman,* Barkow thought as he strode forward until the hall emptied into a dim ballroom. A man wearing a dark-blue frock coat said, "Welcome to the Ballroom of Delights. The custom for gentlemen is to wear a jacket and tie. Enjoy the music and dancing."

"I didn't come for dancing," Barkow said in a gruff tone. "I'm here to see Marie."

"Ah, Mr. Barkow, I presume? Madam Marie is expecting you. She is upstairs, third room on the left. Enjoy your evening, Sir."

"Thank you," he said, his voice a near snarl, as he walked on, glancing about for the stairway. He spotted a bar, complete with white jacketed bartenders, and moved in that direction. Groups of people were milling about near the bar. He approached the near end as a bartender stepped up.

"May I help you, Sir?"

"Bourbon, rocks."

"Certainly Sir. One moment please." An instant later he placed a highball glass, filled with cubed ice and bourbon, on the counter.

"How much?"

"Oh Sir, you jest. Enjoy your evening." The barkeep whisked away to another customer.

Barkow lifted the drink and sipped, found the bitter taste atrocious and set the glass down at once. He turned away and walked parallel with the bar to the opposite end where he noticed a cocktail waitress with red hair. The light from a mirror ball caused her green eyes to flash in a round pixie face as she gazed at him. She smiled and blinked her lashes. *Do I remember her from somewhere?* Barkow moved on.

The dance floor was filled with couples. Music lingered in the atmosphere. He paused and listened as a woman sang the clear, lonesome words of a song:

> *My chains of love are shackled to your heart. Together we are bound eternally....*

Barkow worked his way around the perimeter, watching the people on the dance floor as they dipped and twirled where long shadows slashed across the darkened room.

Eventually, he saw the wide arc of a staircase jutting out over the dance floor and curving back down and under a low ceiling to the final landing on the ballroom floor. He turned toward it, moving straight across the dance floor, dodging the swinging and swaying dancers. He kept his eye on the staircase banister until he came to the portion above the dance floor. He followed it around and found the ballroom floor level.

He started up the stairs. As the stairway curved out over

the marble floor, he paused to stare at the dancers. Below him the blonde whirled, dancing in the arms of a man with shiny black hair. She looked up, her eyes crinkled almost closed as she laughed and waved to him over the shoulder of her date. He nodded, then turned and continued up the stairs. Eventually, he arrived at the top of the staircase and hurried along the wide, carpeted walkway with others who seemed to have definite destinations. After a while, he passed an entry on the right, where several people broke off and entered. He moved over, so he was walking along the left side of the passageway. Perhaps fifty feet farther, he passed another entrance, but on his left. Loud laughter and much chatter came from a large group of people as he slipped past the open archway. *The third room on the left,* he thought. *That's where the man said I would find Marie.*

Later, he passed an entryway on the right where more people departed the hallway. Farther along, at a door on the left all of those who remained turned in, leaving Barkow alone.

He walked along the left side of the hall. On the right, he saw ahead, a small private door. *I will soon arrive at the third room on the left.* He thought. *I will also find Marie and the answer to the strangeness of this place.*

He searched the left wall for an entryway to a room. Far down the hallway he saw no indications of a break. On the right side, he came to the single door, without a knob or lock of any kind. Barkow stepped over and pushed the door, which did not budge. He shrugged and continued on his search for the missing third entryway on the left.

Far, far in the distance, so far he could barely distinguish it, a lone figure was moving toward him. He quickened his steps, walking faster. As he did so, the person approaching began to materialize. They rapidly closed the gap and Barkow became aware of the man's dark hair and clothing. He wore black trousers and a dark red shirt, and was clean shaven with black hair. He appeared to be practically running. Barkow slowed his step and the man also altered speed. The newcomer moved with catlike precision, which announced he was someone to be reckoned with.

Barkow stopped, as did the person. Realization hit him like a sledge hammer. He walked quickly forward and the figure mimicked his actions. Barkow came to the mirror to find dark eyes sparkled with raging anger, a falling bit of black hair on the forehead and a square jaw with thin, compressed lips. The mirror-wall stretched completely across the hallway with no divisions as a single piece of glass.

As he checked the area where the wall met the mirror, he could not find even a hairline separation between the wall and the glass. Both seemed made of the same material. The wall simply met the glass, leaving no trace of them melding into each other.

"Damn it!" He started back, looking for the elusive third room until he arrived at the head of the staircase. He waited at the top of the stairs and when a lone man approached he stepped in front of him and said, "Pardon me!"

"Yes?"

"Can you tell me where the third room on the left may be?"

"Certainly. I am going to the fourth room. I will show you the way."

He stepped around Barkow and started walking. As they passed the first arched doorway on the right, the man pointed and said, "This is the first room on the right." Farther along, he motioned to the next opening. "Here is the second room on the left."

"Wait," Barkow said. "That is the *first* room on the left."

The man kept walking and Barkow followed.

"You seem to be confused." The man sneered. "We have passed two rooms, Sir, the first room and the second room."

They came to the next opening and the man stopped and pointed at the arched entryway. "Here is your third room."

"But this room is on the right side. I want the left side."

The man looked at Barkow with narrowed eyes and spoke in

a low, menacing voice. "If you must have the third room to be on your left side, than walk down the hall a bit farther, turn around and walk back. Good day to you, Sir." He turned on his heel and continued down the hallway.

Barkow, without trying to suppress the anger that arose at the misunderstanding, loudly cursed the man who had shown him directions to the room. His jutting jaw clamped in anger, he strode through the entryway and into a dimly lighted area.

At once, a tall fellow with tight-fitting, black tuxedo fell into step with him. He had a hook nose and long black hair plastered down in a comb-over. "Good evening Sir. May I be of assistance?"

"Where is Madam Marie?" Barkow growled.

"Who is Madam Marie?"

Barkow grabbed the man's lapels and pulled him roughly up close to his face. "I will say this one more time! Where. Can. I. Find. *Marie?*"

The fellow began to struggle, but Barkow easily kept him from breaking away. He lifted the man up until just his toe-tips touched the floor.

From behind him came a voice, clearly female, edged with scorn. "Let Perry go. He can cause you no harm and only wishes to help."

Barkow's smoky gray eyes darkened. "Shut up, Madam! This is not your concern!" Still holding the man, he jerked around to face the newcomer. Before him stood Marie.

MARIE FOUND

MAY 9, 2012, WEDNESDAY, 1:38 A.M.

BARKOW RELEASED THE man, who scurried away. He gripped Marie's upper arm with one large, meaty hand, forcefully guiding her to the side of the room. Placing her against the wall in the dim light, he stood close, his face mere inches from hers. Eyes of hard granite bored into the dark blue pools looking back at him. Knots of muscle bunched on his clamped jaws. "First, you are going to explain exactly what you know about me!" he growled through gritted teeth. "Then you are going to tell me everything you know about this goddamned place!"

She smiled. "Come, Ben, do not be harsh with me."

His grip on her arm tightened and her smile faded. Her eyes flashed cobalt fire as she placed her free hand upon his cheek. Her nails, like raptor claws, were pointed, long and slightly curved. She raked his cheek, leaving three deep, bloody scratches. He grasped her wrist and then slowly drew the arm down to her side.

Her expression dissolved into a mask of hatred. Her arched eyebrows came together as she frowned. "Okay!" she snapped. "Have it your way! Come to my room and I'll tell you what you want to know!"

With surprising strength, she wrenched away from his grip and shoved him away. "Follow me!" she ordered tersely, then turned and walked out of the room.

He followed, immersed in the ambience of trailing perfumed scent as they walked down the hallway and stopped before a door. It opened into the landing of a stairway. "We'll take this back way. There is no reason for you to make an ass of yourself before the people who come here to forget."

"Go!" he growled, giving her a slight push between the shoulders.

They walked up two flights of stairs and again went into a corridor. After passing several doors, they entered one. She turned on him as soon as the door clicked shut. "Okay, Barkow. You are here for no other reason than FalseLife had become too dangerous."

"And who, in God's name, are you?"

"I am Marie Morninggale, your one true friend, enslaved by your love," she said.

He frowned and growled, "Try again. I said who in hell are you?"

"I am your chosen one, lover and confessor. For God's sake, Barkow, can't you look at me and recognize who I am? Do I mean so little since you have been in FalseLife that you don't even know me anymore?"

"What in the hell are you talking about?" he growled in a rising, contentious voice. He glared at her, wide-eyed, slipping into rage. He didn't want to release the pent up belligerence that had been building since he'd first walked in through the door of the mansion. He was aware of, but ignored, the slight prick when a needle was pushed into the pulsing vein in his neck.

His anger was on the razor edge of exploding when the drug reached his brain and began debilitating his strength and vitality. Thoughts accompanied by images began to revolve slowly through the shadows of his mind: a jangling phone dissolved into a night-driving search; a driver in a battered pickup, then a mansion outlined against dark trees. Faster and faster the visions were speeding around in his brain. Jacques flashed by in a tight suit with long arms. Marie with bright blue eyes went spinning past. The aroma of gardenias as a blonde playing a piano shot by, blending into a grand curved stairway. Everything blurred and morphed into sickening, surging waves. His vision zoomed in and out, mixing together like different hues of paint stirred in a single pot, colors fusing, blending into each other as they pulled in the room's furniture, ceiling, floor and walls, all spinning in a gigantic whirlpool, sucking him into its vortex as all consciousness evaporated. He never felt his head hit the floor as he crumpled into a heap.

WRINKLES IN THE PLOT

May 9, 2012, Wednesday, 1:22 p.m.

As Barkow lay on the floor, his mind spun in and out of the maelstrom of conversations whirling by, some near, some far, most unrecognized. He was carried along on various planes of memory with his brain working at twice the ordinary speed, yet fully aware of details within a specific conversation, from the gibberish of blurred speech shooting by in short bursts.

His body did not move except for shallow breathing. Eventually, the spinning visions in his mind began to slow and a sense of action connected with a spoken word, which in turn keyed a memory. Still unconscious on the floor, he sensed a military office and began reliving an episode from years in his past.

He was standing at attention and heard the clarity of a voice speaking with authority, a voice of command, that must be respected, listened to and obeyed.

Full-bird Colonel J. W. Watts, glared at the man standing before his desk. "At ease, Sergeant. I want to know why the best damned man under my command plans to quit the military."

"Tired of killing, Sir."

"Then take some time off, for God's sake. Go get drunk, get laid, travel to some God damned exotic island and lay around a few weeks. Starting right now you got a thirty day leave. Go on, get out of here."

"No, Sir. Mind's made up."

As the colonel stood up he launched his desk chair backward where it crashed against the wall. Red-faced, fists balled, he stomped around the desk to the sergeant and stopped with his face a mere inch away.

"I can order you to extend your enlistment!"

"No, Sir, you cannot."

A deeper shade of red crawled up the colonel's neck and face.

"Turned chicken, eh kid? In the end, Barkow, you're nothing but a shit-faced, goddamned coward." He watched to see what reaction his words would have.

The sergeant's facial expression went flat. The pupils evolved into dead pits of dull, lifeless blackness, fixating on the colonel's eyes with the uncanny holding power of a rattlesnake over the hapless hare. "Do not underestimate me—Sir."

The dead, gray rimmed, penetrating stare coupled with a strange sound in the voiced words, left no doubt in the colonel's mind that the man before him easily could, without remorse, kill him in an instant.

"Permission to be dismissed—Sir?"

The tone of voice carried far more demand than request. The colonel, with an effort, dropped his gaze. "Dismissed.," he muttered, relieved to be away from the relentless holding power of the soldier's eyes.

Sergeant First Class Barkow snapped to attention, saluted, executed an about face and left the room.

The following morning, the youngest Sergeant First Class in Delta Force dressed for the last time as a soldier of the United States Army.

⊙ THE ROOM BEGAN to revolve as old memories swirled through his brain. Flashes of copter flights and firefights spun past in wild delirium while his mind soared through various states of excitement and mental confusion.

Eventually, the turmoil slowed as the vision became like funhouse mirrors, with everything misshapen into weird forms. His mind gradually focused and locked on the memory of his final mission. He'd been assigned to take out the sentries stationed along the back of a warehouse in which four hundred and fifty-six men lay asleep. Barkow silently relived the killing of each sentry, after which a military demolitions expert had slipped in and laid an explosive charge at the foundation of the building.

The killings took thirteen minutes. Six men, two of them still in their teens, lay with throats slashed ear to ear. They died without making a sound or seeing their assailant. The explosives, affixed to the foundation, were wired together along the back of the building in a pre-designed order to bring the entire cement block structure down in a single instant.

At 0330, along the front of the converted warehouse, six sentries, unaware their opposites in back lay dead, also died as the building with four hundred fifty-six men inside was blown into oblivion.

The Delta Force mission ended as three military helicopters rose and veered away into the night.

THE PLOT BEGINS TO BUD

THE MEMORY OF his Army career dimmed, blinked and vanished in gray fog. Barkow lay in a state of unconsciousness as days slipped by. His body had been moved to a sterile room and he was being fed intravenously. The technicians strived to bring Barkow out of his unconscious state.

The fog slowly thinned in his comatose reality as he rode a bus to LA. His head nodded forward, his mind yearning to return to a relaxed state of emptiness. The smell of stale beer and cigarette smoke increased as the familiar click of pool balls and subdued conversation caused him to open his eyes. Lights above two pool tables illuminated the players as they leaned in. He was in a cabaret, secluded and dark, at a table in the corner. He raised one finger and pointed at the table before him. The blonde barmaid understood he wanted more bourbon. A piano player was rolling the blues low down on the bass keys. The music was slow and sad, the way he liked it and the reason he kept coming back to this place. When his drink came, he said, "With the next drink, bring the bottle and leave it."

"One of those nights, eh Sarge?"

"Yeah, I'm celebrating a break-up."

"Oh, are you?" she said with a hopeful ring to her voice. "Hang 'till I get off and I'll keep you company for a while." The subtle fragrance of gardenia was perceptible as he nodded with the semblance of a smile. He lifted the glass to his mouth and drained it.

When she laughed, her eyes seemed to disappear, Barkow thought. He'd nearly finished the bottle, when the waitress said, "Okay,

48

Sarge, let's go. My place is close and we can walk. Do you mind if Jackie, the piano player, comes along for a night cap?"

"No prob," he slurred with little interest. The piano player, with tousled brown hair, joined them as they stepped into the night air. As they walked, the musician and waitress chatted about their jobs.

"By the way, Sarge," the waitress said, "my name's Laura and this is Jackie. We don't normally befriend the customers, but you seemed so sad every time you came in for a drink and you're always a gentleman. We thought maybe you would just like to talk."

"You look different without your uniform, Sarge," the piano player said.

"Call me Barkow," he slurred. "I got a lot on my mind." As he spoke his world tilted and began to revolve on an angle, blurring the street and buildings as voices blended into screeching nonsense, then slowly returned to normal.

The evening slipped away and Laura fixed coffee. "Jackie is teaching me how to pound the keys for a bar crowd," she said.

"She's good too," Jackie replied as he placed a cup of coffee before Barkow.

"Just keep playing it soft and sad," Barkow mumbled.

"Why do you only like blue songs?"

Barkow looked not at Jackie, but through him. "That's where the fucking mystery comes in," he said quietly. "The mystery of sorrows."

Laura said, "So what you going to do now you're out of the Army?"

"Don't know," he whispered. "One thing for sure... gonna change my first name."

"I've seen your ID. What's wrong with George?" Laura said.

"Long an' boring," he muttered.

"Come on Barkow, give us the low down," Jackie said.

"Have some coffee," Laura said and poured coffee into his cup. A lifelong habit of silence broke in the funky fumes of alcohol. The former sergeant was drunk enough to begin reliving his youth.

"Grew up with no father," he said quietly. "His name was George. I got his gold ring. Mom used to sing to me, you know, when she loved me." Ominous music began to swirl through Barkow's mind. "Told me when I was four, Daddy had run off and left us. She brought home a boyfriend named George, when I was around six. He hated singing. No more fuckin' songs for Georgie boy," Barkow mumbled in a thick-tongued monotone as remembrance crawled through the memories of youth.

"Old George beat her an' abused her an' it was the name of the run-away. Took less'n a year an' Ol' Fuckin' George moved in." His words slurred as his chin sank down on his chest.

"Always called him Ol' Fuckin' George 'cause he got Mama hooked on drugs. I spent as much time hiding from him as I could an' he grew meaner. We moved a lot, always some cheap-ass, dirty dump, one jump ahead of the law."

The couple stared at Barkow with concern as his past unfolded. They kept urging him to drink coffee.

"I's thirteen when Mama had a nervous breakdown an' couldn't do nothin'. The son of a bitch beat her so bad 'cause of it, she died. Came home early, cuttin' school as usual, found her in a puddle of blood." Tears ran down both cheeks.

"Oh my God!" Laura whispered.

"Then what?" Jackie said as he leaned closer.

"Covered Mama with a dirty sheet, took the gold ring and house keys. Never went back," he mumbled. "Crime's common in the ghetto. Took the bastard's jackknife too, an' never heard a thing about what I did."

"Where'd you go?" Laura said as she set a fresh cup of coffee before him.

"Home-schooled on the streets with the homeless, hookers and pimps. Hell, I survived on soup lines and mission meals. Could lie better'n I could tell the truth, an' I learned how to fight."

His head lolled and out came a bitter laugh. "It's a sorry fuckin' mystery."

"It's all behind you, Sarge." Jackie said. "You got a new life ahead of you now."

"Gang punks used to beat the crap out of me for sport… until I learned the way of street fightin'." Barkow's speech lagged. "Never allowed to be called George either…. When I looked old enough, I bought a phony ID and joined up."

Barkow's speech was hesitant and becoming a drawn-out drawl. Jackie and Laura were straining to understand his words. Jackie smiled at Laura, winked and said, "He's about gone, probably going to pass out."

"Ina Army… I was a ring-tailed, fuckin' killer… having had prior experience." Again, he uttered the short, disrespectful laugh. "Another fuckin' mystery… I was picked for Delta Unit."

While he was speaking, the room slowly turned sideways in a sickening angle. The blonde barmaid and musician swirled sluggishly past, along with the furniture and walls. Everything lost cohesion and melded into a multicolored mass that slowly faded into the emptiness of unconsciousness.

"Man, that dude is out colder than a mackerel," Jackie said. "What do you want to do with him?"

"Help me get him on the couch." Together they lugged Barkow to the couch. "He can stay here until morning," Laura said as they stood looking at the former soldier.

"You sure you want him here?" Jackie said, concern in his eyes. "Heck, Laura, you don't know what he'll do when he wakes up."

"It'll be okay, Jackie. I'll be alright."

"You want me to stay with you tonight?" Jackie said hopefully, with a smile.

"Nah, go to your steady, she'll be waiting for you."

"Okay Hon, you take care and call me in the morning. I mean it, Laura. You call me early in the morning, or I'm coming back with a tire iron."

"Okay, okay. I'll call first thing," Laura said as she opened the door.

Jackie slipped out the door and was gone.

Laura cleaned up the cups and went over to Barkow, who was snoring on the couch. She removed his shoes and loosened his tie, causing him to snort twice, then fall into quiet breathing. She placed a lightweight throw over him and thought how innocent he looked while relaxed in sleep. He had always seemed so unhappy when he came to the bar, always alone and not very sociable.

In the confines of her bedroom, as she undressed for bed, she wondered, *Who does he sleep with? A man that handsome has to have someone. He's got the magnetic attraction that all women notice. No wonder he's so unhappy, the way he was brought up.* "Oh well, he doesn't belong to me," she mumbled as she climbed into bed. *Damn it anyway, he'll never belong to me.*

In the pre-dawn hour of darkness, Barkow awoke with a hammering headache and wondered where he was. The muted scent of gardenia lingered in the air as a patchwork of partly remembered events of the evening returned. He picked up his shoes and slipped silently away, ashamed. It was the first time he had ever spoken about his youth.

THE BUD BECOMES A BLOOM

"JACQUES, COME QUICKLY!" Carrie called.

The hard looking man with long arms burst through the doorway. He stood with Carrie as they looked down at the naked man on the bed.

"At last," she murmured. "He's coming out of the coma."

"I figured him a goner after two weeks a vegetable," Jacques muttered.

"Take him to the Lavender Room," Carrie ordered. "He's beginning to shake off his FalseLife role."

Jacques bent and picked up the two hundred thirty pound Barkow like a stuffed doll. He carried him through another door, where he dropped him on a bed.

"Thank you, Jacques. I will tend him."

"You're the boss," Trifle grumbled as he turned to leave.

"You're damned right, I am," Carrie snarled as she glared at his back. "And don't forget it. You have a place now, but it can disappear the second I say so."

Trifle kept walking, pretending not to hear.

Carrie kicked off her shoes and knelt beside the bed. She ran her fingers through Barkow's thick, black hair and then paused to feel his forehead. It was wet with perspiration. He groaned, but his breathing was consistent. She leaned over, kissed his triple-scratched cheek and drew her lips back and forth across his closed mouth. "Forgive me, Barkow," she cooed. "The game had to stop for both our sakes. I have so missed you, my darling." She laid a gentle hand on his chest, checking the rise and fall. "Did

53

Marie bring you back too fast?" she murmured as Barkow rolled onto his side. She smiled, thinking it was time to put her plan into action.

She left him nude, stretched out on the bed, went to the bathroom and stared in the mirror at her image, then began removing clothing until she was naked. She withdrew the pins that held her hair in place, letting it fall. Bluish-black tresses, dividing at the shoulders, dropped on either side of her face and over the swell of her breasts. For a moment, she admired her gleaming black hair and how it set off her pale skin.

She took Barkow's clothes from a linen closet and placed them on the counter. Then, with a feral smile, she skipped from the bathroom and slipped onto the bed with Barkow, folding her soft white body against his hard, muscled back.

Sometime later he awoke. Outlines of memory drifted by in a colorless haze. Partial thoughts of Army life hung in his mind. He lay on his side as his mind started to function. His eyes moved from side to side behind lids lowered to mere slits. The room began taking shape in shades of lavender. Surprised, he realized the warm contact of flesh pressed against his back. He opened his eyes, shifted away and turned with caution toward a nude body. A mass of jet-black hair almost concealed her face on the pillow. She lay on her side facing him, one hand resting on her thigh. He edged closer and leaned toward her. His mind was still in disorder as he reached across and pushed the hair away. With an involuntary intake of breath, he breathed the question. "Mary?"

She moaned and rolled onto her back.

Still lethargic and on one elbow, he looked at her face and bent to kiss her cheek. Nestling his face in her hair he spoke low in her ear. "Mary?"

She awakened and wrapped her arms about him.

"Good morning, precious. Your Marie loves you. How do you feel?"

"Sluggish," he grumbled, "like I've been drugged. Maybe it's a hangover. How did you get here?"

"You've been in FalseLife," she murmured. "You were trying to evade Trifle and his thugs. I knew the place was addictive, but I had to trick you into going there to save you."

"I can't remember anything. Who's Trifle? What happened?" His mind reeled as he tried to understand why Mary Cruthers was in bed with him, naked.

"I was waiting until you were close enough to a portal, in order to entice you to come to me. Trifle was on your trail in FalseLife and I was afraid you would not recognize him as an enemy."

To Barkow her voice grew into a screech as it wavered in unpredictable heights, then dropped to a croaking bass and crawled up the scale to hover in a near-normal range.

"A portal? What portal?"

"A stone mansion on the coast of Washington."

"What in the hell are you talking about?" he barked as awareness ignited in the full impact of her being here. "How long have I been in this FalseLife?"

"About four weeks in TrueLife time, but several months in FalseLife time. I love you, mon amant."

The room toppled sideways and began to turn. Furniture blurred as the speed increased. Barkow tried to sit up, but the imagined centrifugal force of the spinning room kept him pinned on the bed. "What's happening?" he yelled.

"Hush now, Cheri. It is the effect of coming out of FalseLife."

With something akin to nonhuman strength, Barkow forced himself to bring his legs over the edge of the bed. Every muscle and bone ached as if he had run a marathon. He lay back in exhaustion. When the room slowed, he stood, swayed, almost fell, and then lurched to the bathroom. "My God!" he uttered as he looked in the mirror. His face was beaten and battered, and there were dark pouches beneath his eyes. Three scabbed furrows arced from his left cheekbone toward his mouth. A web of wrinkles spread from the corners of his bloodshot eyes. He needed a shave and was stark naked. Large welts and bruises were scattered over his body. Holding on to the countertop, he turned to the doorway and staggered back through the swaying room to collapse on the bed.

"No, no my love, you must fight to regain your strength and good looks again," she said. "I have so much planned for us. Together we can rule the world."

"I'm sick," he groaned as he curled up on his side and the room started to revolve. "I need to sleep."

"Yes, you go to sleep!" she hissed. "I may or may not be downstairs if you ever decide to wake up again."

Through slitted eyes, he watched as she pulled on a thin robe and stormed out of the room, slamming the door behind her.

Forcing himself to take control of his mind, he closed his eyes and started a slow breathing exercise to calm himself. The room slowed and stopped turning. The dizziness in his mind cleared as imagined cobwebs, clouding reason, were pulled away. A strange tranquility began building a gentle umbrella above him. He let his body and mind relax as the tension drained away. When he reached a state of comparative self-controlled comfort, he tried to recall what he could remember. *Years ago I fell in love with Mary Cruthers when we worked together on the story she wrote about Delta Force. I thought she loved me too until I realized she had used me to get the information she wanted. My pride and bitterness would not allow me to go begging for her love.* His mind started to work with more speed and precision as he continued to catalog his memories into order. *I worked as a claims adjuster by day, drank rotgut whiskey in cheap bars by night and carried the torch for Mary. Later I won the Arizona lottery for ninety-six million dollars and after taxes walked away with forty-three million in cash. From that day forward, I only drank the best—Blanton's Single Barrel Bourbon—and changed to a life of refinement.*

The odd situation and condition in which he found himself, began to solidify in his mind. *It all started with a strange phone call at the hotel in Seattle,* he thought. *No.... Before that, a claim about a boat fire.* His mind was grasping at an elusive figment: *In the Blue Note Bar. There was a fight.* He mentally began to sort and catalog new memories. All of a sudden, like a musty, old machine brought out of storage, his brain burst into life. With perfect clarity, a single thought formed: *The woman named Marie appeared to be made up to resemble Mary.* Realization exploded in his mind. *Something's off.* A vague impression of an actress playing a part and the answers piled one upon another. *Her speech patterns are skewed, her behavior makes instantaneous changes and she has a temper that ignites in a split second.* Of one thing he was certain: the woman with black, dyed hair and a French accent was *not* Mary Cruthers.

MARY CRUTHERS

MAY 22, 2012, TUESDAY, 1:15 P.M.

BARKOW LAY IN bed, weak, battered and bruised, but functional. He recalled his past life. *My youth was a fucking mess and, life on the streets was just as destructive. The Army? Yeah, I remember that shit too. I got blind drunk on the day I was discharged.*

Some thoughts arrived in crystalline sharpness. *I met and fell in love with Mary Cruthers. Hell, I still am and I'm still working for Great Metro.* His mind picked and pried at vague memories. *Everything is clear right up until I fought with the two guys at the Blue Note. Memories get fuzzy around the edges from that point on.* Scraps of memory materialized and faded into obscurity. Seattle and something about a search welled up from the murkiness of memories, shrouded in cobwebs. A fog swirled in his mind, clouding remembrance until he awoke with the woman who resembled Mary. *Get up! Get out!* The constant awareness churned in his brain cells. *Get up! Get out! Get up now and get out!*

Realization connected with understanding and exploded into knowledge. Clearly, everything that had occurred since the fight at the Blue Note had happened not in reality but in his drugged mind. *Get up! Get out! Get up now and get out!*

⊘ MARY CRUTHERS WAITED three floors below for the Personnel Manager of Axelwood Labs to make an appearance. The time was 1:36 p.m. Her thoughts strayed to a point in time, several years ago, when she had received a bonus of five thousand dollars.

"Thank you, Sir. I am also pleased with the story. It was easy to write once I had all the facts."

"Yes, but getting the facts and putting them in your own style of writing was superb. That's why you were given the task. The same may be said for why you are now the Featured Writer on Socialite Magazine."

"Thanks again." She had smiled at him.

"A bonus for a job well done."

"Thank you so much, Mr. McCormick."

That had happened four years ago. The phrase lingered in her mind as she glared at the wall clock showing 2:05 p.m. *Why is he not here? I have my career and I'm famous in a modest way.* She recalled the restaurant, where she had gone and called her best friend. "Hi Rusty, I'm at a fabulous restaurant," she had said. "You want to join me?"

"Sorry Hon. I can't. I'm involved in a shoot that might go on for hours."

"Aw. I wanted to celebrate my bonus with you. My treat," she had said hopefully.

"Sorry sweetheart, I just can't. How about we go out tomorrow night?"

"Okay, she'd said. I'll see you then. I love you."

"Love you too."

Mary was aggravated. The time showed 2:34 p.m. and the Personnel Manager had yet to make an appearance. Her thoughts skipped to the reason she was here. She had awakened in the wee hours of morning, wondering why. *Why do I even think about him anymore? So he had been hurt, so what? My plans do not include being involved with anyone except Rusty, regardless of Barkow's looks, or his feelings.*

She'd written the story. It had been featured in the SM and became a blazing success in a six-part series. *Barkow was the perfect fit to provide the details I needed to make it a perfect story. Of course, I had to pretend I was falling for him, in order to get the facts. I got my bonus and kudos from the big-guy himself.* All had gone according to plan. Facts were the essential thing. *How else can my fans understand the precise way to slit a man's throat or kill four hundred and fifty-six men in the space of a few seconds? He'll get over it,* she thought, *but will I? Heck, he might even be married by now.*

It had happened after his discharge from the Army. They'd spent six weeks sharing a suite of rooms at the palatial New York Four Seasons Hotel. The SM paid all expenses. She had her set of rooms and he had his, each off a central living room. Locking doors to their own rooms allowed both of them privacy. Each suite had a personal exit door to the hotel hallway.

Deep in my heart, I knew he was falling for me, but he is a gentleman and would not press. I showed just enough of myself to lead him into telling me everything. A few hugs and kisses that I thought meant nothing, at least to me.

For the ten-thousandth time, she thought of how she had ended the relationship. Nonchalantly, she'd said, "Well, this is the end. We finally got the job done. It's been fun and I hope you have a wonderful life."

"Wait a minute," he'd growled. "Are you just going to walk away without another word?"

"Hey, I have a career to look after." She'd opened the door to her suite.

"Mary!" he had exclaimed as she was shutting the door.

"I love you!" she heard as the lock clicked shut.

She'd left her room, going down the hallway to the elevator. While the doors were opening, he had appeared in the hall.

"Wait!" he'd called as she had stepped into the elevator and pressed the button, cutting off his final words.

"Mary, I love—"

That was the last time she'd seen him. He'd never called or tried to contact her as she'd expected he would do. Later she began a relationship with Rusty, but Barkow had haunted her thoughts through the years. Now, before she moved in with Rusty, she needed to talk with Barkow and make absolutely certain she had no feelings for Barkow.

IN THE LUCKY DUCE TAVERN

AT THE BACK of a sleazy Chicago tavern sat a heavy, robust man. He slouched at a splintered, shopworn table, unshaven and rumpled. He had black hair and a bronzed face, weather creased from working the docks. His short fingers spread from calloused palms. He drank the last of his beer and bellowed: "Another damn beer here!"

The bartender shuffled over and set a bottle before him. "That'll be three bucks."

The customer drew crumpled bills from his pocket and slewed them across the table, along with some change. The barkeep sorted out three dollars and returned to the bar.

A slow-moving paddle-fan gently ruffled the blue haze drifting in the room. The entrance opened, revealing a woman who quietly pulled the door shut. She moved with a lithe grace through layers of shifting air currents to the bar, her high heels clicking across the dirty concrete floor.

"What'll you have?" the bartender asked, sizing her up.

"I'm looking for a man named Trifle. Is he here?"

The men seated at the tables along the wall, gawked. Each was thinking of the body filling out her tight black skirt. Her hair was tied back by narrow side braids joined in back and lost in flowing waves of bluish-black hair. She wore a smart little wool cap, set at a jaunty angle, and a fitted jacket of black suede, the top three unbuttoned and bursting with the swell of breasts, which seemed to have mesmerized the bartender.

"Well?" she demanded.

"I might know him. What's it worth?" he murmured, leering at her cleavage.

She fixed her cold, ice-blue eyes on the barman. A stare of unrelenting penetration bored into him until he raised his eyes.

For a moment, he looked at her face, then made his decision and flicked his gaze away. "Table in back." He muttered.

She turned and walked to the table, where the brutish man was sitting. "Is your name Trifle?"

"Who wants to know?" he said as he brought the bottle up to his lips. He looked from little pig eyes as he let a swallow of beer flow into his mouth. He had a weather-beaten face and massive bone structure forming an overhung forehead with thick eyebrows. A bent and flattened nose, having been broken more than once, set above meaty lips. Deep creases lined his face, accentuating the square jaw and bull-nosed chin. He was muscular, with long arms.

She stood opposite him and leaned forward, showing ample cleavage. "I do. I understand you know how to handle men. Is that true?"

"That's me, lady. You got a job for me, eh?" He spoke in a low, raspy voice that could peel layered brass from a doorknob.

She looked him over like a rancher assessing a prize bull at a livestock auction. She noted the scarred knuckles, his calloused palms, the bulging biceps on his long, thick arms and his battered face. She nodded. "You'll do." She fixed him with a piercing gaze. "If you'd like to make more money than you've ever imagined, you'll be at this address, ten o'clock tomorrow morning." She laid a card on the table.

"This job is for as long as you can take orders and keep people in line. You'll be given an open expense account and furnished with housing, clothing and food. You may drive any brand of car you prefer, with a new model every year. You will take orders directly from me and keep your mouth shut about everything you see or hear while you're my employee."

She turned away before he said anything and walked back

toward the front door. The beer guzzlers gawked in appreciation as she tapped by in the slow, rolling gait of a woman advertising her sexuality. One man openly leered, showing yellow-stained teeth. Another in a filthy tank-top, his arms covered with prison tattoos, blew a low wolf whistle as she reached the door.

Trifle also watched her leave. The scent of perfume hung in the stale air around his table. A furtive smile cracked his thick lips for an instant as he gathered up his change, downed the remaining beer and tucked her card into his shirt pocket. He stood up, pushing his chair back, sent a sideways, backward nod toward the tables near the wall and left by the back door.

Throughout the episode of her arrival and departure, no one had noticed the small, plain man with a hatchet face who had entered directly after the woman. He was lacking distinct or individual characteristics and appeared dull and uninteresting, with a wide-brimmed fedora pulled low on his forehead.

Had anyone seen his eyes, below the brim, they would have been startled at how baleful they appeared as his gaze swept back and forth across the room. His right hand remained in the pocket of his trench coat as Cain Martin quietly left the Lucky Duce, shortly after the richest woman in the world had departed.

CARRIE AXELWOOD

IN PHOENIX, ARIZONA, Carrie Axelwood stood at one end of a polished bar in an upscale hotel. She had indigo eyes that could read a man like an x-ray as she watched their faces while they appraised her curvaceous body and perfect make-up. Her dark brown hair, now dyed black, hung in waves that parted at the shoulders, leaving tendrils of curls to play about her throat. The dark blue, sequined cocktail dress hung to just above her knees. The faces watching her were a study in desire, some hungry, some dominant and some literally drooling as their eyes feasted.

Some women have the ability to make men lust for them just by being what they are. Other women have the ability to make men consider them unschooled in the art of deception, and there are a few women who have both the foregoing effects at the same time. Carrie Axelwood was such a woman.

She was thinking of Trifle and how and where she had found him. Her plan required someone of his background and abilities. Positive that her natural instincts had picked the right man for what she had in mind, she had mentally thanked Cain Martin for giving her the tip of finding him in that Chicago tavern.

"Miss?" the barkeep said as he approached her end of the bar.

"Lemon-drop," she said in a soft voice that hinted a French accent. When the drink arrived she laid a twenty on the bar.

Drink in hand she once more scanned the room in search

of *his* face. With a soft sigh, she slowly walked through the lounge with the undulating gait of a woman on the make, but in truth, she only wanted *him*. Carrie enjoyed having handsome men watching her. She not only used, but also abused, many of them.

Let them drool! She thought as she purposely threaded her way through and around the upturned faces. Her perfume left a trail of delicate scented air through the cocktail lounge and into the lobby of the Phoenix Grand Hotel.

⊘ CARRIE AXELWOOD, RICH beyond the means or expectations of a large number of the world's governments or their populations, was used to having her own way. The handsome man who came to work on the claims adjustment issue, had at once commanded her full attention. Great Metro had sent him when she was suing them for the sum of four million dollars, which was small by her standards.

It was certainly not my fault, she thought, *that some ridiculous paper was not signed at the time the insurance was taken out.*

When the claims adjuster G. B. Barkow arrived, she had taken one look into those fierce gray eyes and knew he was the one meant for her to love and cherish for as long as she desired. She held the key to winning his love right there in that little four million dollar lawsuit. She dangled the settlement in front of him like a carrot, all the time having dinners and lunches with him on the pretext of getting the lawsuit settled.

Carrie was beautiful and wealthy. She was sought after by many powerful men but had never developed an interest in marrying anyone. She enjoyed many one night stands, always being the dominatrix, refusing to allow anyone to take control except with her permission. After all other attempts to win Barkow's love or adoration failed, she eventually offered her body, which he cautiously refused. Carrie was stunned by the fact that there was actually a man she could not have. Previously, her wealth had purchased anyone she desired. Barkow became her first failure, which only intensified her craving for him.

Then he had found the loophole that destroyed all her plans. Carrie cared nothing about the money. She had more money than she would ever need. It was the man she wanted. She had convinced herself that he would be her boy-toy to use as long as she desired.

With the development of FalseLife, Carrie could have anything the world had to offer. Why Barkow, this sexy, good-looking man, would not fall into the pattern of bowing and scraping like all the rest, she did not understand. Her craving became a fixation.

Carrie was not only a beautiful woman, but also highly intelligent. She was an authority on psychology as well as mastering the internal mechanisms of electronic role-playing avatar games.

She had designed, engineered and developed FalseLife, a virtual environment in which the player assumed the form, attributes and aspect of a highly sophisticated avatar while playing the game that had become a worldwide leading pastime.

FalseLife was more realistic then life itself and certainly more exciting. Everything was perfect because it forced your course of existence to be whatever you wanted it to be. Designing and building your avatar was as effortless as thinking it. This animated, digital object produced by thought and imagination became the embodiment of the user, functioning in a virtual environment, controlled by computer software.

In the beginning, anyone with a computer could avoid the actual world and enter a fantastic world of make-believe. It realistically created life in any desired scenario. In the game, you literally became whatever you wished to be, although in truth, your body was actually controlled by scents, desires, wants and needs.

The only drawback was the power of its opium-like seduction, which drew people like a magnet draws iron filings. Governments passed laws attempting to snuff out usage and ownership.

Carrie's answer to those laws became the patented FalseLife Portals, which now dotted the landscape of many countries. They were small constructions that resembled motels or hotels. They were made up of small rooms that contained the full control apparatus, connected to a central computer, and operated for a period of three hours per session. The period of time could seem like weeks in the maze of FalseLife.

The Portals operated on Tuesdays, Thursdays and weekends. Sessions were available, for a price, to anyone who wished to escape into a make-believe existence, unrestrained by convention or morality.

The Portal system was designed and built by Axelwood Inc. People had been known to return to reality with a vastly changed persona.

FalseLife Portal procedures were negotiated with and approved by the United States government. Carrie Axelwood had quickly become the richest person in the world.

It was rumored in dark places that black market, full time hook-ups could be obtained, complete with enhancement drugs and perfumes, for a price affordable only to those who were wealthy and had influence.

Carrie's obsession with avatar role-play eventually transferred itself to a desire for the love of a man. Not any man, but a certain man she had set her heart on. All she required was a way to persuade him to come to her. She needed to manipulate his life so he would love her and only her. She simply had to set her mind to the problem, which would allow her intelligence to produce the desired effect.

By having the subject use a combination of FalseLife role play, being detached from a computer and using a form of cyborg kinetics, she was certain the details would work out to her satisfaction. Axelwood technicians feverishly worked to perfect those techniques.

THE MELTING POT BUBBLES

MAY 22ND, TUESDAY, 10:00 A.M.

MARY CRUTHERS LANDED at Phoenix Sky Harbor on a bright sunny morning. After obtaining her luggage, she taxied to a Four Seasons hotel.

Here, she would begin searching for information about G. B. Barkow. She needed his routine so she could accidentally bump into him. In the phonebook, she found the address to both the Great Metro office and Blue Note Bar & Lounge. Picking up the phone she punched in Room Service.

"This is Mary Cruthers. Please send up a pot of coffee and today's local paper."

MAY 22ND, TUESDAY, 10:15 A.M.

Unknown to Mary, Carrie Axelwood's private jet had landed shortly after Mary's plane arrived. A single passenger in a brown suit and trench coat had deplaned quickly. A chauffeured limousine waited to whisk Cain away from the airport, past dusty mesquite trees and cactus, to a location deep in the desert.

MAY 22ND, TUESDAY, 10:15 A.M.

Barkow lay on a bed in the lavender room, having come out of FalseLife and was clearing the fog from his mind as memories were returning. He had no awareness he was in a research and development complex known as Axelwood Laboratories.

He could recall his early home life, Army service and time

spent with Mary Cruthers. It was the time from the fight in the Blue Note that still had missing parts. He vaguely remembered sections of time that seemed real, yet surreal.

He knew he was the senior claims adjuster at Great Metro. He was also aware of having been drugged and that it caused him not to remember certain things. His mind kept regressing to the thought that he desperately needed to get himself away from his present location. "Yeah, that's it," he muttered. "Got to get up, get dressed and get out." He was clumsy in raising himself up and pushing his legs over the side of the bed. He forced himself to stand, fighting the wave of nausea that swept over him.

Struggling to keep his balance, Barkow swayed back and forth as he stood beside the bed. His legs began to tremble, then to shake uncontrollably and he knew if he tried to walk he would fall. He sat on the bed, thoroughly exhausted. All he wanted to do was to lie down again, but regardless of how his body felt, his subconscious mind demanded he get up, get dressed and get out. Bleary eyed, he stared across the room. He saw a wavering door, forced himself to stand and then staggered toward it. He grasped the door handle for support, pulled it open and saw his clothes on the bathroom counter. He slowly gathered them up and lurched back to the bed. Waves of queasiness washed across him as, like a sleepwalker, he pulled on his clothes. His mind was locked on the single action of getting out of the room and away from this location.

MAY 22ND, TUESDAY, 11:59 A.M.

Two floors below the nauseated Barkow, Carrie Axelwood was enraged because the innovation she'd used to seduce Barkow had failed. She strode into the recreation room and glared at the employees lounging about in comfortable, overstuffed chairs. A stereo was blearing insane rock music, which reverberated from the ceiling and walls. Along the bar-top stood open bottles of alcohol and empty glasses.

Carrie looked around the room, noting how the people were slouched here and there. Most were paying little attention to anything, appearing to be in a stupor. Her gaze eventually settled on Jacques Trifle. He was sitting in a relaxed posture, drink in hand, head resting on the back pillow with his mouth open, as labored breath wheezed in harmony with the rise and fall of his chest.

Carrie walked behind the bar and cut the power to the stereo, plunging the room into silence. She walked the length of the back-bar, one arm sweeping everything away, sending bottles and glasses crashing to the floor. The group quickly became aware something was wrong. Trifle leaped up, letting his drink drop to the floor as he crouched into a street fighter's stance. Some people quickly looked up and others sat up straight. All eyes turned toward the bar.

"The game's up!" Carrie said loudly. "Jacques, Butch, Rollo and Bert will stay. Trifle, you are to pay off and fire the rest of them."

"Fire them? Why in the hell you gonna fire them?" Jacques said in surprise. "For Christ's sake Marie, these are damn good men!"

"Listen to me, Trifle. You do as you're told, or you and your entire pack can get your fat asses off my property! And don't call me Marie anymore! Understand?"

"Well crap, I just think—"

"You're not paid to think! You're paid to follow orders! Now move it! Get them paid off and on a bus out of here within the next ten minutes or you'll be going too!"

Carrie picked up the phone and touched Security, which connected her to Axelwood Patrol, her private security company. Almost a small army, it guarded the many properties she owned throughout the world.

"Captain, have a security bus brought around to the side entry and then stand by at the Controller's Office with a squad of men. Your team is to accompany the passengers to Sky Harbor Airport and then return here."

"Yes, Ma'am. Right away, Ma'am!"

"Another thing, Captain. Alert the main gate and tell them I am expecting a visitor by the name of Cain Martin in the limo. Have them take him to the Blue Room."

"Yes, Ma'am. Right away, Ma'am!"

The group of actors and make-up artists, somewhat shocked and bewildered, followed Trifle into the main office of the building. The Controller for this particular Axelwood complex was used to things changing quickly. After consulting his records, he paid each person $1,500 in cash as six well-armed guards of Axelwood Security stood by. When they were all aboard the bus, Trifle gathered up the other three and went to the owner's private office.

Carrie was at her desk, leaning forward, writing notes on an inside page of a folder. She did not look up when Trifle and his men entered, but continued to scribble notations.

Trifle knew, in her frame of mind, not to interrupt. He and his men waited, knowing she was deliberately ignoring them. After several long, silent minutes, Carrie stopped writing. She shut the folder, pushed it to the center of her desk and then leaned back in her chair and looked at the four men.

"What you want us to do, Boss?" Trifle said. "Are we gonna keep Barkow going in circles?"

"For God's sake, you idiot, it's over! If these two loony-birds of yours, hadn't screwed up the fight in that bar, everything would have gone as planned."

Glaring at his employer, Butch mumbled through his swollen jaw, which was still wired in place, "How'd I know he was a fighter, Ms. Axelwood? If I'd been told he was a scrapper, I'd've been ready for 'im."

"I told you Butch, y'should've used brass knucks on him," Rollo said in a falsetto voice. His mashed nose was swollen and veined with bright scarlet lines, causing his voice to sound high pitched and strange. He walked with a limp, favoring his aching knee, which was bundled in a soft cast.

"Shut yer mouth," Butch said through clenched teeth, "or I'll close it for ya permanently."

"Shut the hell up!" Trifle growled, pushing them apart.

"Instead, you both got your butts kicked!" Carrie complained, staring at the two. "The strategy was to put him in the hospital where I could have had him worked over and led him into FalseLife under control. But no, you bozos are simply too dumb to handle one drugged man. He was pushed too fast. Barkow has so damn much self-confidence he was never wholly under control."

Trifle turned toward the desk. "I did my best with those false identities."

"You did well Jacques," Carrie mused. "I thought we had him when he came to the mansion."

"I often thought," replied Jacques, "he was going to pop back into reality at any second."

Carrie was silent, thinking of how they had led him around under the drugs he was getting in his coffee, booze and food. She plotted a plan of action. *I still need Trifle, and I'll keep his two goons because it makes him think all is well. Bert has also been useful. Barkow actually thought he had flown to Seattle and inspected a damaged boat. He never realized he was walking and talking in the enhancement rooms of this complex.*

Carrie's mind quickly skimmed the facts. Descriptions had been fed into Barkow's brain. Exotic, life-like scents had increased the sensation of reality. He had been in a mock-up car at the gate of a nonexistent mansion. Her technicians were masters at the art of make-believe.

The mansion and all its oddities were made up well in advance of putting those thoughts and feelings into Barkow's mind.

Some people he thought he talked to were merely actors

in make-up, modeled after individuals he knew. The butler, the servants and others were performers, made up and enhanced to execute as designed, to create a feeling of realism.

Everything except the bar fight had taken place here in this complex of Axelwood Laboratories in the desert on the outskirts of Phoenix.

The problem had been Barkow himself. He was strong willed and would not, in the deepest part of his soul, believe the world as it had become. His sub-conscious kept rejecting things that could not happen, even when his drugged conscious mind told him it was true. As events became more bizarre, caused by the technicians in their attempt to fully pull him under, his rejection became more pronounced. He seemed always on the defining edge between reality and FalseLife.

From the time he got out of the mansion he began to reject what was happening. That rejection was replaced with anger. The techs were desperately trying to maneuver Barkow into a false reality, but that only increased his wrath as he resolved to get at the truth of the strange happenings.

Carrie closed her eyes, rubbing the high bridge of her nose, trying to massage away the ache in her head. Her thoughts still lingered on Barkow: *I wanted him to believe I was Mary. He should be in my bed, loving me as I would love him. But no way! He had to be snotty about the whole thing and then became aggressive. And that stupid quick-release drug didn't work either. Now he's half out of his senses. Will he return to normal or become an imbecile?*

She sighed. The time had come to get rid of G. B. Barkow. She opened her eyes and looked across her desk at the four men, silent before her. With meticulous precision, her mind presented the necessary steps to be taken. "Bert, go get Cain Martin from the Blue Room. Bring him to me." Bert nodded and quickly left the room.

"You two, Dumb and Dumber, get Barkow from the Lavender Room and shackle him with chains—not ropes—then gag him and put him into the black SUV in the garage. Now listen carefully: use extreme caution, he is out from under the influence of drugs and may be volatile. Make sure he is totally controlled."

"Jacques, you stay with me. I have a little chore for you."

She stood up, shaking her head, and glared at Butch and Rollo. "Well, don't stand there, you fools, get to it!"

The men quickly hobbled out of the room.

Bert brought Martin into the office, then turned and left.

"You want me for something, Carrie?"

"Yes Cain, matters have become serious and I wanted to tell you in person." Her stare bonded itself to the flat black pupils of the unpretentious man. "I have an important job for you to do in a short while. Be prepared for action at a moment's notice." Carrie turned and began putting some folders away. "If you want anything, anything at all, just call Supply."

"I will await your call," Cain said in a monotone as he slipped out the door, closing it softly.

"Come, Jacques" she snapped, stepping from behind the desk and walking quickly out of the office, with Jacques following like an obedient dog. The time was Tuesday 11:50 a.m.

MARY ON THE PROWL

Mary Cruthers was eating lunch and skimming the paper. A small advertisement caught her attention: *Wanted: Persons knowledgeable in cyborg kinetics. Highest prices paid. Contact Axelwood Laboratories.*

Her reporter's instinct sounded the alarm in Mary's head. The smell of a story distinctly hovered around the ad for cyborg kinetic technicians; however, it was the name of Axelwood that set off the alarm. Mary recalled a newspaper article stating that Axelwood Inc. had filed suit against Great Metro Insurance. She was interested because Barkow had been assigned to the claim. She had followed the story in later articles and observed that Carrie had an obsession with Barkow.

During the ensuing lawsuit, he'd testified that he had refused to allow a relationship to flourish because she was a client with a bogus claim.

The truth was, because he ignored her advances it had only increased Carrie's desire to have him. He was grateful when he could prove the claim fraudulent and end contact between them. Even so, she had kept popping into his life, from time to time in the guise of chance meetings.

Mary picked up the phone and dialed the number in the ad.

"Good morning. Axelwood Labs," someone with a cheery voice said.

"Good morning. I would like to inquire about the ad for cyborg kinetic technicians."

"Of course, please hold while I put you through to Personnel."

In a moment, someone said, "Personnel."

"Hello, I'm a reporter for SM magazine, working on a story concerning cyborg kinetics. This is in regards to a human whose body has been taken over in whole or in part by electromechanical devices. Is it possible for a person to be controlled by a machine, thinking they are an integral part of the machine, or is the machine simply a part of them?"

He laughed. "We are delving into such matters only in a temporary capacity. Our founder has become interested in it and has been asking for experts on the subject."

"I see. Any particular reason for the interest?"

"Only that she wishes more research on the theory of Cyborg Kinetics.

"Thank you so much. Perhaps I can come out and speak with someone who could answer a few technical questions."

"Of course. I'll hand you over to my secretary who can give you the particulars on our location and so forth."

After gaining the information, Mary hung up. Next she took a cab to the Blue Note Bar and Lounge. It was just past noon and the place was deserted. She stepped from the lobby through the blue beaded curtains into club central. Inside, she noted the bar to her left, along the back wall. Tables and chairs were placed around a small dance floor, looking across to a raised section in the corner, which held a parlor grand piano. The only person on duty was a young man behind the bar.

"Hi, would you like a drink?" he said.

"Too early… can you tell me if G. B. Barkow has been in lately?"

"Sorry, I'm Bobby, the day fill-in. You could stop by later and talk to the night barkeep. He may know."

"Okay, thanks." Mary smiled and walked out of the bar. The cab she had come in was nowhere in sight. Here in the suburbs there would be no taxi stands so one would have to be called. She retraced her steps into the Blue Note and asked if she could use a phone book.

"Of course," he replied as he laid the book on the bar top.

"Thanks, Bobby." She flipped through the pages in search of a car rental. Finding one, she drew her cell phone out and called the number.

The reply came in a metallic voice. "Hertz Rental."

After she told them she wanted a late-model Lexus, they advised her it would be approximately twenty to thirty minutes before a car could get to her location.

"Thank you and will you please send a map of the city along with the car?"

"Yes Ma'am. A built-in GPS comes with the car."

"Thank you, I'll be waiting." She snapped the phone shut and replaced it in her purse. "Guess I'll have that drink after all," she said to the barkeep. "Make it a lemon drop."

He nodded, took a small goblet, and prepared the drink. He placed the glass with a sugar coated rim before her on a napkin. "Not many people order that anymore, although lately, there is one who does."

"I have always enjoyed the sour-sweet taste of it. Your customer must be a woman; it's definitely not a man's drink."

"Right on. Ms. Axelwood is very partial to that drink."

"I see! Does she come here often?"

"Well, she actually hardly ever comes in on my shift, but Bert, the night bartender, once said she had been coming in quite regularly. I think she even hired him for some part-time work."

"That's very interesting." Mary said. "I had just called Axelwood Laboratories today, seeking information on a story I'm doing."

"You a writer?"

"Yes, I just flew into town today." A long blast of a car horn sounded outside. "That's my rental. How much for the drink?"

"For a new customer, it's on the house!"

"Thanks Bobby. I gotta run. See you around." Mary stepped

through the beaded entry into the small lobby and outside to the waiting car at the curb.

The driver took her back to the rental office, where she filled out the necessary paperwork and took possession of a white Lexus sedan. She plugged the address for Axelwood Laboratories into the GPS and soon was heading out of the city.

It was May 22nd, Tuesday, 12:20 p.m.

OUT OF THE FOG

BARKOW, HAPHAZARDLY DRESSED, still dizzy, but starting to function somewhat like his old self, looked around the lavender room for a weapon. The entry door was locked from the outside and he was aware danger lurked from unknown opponents. Scanning the room he spied a desk chair. It was rather elegant looking with a carved scroll back and short, curving legs.

He laid the chair on its side and with a single stomp, broke off one of the legs. He stepped into the bathroom and splashed cold water on his face and over his hair. Feeling awake and more alert, he abruptly stopped short, head slightly bent, and remained that way for a long moment. He had recognized the sound of scuffing outside the room. With a rush of adrenaline, he stepped to the door of the bath, which was ajar, waited and listened. There came the small, unmistakable brattle of a key being inserted, followed by the releasing click of a lock as the entry door opened and into the room stumbled two men.

"Probably passed out in the bathroom," one of them said in a clipped, crusty voice.

The other answered in an odd falsetto. "That shot was enough to kill a mule."

"What the hell? Who broke the damn chair?" the first man said.

"That would be me." Barkow stepped out of the bathroom, chair leg in hand.

Standing before him was an odd looking pair. Rollo's huge swollen nose was webbed with small veins like a road map.

79

Draped over his shoulder, in loops was a small-linked, steel chain. The knee of his right leg had a soft cast on it, making him walk stiffly. His eyes were bright and wide open in surprise. His shirt with sleeves cut out at the shoulder-seams showed thick, fat arms covered with hand-pecked prison tattoos.

The other one, Butch, with his mouth bandaged where the jawbone was wired shut and eyes mere slits in a swollen face, held a pair of cuffs in his right hand and a bottle of beer with a protruding straw in his left.

Barkow recognized them as the pair who had attacked him a month earlier in the Blue Note.

Rollo took the length of chain from his shoulder and advanced, swinging it around his head.

Barkow threw his make-shift club directly at Rollo's face and quickly moved toward Butch, who seemed rooted to the floor. Grabbing the handcuffs as he went past, he pulled Butch's arm up behind his back. Barkow's Army training returned as he gripped the other arm and quickly snapped the cuffs onto the wrists while using him as a shield. He shoved Butch into the advancing Rollo, who, not wanting to hit Butch with the chain, checked his swing. A moment later they collided.

Barkow kept pushing and the two would-be assailants fell into a heap on the floor. A vicious kick to Rollo's head put him out of commission as Barkow grasped the chain and quickly tangled them together with it. He turned, seeing the key still in the lock of the open door, grabbed the phone, ripped out the cord and dropped the receiver on the floor.

He quickly slipped through the door, pulled it shut and locked it. A wave of nausea swept over him and he leaned against the wall for a moment until it passed. Seeing a potted palm, he stepped over and buried the key in the potting soil. At 1:40 p.m. he bypassed a recessed elevator and continued down the hallway to a door marked *Stairs*. He slipped inside and soon arrived at the bottom of the stairwell at a door with a small window to the outside. He peered through the window as a busload of men drove past.

He cautiously opened the door and looked in both directions. An incoming black limousine was stopped at the gate. To his right, he assumed, was the front of the building. He slipped out the door and ran left, along the side of the building toward the back.

There, freight trucks were backed up to a dock. The truck doors were painted with the Axelwood logo. He decided to be bold and act as though he belonged here. The sun was hot and high in the sky. He walked the length of the dock. At the corner, a short set of concrete steps led down to a sidewalk, which ran toward the front of the building.

A white Lexus was parked in the visitor's parking lot. He noted the small number decal on the back of the car, identifying it as a rental. With the confidence of luck, he strolled to the car. Finding a back door unlocked, he slipped into the car.

The heavy tinted windows were excellent cover. The scent of new car was unmistakable. He also was aware of the slight fragrance of cologne and wondered why it had been left unlocked. The dash clock read 2:00 p.m.

Because it was in the visitor's parking slot, chances are that whoever rented it would come back before long. He hunkered down on the floorboards to wait. As he waited, the thought of it being unlocked led him to believe the person must have been in a great hurry. Like a dose of cold water, the thought entered his mind. *Perhaps the keys are also in the car.*

He looked over the driver's seat and sure enough, the keys were still stuck in the ignition. Barkow looked at the guard shack by the gate. The wooden gate arms were lowered for both incoming and outgoing lanes, with the guard shack to one side. No guards were visible, which put them all inside the shack.

This was too good a chance to pass up. He climbed over the center console and plopped into the driver's seat, started the engine and slowly backed out of the parking slot. Slipping the shift lever into drive, he began rolling slowly toward the guard shack. No one was near when he stopped at the gate. A guard at the window waved him through without stepping outside. The gate arm went up and Barkow was free of the complex. As the powerful engine gathered speed and roared down the highway, a tight smile of satisfaction spread across the dry, cracked lips in the bruised and swollen face of G. B. Barkow. It was May 22nd, Tuesday, 2:20 p.m..

THE OTHER SIDE OF CARRIE

CARRIE WALKED OUT of the room with Jacques trailing behind. She strode down the hallway to a set of elevator doors and placed her thumb in the scanning device. With a click and a whir, the doors slid open. She stepped inside, then looked back. "Well Trifle, get in here!"

He entered the elevator and Carrie pushed a button for the basement. When the car stopped and the doors opened, she stepped out, turned to the right and walked past several doors. Eventually stopping at one, she produced a ring of keys. Locating the correct key she opened the door and motioned Jacques inside. Stepping in behind him, she relocked the door and hung the keys on a hook next to the door frame.

The room, dimly lighted by several faint reddish glows, left most of the area in darkness. Jacques could make out some obscure contours of apparatus. A large X stood beneath the red glow of a small flood light. Locking straps dangled from the arms, legs and center of the cross. Beyond, barely visible, was a table of sorts with buckles and belts hanging from the sides. Out of the darkness above hung chains and shackles.

"Over here!" Carrie said sharply as her high heels clicked across the tiles to an open space and a massive, wooden chair. It had a padded leather seat, a straight back and no arms. Above the chair hung a single small bulb, directing a hazy red cone of light directly down.

Carrie held a small object with a digital readout. "Sit down, Jacques," she said in a hard voice. "You are going to be unleashed for the space of one hour. All the rules are revoked for sixty minutes, at which time this device will ring a bell and you are to stop whatever you're doing. Do you understand that simple concept?"

"Yes," he said with narrowed eyes, although his expression was one of confusion. He watched as she pressed a button and set the timer on the floor.

She spoke scornfully. "One thing I cannot abide is failure to achieve an objective that, with proper planning, is obtainable."

"I did every damn thing as instructed," he growled. "By *you* Carrie! "

"Of course you did." She sneered as she began to unbutton her blouse. "I have seen no shortcomings in your work." She slipped the blouse from her shoulders and let it fall to the floor.

"You have been much more patient with those two clowns than I would have ever been, but now it is time to take care of business. This mission failed because I failed." She toed each high-heeled shoe from her feet and kicked them away. "I made a gross misjudgment regarding Barkow's mental strength. For that error in judgment, punishment is required." Reaching behind her, she unbuttoned her black skirt, letting it fall to the floor.

Trifle stared at her. He wondered what she was leading up to as she stepped out of the puddle of her skirt and kicked it away.

She glared at him. "Unsnap the garters from my stockings, now!" As he reached forward, she took hold of his hands. They had thick, stubby fingers that spread from heavily callused palms. His long arms, corded with muscle, ended in thick wrists. She softly caressed his fingers and the thick, hard skin of his palms. "Since when do you take orders from a woman?" she said in a grating, contemptuous voice. "Are you some kind of a god-damned mama's boy?" In the surreal red glow, his overhung brow left both eyes in darkness. His shadow-lined lips drew back as the corners turned down.

She dropped his hands and slapped him across the mouth. His face smarted from the slap and as she swung for the second one, he blocked the blow and then clamped his hands onto both slender forearms.

"You're ugly!" she snarled. "Ugly and stupid! You don't know how to keep a woman in line anymore than you do men." She spat in his face and tried to bite him as he held her arms at her sides and turned his face away.

He pulled her close to him, then dropping his hold, quickly wrapped long arms around her body, pinning both arms at her sides. Still seated, he held her to him and buried his face between the cradled breasts in her bra. He found the garter-belt behind her back; he roughly pulled it apart. The fabric ripped as he tore the seams open and pulled it down her thighs on either side, bringing the stockings with it. Then he shoved her away. She staggered backward, the silk stockings tripping her as she fell into a sitting position with a thump.

Carrie peeled the mangled garter belt and stockings off her legs. With a hiss and the grace of a cat, she leapt up and unhooked her bra, tossing it to one side. The soft, ripe, fleshy bulbs of her breasts swayed away from her body as she leaned forward, pulling her panties down and kicking them away. "Punish me!" she hissed, "Spank me with those big hard hands, you ugly bastard, or I'll claw your goddamned eyes out!" Her face contorted in shadowed rage and hatred, and she spit in his direction. "You're nothing but a big fucking pussy cat!"

Trifle leapt from the chair and rushed her. His deeply creased face contorted into a twisted mass of ugly hatred. She began to back away, literally hissing and spitting, but he grabbed her by the hair and half-pulled, half-dragged her back to the chair. He sat down and roughly forced her face-down across his lap. Locking his left hand in a twist of black hair, he easily held her in position. With his forearm across her back, he brought his right hand down in a hard slap on one white, rounded cheek.

She screamed. "You son of a bitch, don't you dare! Don't do it! Goddamn it Trifle, stop! You've hurt me!"

Again his palm smacked down on the stinging red hand

print. A following blow landed on the opposite side and brought more shrieking, punctuated by demands to stop. He continued, alternating slaps between the left and right cheeks.

She screamed vile oaths at him and thrashed her legs. She vowed to have him killed. Soon both cheeks, visible in the abnormal light, were dark red. The louder she screeched, the harder he spanked until at last she began to thank him, while promising never to be wrong again.

"Stop Jacques... please stop."

Whack!

"Please, honey, I'll be good."

Whack!

"Please stop and I'll be special for you."

Whack!

"I'll be more careful in the future."

Whack!

"Thank you for teaching me to behave."

Whack!

"Thank you, Honey, thank you so much." Her voice grew quieter and quieter until she began to cry. At last, he heard only trembling sobs as each blow landed on the puffy, tumid flesh. When, with each slap, she involuntarily shuddered, he slowed so a greater amount of time elapsed between each blow. *Whack! Whack! Whack.* He finally stopped as she lay like a sack of sand across his lap, whimpering but unmoving. He pushed her off and she crumpled to the floor, then curled into a fetal position.

Jacques knelt, grasped a fist-full of hair and pulled her face around. Then, putting his mouth close to her ear, he growled in a raspy voice, "Never, bitch, be wrong in my presence again!"

He roughly shoved her head away, walked over to the door and unlocked it with the keys, then dropping them on the floor, left, slamming the door behind him. The time was 1:00 p.m.

Ding! Ding! Ding! The timer announced the hour of punishment had ended.

MARY'S PREDICAMENT

MARY DROVE THE Lexus to the entrance of Axelwood Labs and stopped at the guard gate, unaware the man she was looking for was, at that moment, in the process of making his escape. While she waited for the gate arm to lift upward, a gray bus rumbled outbound and then the guard came over to her car. After she stated the reason for arrival, the guard waved her through.

She drove to the visitor's lot and parked the rental. Gathering up her purse she opened the car door and turned in the seat, put one foot out on the pavement and then remembered she should make a phone call. She dug a cell phone from her purse and punched in the number for the Phoenix Branch of Great Metro Insurance.

"Great Metro." It was a male voice.

"May I speak with Judy?"

"One moment, hold please."

"Hello, this is Judy speaking."

"Hi Judy, it's me again, Mary Caruthers."

"What's up?"

"I am at Axelwood Labs, just outside of Phoenix."

"Wow, you sure get around. What can I do for you?"

"I'm hunting for a lead on where I can find Barkow."

"What in the world would he be doing there? We don't have any claim with them that I know of."

"It's a long story, but listen. I know Carrie Axelwood has been spending a lot of time here and I think she may know the whereabouts of Barkow. Were you aware they had a relationship of sorts years ago, when he was working a claim she had against Great Metro?"

"All I heard is that, at the time of the claim, he didn't like her very much," Judy said. "He mentioned she was a pain in the ass to work with."

"Okay. Hey, you want to catch dinner tomorrow night?"

"That would be great. Where?"

"How about the restaurant in my hotel? I'm at the Four Seasons and it looks pretty good."

"Sounds like a plan."

Shoving the phone into her purse, Mary pushed the car door out wider and, ignoring the softly dinging alarm, got out. In a hurry to see what facts she could dig up about Barkow and his whereabouts, she quickly walked up the wide steps and through the double entry doors.

A woman sitting behind a small lacquered desk was shuffling papers. She looked up. "Hello. Welcome to Axelwood Labs. What can I do for you?"

"Hi, my name is Mary Cruthers. I'm a reporter for the New York Socialite Magazine." She laid her business card on the desk. "I called earlier and made arrangements to speak with someone about the technical side of cyborg kinetics."

"One moment and please sit down while I find out who you are to meet with." She slipped out of her chair, picked up Mary's card and left the room. Returning a few minutes later, she said, "Mr. Hansen will be with you shortly."

"Thank you," Mary said. The clock on the wall read 12:45 p.m.

At one o'clock, the secretary said, "I'm sorry to tell you that Mr. Hansen is delayed in some company business. He is not sure when he will be free but assures you he will get to you as soon as possible. If you would care to make an appointment for a different time, I can arrange that now."

"No, thank you. I'll wait if that's all right."

An hour and forty minutes later, a tall, thin man in a business suit entered the room. "Ms. Cruthers?"

"Yes," Mary said as she stood up.

"Mark Hansen." He offered his hand. "Please follow me." In Hansen's office, he explained he was the Director of R&D and apologized for her long wait. He asked what information she was looking for.

"I just need general information regarding how and whether a human being could be controlled by an implanted machine-like device, if that's what you are working on here?"

"I am the Director of Research and Development at Axelwood Labs. I am aware of various projects that are in the projected stage, although I can be of little value as far as technical information goes. It is the policy of Axelwood not to provide information of, on or about the projects that are being considered or studied in any way. Is there any other matter of which I may be of service to you?"

"Apparently not." Mary spoke sharply as she stood up to leave. "Thank you for what must be your very valuable time."

While digging into her purse for the car keys, she walked out of the building and over to the visitor's parking area. Still struggling to find the keys, she looked up and stared at the empty parking space. "What the hell? Where's my car?"

Seeing the guard shack at the gate she walked over and demanded from the first guard, "What did you do with my car?"

"What car?" He looked closely at her.

"The white Lexus I drove in here a while ago."

A heated discussion began with the guard claiming the Lexus had already left and Mary demanding to know who was driving it.

"What was the license plate number?"

"How should I know, it's a rental!"

"Okay lady, please calm down and just show me the papers."

"The papers are in the glove compartment."

"Give me the keys, there are identifying tags on it."

"I can't find the keys."
"For crying out loud lady, what did you do with them?"
"I must have left them in the car."
"Aw shit, lady." The time was 2:50 p.m.

CARRIE'S RAMPAGE

MAY 22, 2012, TUESDAY, 1:30 P.M.

EVENTUALLY, CARRIE UNCURLED from the fetal position. She flinched as she slowly raised herself to her hands and knees. Using the chair for support, she pulled herself up to a standing position and quickly sat down on the chair, which also brought a grunt of pain. Her head was throbbing and her body ached. The soft glow of the dim red light left much of her body in deep shadow. The unlocked entry door suddenly swung inward, throwing a long, angled block of glaring light across the floor. The black silhouetted shape of a wide, simian body with gibbon-like arms stood silently at the entrance.

"Close the door!" she croaked.

The silhouette backed out and the door closed with a soft click.

Carrie, alone in the room, forced herself to put on her clothing. She dropped the mangled garter belt and silk stockings in a waste-can and then hobbled over to the exit. She picked up the keys from the floor and opened the door. Head down, she stepped through, pulled the door shut and locked it. She limped to the elevator and Trifle, without a word, fell in behind her. She placed her thumb in the scanner and the elevator door slid open.

In the elevator, Carrie said in a nearly inaudible voice, "Get Bert and tell him to come to my office. Go find Cain Martin also and bring him."

"Okay," Trifle said. "When I left the room I couldn't get out of the hall. The elevator doors wouldn't open and the only stairs had a thumb-scanner."

With a look of contempt, she said, "I know that, for Christ's sake. I own this damn place. Now go like a good boy and do as you're told."

She entered her office and gingerly sat on the padded desk chair, flinching as a tight smile crossed her face. The phone began jangling, and she picked it up.

"Axelwood!" she breathed into the mouthpiece.

"This is Commander of Axelwood Security." A deep male voice said. "We have a lady in custody named Mary Cruthers, not connected with this complex, who says her car, a white Lexus, has been stolen from our parking lot. She apparently came in a rental and left the keys in it. The guards at the gate allowed it to be driven out a half-hour ago without checking the driver because it had just arrived a while earlier. I have sent two patrol cars to try and catch it. I'm keeping the woman here in Patrol Headquarters at the present time."

"Have you notified the police yet?"

"No, Ma'am. I am waiting 'til I hear from the cars I sent out."

"Very well. Do not call the police, but keep me advised." She hung up, then called the Director of R&D. "Mark, did you interview a woman this afternoon named Cruthers? If so, fill me in on what was said."

Mark Hansen quickly told her of his five minute discussion with Mary Cruthers.

A knock at the office door caused Carrie to call in a throaty voice, "Come in."

Bert entered and stood before her desk, waiting for her to speak.

"Bert, I want you to return to the Blue Note and continue your position as bartender," Carrie said hoarsely as she hurriedly jotted notes into a folder. "You will be under the same salary, working for me, undercover. You will keep your eyes and ears open for any gossip, no matter how trivial, concerning me, Axelwood Labs or Barkow and report directly to me." She stopped writing and looked up at him, holding him with her gaze. "As far as

Trifle or anyone else is concerned, you have been fired. Only you and I know that you are still my employee. Is that clear?"

"Yes, Ms. Axelwood, perfectly clear."

"Very well. Your car is in the garage. Take it and leave as though you have been fired."

"Yes Ma'am." He turned to leave and, as he opened the door, almost collided with Cain Martin. He nodded to the man as he stepped past him and headed to the garage.

The rather small man with a hatchet face, wearing a trench coat and an old fashioned felt hat stepped forward. His dead black snake-eyes shifted back and forth until his gaze settled on the ͏man seated at the desk.

the door and take a seat. I have a job that
wi ͏d as she carefully relaxed
in

and sat down
͏s sheathed in
as if to display
͏ed wingtip. He
able except for a

͏d at the door of
at Cain, croaked,

in, out of breath.
"I have something
͏arrie, then Cain and

͏ in a subdued voice.
the room to another
, she said huskily over
͏ the ultra-private back

Trifle said, "Barkow has
͏t him get away. I found

them locked in the Lavender room, where we had left him. They said he caught them by surprise and got away." He glanced at his Rolex. It was 3:05 p.m. "It happened about a half-hour or forty-five minutes ago."

"Jesus H. Christ! It's gone too damn far now. Those two idiots have done nothing but screw things up every time they get involved."

"I alerted the Captain of Security and he has men combing the buildings and grounds." Trifle growled.

"Shit." Carrie muttered. "Call Security and have them stand down. He's already gone. That little slut left the keys in her car so he could make his getaway. But we still have her."

Trifle, his face blank, stared at her. "Then what?"

Her face twisted into a mask of hatred and fury. "Get out! Go get those two baboons of yours and take them to the black SUV in the garage."

"You want me to call Security first?" he said.

"Get out! Get out and do as you're told! I'll take care of Security!"

As Trifle hurried from the room and into the outer area, he brushed past Cain without a word and quickly left the office.

She called Cain into the inner sanctum. He came in, closing the door softly. Carrie was in the center of the room staring glassy eyed at nothing.

He waited.

In a monotone she said, "There is a black SUV in the garage. You will find Trifle and two other men waiting. I want you to take those two men somewhere and kill them. I want it to be done quickly and efficiently, with no evidence left that can in any way involve Axelwood Labs. Tell Jacques nothing of this, but he is to meet me back here in thirty minutes."

"No problem. Anything else?"

"Yes. I will alert the gate to allow the SUV to leave and return without hassles."

Plotting, she turned tiger eyes upon him. "As usual you will speak to no one of the duties you perform for me. Jacques will have a package for you when you finish the job with the two goons. You will deliver the package, tonight, to my private retreat on St. Lucia via Axelwood jet. After you have safely delivered the package into the hands of Kojo, you will return to Chicago and await further instructions."

"I understand." he said, "My fee?"

"Your fee will be deposited into your private account as usual when the entire set of instructions have been followed and completed."

"Until we meet again." He turned and left the office.

Carrie called Security and told the commander to stand down in the search for Barkow. She also informed him to tighten security at the gate and fire the men who allowed the Lexus to drive through without being checked. "By the way, Captain, the company's black SUV will be departing soon. Alert the gate that Mr. Cain Martin has requested to use the SUV once again in order to take care of more of his personal business. You are to allow him to leave and return without any questions."

"Yes Ma'am, understood."

"And Captain, have Cruthers held in a locked room, incognito, until Mr. Trifle arrives to take control of her."

Next, Carrie called Axelwood Retreat, using Kojo's private number.

He answered on the second ring. "Kojo."

"I am sending you a package, tonight. It will be delivered by Mr. Martin. I want it held without questioning, as a guest, until such time as I contact you again. Do you understand? No harm is to come to the package until we speak again."

"Kojo understand, Madam. Of course, no harm."

"And she is to be told nothing pertaining to information regarding me or Axelwood holdings in any way.

"Yes, Madam."

"Repeat it! Say it, Kojo!"

"Kojo no tell information on you or Axelwood."

"And?"

"And no harm her any way and treat like guest."

"Very well, Kojo. I will be in touch with further instructions."

"Thank you, Ma'am. Kojo thanks Madam."

"Goodbye Kojo."

"Goodbye Madam."

Carrie pulled out a diary and began adding notations. *Cain Martin asked AGAIN to use the SUV for personal business. I am becoming suspicious of him. He is also hinting for the use of the Company jet.* She wrote in her bold handwriting. *Could he be up to some skullduggery and using the Phoenix Lab facilities as some sort of base?* As she was putting away the diary, Trifle knocked on Carrie's office door.

"Come in," she murmured.

Trifle at once opened the door and entered. "Mr. Martin said you wanted me here in thirty minutes."

"Yes, Jacques. I want you to go and get the woman who is confined at Security. Tell her we now have possession of her car and will bring it to her. That is all you need to say. Then take her to the Red room and lock her in it. These are explicit instructions. You are not to carry on a conversation with her. Understand?"

"Okay, Ms. Axelwood."

"You are to sit in a chair outside her room in the hallway until Cain Martin comes to get her."

"Okay."

"Okay what?"

"Okay, Ms. Axelwood."

"Very good, Jacques. By the way, your two friends have been paid off and sent back to Chicago. I was so mad I had both of them sent out right away. I say good riddance."

"Okay, Ms. Axelwood."

"Come now, Jacques. Don't be so glum. We will soon be going on a nice vacation to the Caribbean together. It will be fun." She watched as the man with long arms waited for her to tell him to leave. "Now you may go. Remember, take her to the

Red Room and lock her in. Simply tell her we are bringing her car back and that soon a man will take her to it."

Jacques nodded and left as Carrie picked up the phone. She called the pilot of the company jet.

"Bob Simmons."

"Robert, Mr. Cain Martin has personal, urgent business and must leave today. Get the plane ready for take-off ASAP. Do not hold a conversation with him. Just do as he says and take him wherever he wishes to go. Log in the hours and file a report to my attention on flight hours, mileage, destination, et cetera. Also contact an ambulance company and have one sent to Axelwood Labs to arrive two hours from now. Just say it is requested by a Mr. Cain Martin to pick up a patient. All they are to do is deliver the patient from here to the airport."

"No problem at all, Ms. Axelwood," Simmons said, trying to sound important. "The plane is ready to depart anytime and I will take care of the rest."

"I know you will, Bob." Carrie said with guile. "This is Cain's business. The more you keep the name of Axelwood out of all matters, the better."

"You can count on me, Ms. Axelwood."

"Then, Bobby, I leave it in your unusually capable hands."

MURDER AND MAYHEM

MAY 22, 2012, TUESDAY, 2:15 P.M.

CAIN MARTIN WALKED to the garage. As he approached Trifle and the two other men he said, "Ms. Axelwood has a job for us to do. She wants Trifle to check back with her in thirty minutes. You other boys are with me." As Cain watched Trifle walk away, he spoke to the other two. "Gather up a bag of lime, two shovels and a pick. Bring them here to the SUV and we can get you back in her favor. You know she's a little upset with you guys for letting Barkow escape."

"I tol' ya, Butch. I said she was gonna be really pissed at us for letting him get loose," Rollo whined in an odd, high pitched voice to his confidant.

"Come on, Stupid, less get the stuff and get the job done. My jaw is killin' me," Butch mumbled in a low, tired voice.

The two men left to go to the contractor's tool shed. They picked up a wheelbarrow, a bag of lime, two shovels and a pick and then started back to the garage.

"What ya suppose we gonna do wid dis stuff?" Rollo said.

"Who gives a shit?" Butch mumbled. "Less jess do it."

After returning to the garage, they loaded everything in the back of the SUV and climbed in. Cain had been waiting in the driver's seat. He started the engine without a word and drove out of the garage and over to the guard gate. He rolled up and stopped where a guard held his hand up. The guard looked inside the car and nodded to the three men.

"You've already been cleared to leave, Mr. Martin," he said as the gate arm rose. Cain nodded and then eased through the exit lane and down the highway. He drove about a half mile and slowed down, searching for a small dirt side road. Finding it, he turned to the right and continued along the fence of the property line.

"What we gonna do?" Rollo grumbled from the back seat.

"Gotta dig up a box of buried gold," replied Cain. "Something Ms. Axelwood wants done right away."

"What's the lime for?" Rollo demanded.

"Damned if I know," Cain said. *Unbelievable stupidity.* "She just said to dump it in the hole before we covered it up."

They drove on in silence until they came to an unused gate in the fencing. The ground was covered with weeds, wind-blown sand and cacti.

"Get out and open the gate." Cain said, handing him a key. "As soon as I drive through, close it, but don't relock it." *Good thing I lifted that gate key when I cased Carrie's office a while back and had a copy made.*

When Rollo was back in the SUV, Cain began driving across the desert toward the southwest corner of the property. The land was rolling hills of gravel and sand, covered with prickly-pear cactus. Scattered randomly here and there were mesquite trees and greasewood bushes. The buildings of the lab complex were soon lost from view.

"Here we are," Cain said as they came over a hillock and the ground dipped sharply down. "She brought me out here to show it to me earlier. Said it was about eight feet down in a metal box."

"Why are we here?" Rollo said.

"You boys gonna do the diggin'," Cain said with a grin.

They all three got out of the car. Butch lifted the back hatch and removed the tools from the back. Cain made a show of holding a portable GPS in his hand while walking, followed by Butch with Rollo pushing the wheelbarrow of tools. When he was about fifty feet from the car, Cain picked a spot that had a mild depression by a drifted ridge of sand and said, "This is the place. Start digging here."

In the bright light of the sun, still high but past the zenith, they started shoveling the windblown sand away and slowly worked their way down to where a caliche layer had formed, which fortunately was only about eight inches thick, but the pick was required. One would swing the pick until he had cracked and broken some of the hardpan and then the other would move in and scoop it out with the shovel. As the shadows began to lengthen, the air was thick with the heat of the day and both Rollo and Butch had worked up a sweat. They removed their shirts and kept deepening the hole.

"Why in the hell did she ever have it buried here?" Rollo puffed.

"Just keep diggin'," Butch mumbled through his wired jaw.

The two, sweating from their labors, were finally past the caliche deposit and dug until the clay became so hard that even the pick could hardly gouge it.

Butch said, "This ain't never been dug up before!"

"Look here," Rollo said. "I've struck solid rock. Hey Cain, C'mere and look at this."

Cain at the top of the pit looked down at the men, whose shoulders came just about the level of his feet. He looked out of place in his trench coat and outdated snap brim hat. Only his rattlesnake eyes hinted at the treachery of which he was capable. "Get down on your knees and wipe the loose dirt away from the rock so I can see it."

As they began brushing the dirt from the rock, Cain removed a nine millimeter, semi-automatic from his pocket. He slowly screwed a silencer on the end of the barrel.

"Just a little more." He aimed at the back of Butch's head and fired.

"Hey!" Rollo looked up and received the second shot in the center of his forehead.

Cain dropped the gun, silencer and all into the pit. He gathered the shirts of the two men and threw them in after the gun. He took a pen knife from his pocket, slit the top of the bag of lime and poured it over the bodies as a cloud of lime dust arose. Tossing the empty bag into the maw of the grave, along with his gloves, he picked up the remaining shovel that was lying by the mound of excavated sand and gravel and quickly began shoveling that material into the hole. It was loose and easy to scoop and push into the pit. Soon the two bodies, as well as the pick and the shovel, were covered.

Cain tossed his shovel aside and began gathering larger rocks and dropping them into the pit until he had a rough layer, then using the shovel again, scraped all the loose sand and gravel around, into the remaining depression. Lastly he dug up a few cacti nearby and roughly pushed their roots into the loose sand above his handiwork.

"That should do it." He muttered, sweat running down his face as he picked up the shovel and returned to the black SUV. Tossing the shovel along with his hat and coat into the back of the car, he slammed the hatch closed, then quickly slipped into the driver's seat. Backing the car around in a tight half-circle, he drove back through the late afternoon, the same way they had come in. He turned the air conditioner up and arrived back to the gate where they had entered and driving through, stopped. Leaving the motor running he got out and pulled the gate closed; only to find the padlock was locked through a link in the chain.

"That stupid shit! The key is in his damn pocket buried in the desert." He wrapped the chain around the gate and returned to the SUV. Within twenty minutes of leaving the grave site, he was driving up to the guard gate.

The guard came over with a clipboard to the rolled-down window. "Please step out and open the back for inspection."

"No problem," Cain said realizing this was the same guard who had checked him out earlier. He cut the engine then opened the car door and stepped out.

The guard followed him around to the back of the car and waited for the hatch to be opened. As he followed, he noticed Cain's trouser legs were lightly coated with a white powdered substance from the knees down. Looking inside, he noticed the shovel, coat and hat lay in a dusty, tangled heap. "You're checked back in Mr. Martin, drive on."

As the big SUV drove away, the guard realized his uniform was smudged with dust wherever it had touched the side of the car. He jotted a notation beside the log-in time of 4:10 p.m. *Vehicle and driver's legs coated with dust and white powder. Three men left earlier in this car, only one returned.*

New orders had been issued, that all vehicles and occupants entering and leaving the complex had to be carefully looked over for any out of the normal appearance.

The balance of the day passed without further incident at the gate. When dawn pinked the sky, the sun slowly rose behind the mountains, heralding the day, as its first rays glinted on the painted sides of a bright red construction wheelbarrow, forgotten and left near the final resting place of two Chicago thugs.

BARKOW IN RETALIATION

A S HE SPED down the blacktop road that connected Axelwood Labs to an Arizona State highway, Barkow felt a vast sense of satisfaction and contentment. *How lucky to find this car with the keys in it.* His mind was smoothly efficient as he considered the recent past. He smiled, thinking of how his drugged confusion had cleared just in time to foil the attempts of the two bozos who had come to get him. *I've got to ditch this ride as soon as possible. It has a GPS unit.*

He flashed past a road sign that indicated he was now on an Arizona State highway, speed 65 mph. He slowed the car down and drove through the afternoon sunshine until in the distance an overpass and several buildings came into view.

Coming to where the highway continued under a freeway overpass he took the exit and pulled into a Flying J truck stop. A few tractor-trailer rigs were fueling and many more were parked in rows out back of the restaurant lounge.

Along the side of a building, a number of men were standing around laughing and drinking beer. He skidded to a stop close by the group, leaving the engine running, got out and sized up the situation.

A lot of loud talk was happening between some young Hispanic men and some others wearing black leather jackets. It seemed most everyone was holding a beer bottle. Plotting, Barkow noticed the motorcycles leaning on their kick stands, at the back of the building. He knew right away, there was going to be trouble between the two groups. He began to stagger toward the beer drinking men.

"Hey, yoush guys! I gotta get this car to the Phoenix Airport." He stumbled and almost fell down but grabbed onto one of the Latinos.

"Get the hell off me, man!" the Latino cried as he pushed him away.

"Lishen Buddy, y'wanna make some mucho dinero?"

Everyone was watching and listening. The Latino boys were grinning. The bikers were starting to draw together.

"Fer Crish shake, doan nobody wanna drive this fuckin' car to the airport for me?"

"How much?" said a heavyset man in a black leather jacket.

"Two hunnert, an' there'll be a hot chick t'take it off yer han's."

"I'll do it for three hundred," the biker said.

"Wait a minute, man," It was the Latino. "He asked me first."

"Shit man, I don't got no cash, but Tina'll give y'two C notes," Barkow muttered as he staggered and nearly fell down. "Jessh go ina airport parkin' lot an' ash the ticket-taker for Peggy."

"Which airport?"

"Sheesh, the big one, y'dumb shit." Barkow began to lurch to the door of the restaurant. "I'm gonna be shick!" He staggered, half bent over and pushed his way through the door.

The biker caught up with him and grabbed his collar. He pulled Barkow around. "You jerkin' me around?"

"Screw you, I'm gonna heave." Then Barkow laughed. "But ol' Peg'll do that for you and yer fuckin' buddies too." Cramped over he started for the restroom.

The biker turned, pushed through the door and went outside. "Leave my ride in the back and follow me to the airport. We gonna get drunk," he said to his friends as he got into the Lexus. With the squeal of spinning rubber and in a haze of blue smoke, he took off as all of the bikers rushed to their machines, generating a cloud of dust and roaring engines as they sped after the taillights of the receding white Lexus.

From inside the building, Barkow, peeking through a window, grinned. *They're going to be in for a rude awaking.* He didn't know the Lexus' glove compartment held the rental papers of Mary Cruthers. He made his way into the driver's lounge to beg a ride from some trucker who would hear whatever lie he thought up.

He took a seat at the counter next to a burly man with a full beard. He spun the stool around and faced the room, his elbows on the counter, and surveyed the customers.

The man next to him looked at his beat-up face with the three deep scratches and said between mouthfuls of ham and eggs, "Where ya headed?"

"I gotta get back to Phoenix some way." grumbled Barkow. "Dang woman took off with my car, my money and everything."

"You hungry?" the big man said.

"I sure could use some grub."

"Eat up on me, friend. I'll give you a lift to Phoenix since I'm headed that way."

"Hey, all right!" Barkow spun the stool around. "I don't have any money, but I can pay you back if you give me an address to send it to."

"No need. I been where you're at. Glad I can help out."

After a meal of ham and eggs, toast and coffee, the two men left the restaurant and walked toward a Kenworth tractor coupled to a set of doubles. Barkow looked the driver over as they walked to the truck. He was a huge man in black Frisco jeans, held up with wide workmen's suspenders, built like a tree trunk with a large head and a ponytail of gray hair hanging through the hole in the back of a greasy baseball cap.

They climbed up into the cab and the driver started the engine. As the driver shifted through a series of low gears and the truck picked up speed, he said, "So tell me, where'd y'steal the Lexus?"

Barkow looked at the man sitting next to him. "Is it that obvious?" he said as they rolled out of the truck stop. He noticed with a smile, two Axelwood patrol cars came roaring into the parking lot and skidded to a stop.

"Naw. Saw y'drive in and overheard your little act with the biker. I near fell off my perch when that guy took the bait." He roared with laughter and Barkow fell into laughing with him.

The driver chuckled. "I was sittin' on a stool just outside the door 'cause I thought there was gonna be a fight between the bikers and the Mex."

"Yeah, I was beat up pretty damn bad and trapped down there in that Axelwood outfit." Barkow grumbled. "I couldn't believe my luck when some dunce left the keys in that car. It had a GPS in it and I knew as soon as they found it gone, they could trace the whereabouts of the car and come after it."

"Well, you're some fine actor, you are." The driver laughed again as the rig attained a speed of seventy miles an hour.

⊙ In Phoenix, Barkow said, "Thanks for the lift, Buddy, and I want your address 'cause I'm gonna make it up to you for helping me out."

The big man pulled a faded business card out from where it was wedged in the windshield molding and gave it to Barkow.

"There y'go, but it ain't no need for you to send anything. Heck, the dang show was worth the price of a meal and a ride."

He dropped Barkow off at a corner near the Blue Note Bar, a place he was very familiar with. He went inside and parted the beaded curtain but remained in the lobby. After getting the attention of Terry, he motioned for her to come over.

"God, Barkow, you look terrible! What happened?"

"No time to explain now," he said speaking quietly. "Can you lend me your car? I'll get it back to you in a few hours."

"Of course. Hang on while I get the keys from my purse." She returned in a minute and handed him the keys and the remote. "It's out back, a blue Chevy club coupe. You're lucky I had to come in early today."

"Thanks a load Terry. I'll get it back in a little while."

"No problem. Glad I can help."

"By the way, don't tell anyone you've seen me, okay?"

"Sure thing. See ya later."

He slipped out the door, found the car and headed for his apartment. He pulled into the lower parking garage and drove to his Mercedes. Parking beside it, he locked the Chevy and walked to the elevator for the lobby of the building. When the doors slid open, he stepped out and went to the counter where a doorman was reading a paperback novel.

Hank Harrison was a retired police officer. The man looked up. "Hey Barkow, you've been in a fight, ain't'cha? You need some help or something? How y'doin'?"

"Same old thing, Hank," Barkow said. "Anything going on here?"

"Nope, just people coming and going."

"Okay, I just got in from a trip and I have to go out again. Has anyone been around asking for me?"

"Nope, not a soul. Are you in trouble?"

"No, I'm not in trouble; you can get back to your book. See y'later."

Leaving Hank with a puzzled look on his face, Barkow took the guest elevator to the top floor; his penthouse occupied that entire level.

He entered, making no sound, and carefully checked all the rooms and found nothing out of place. He stopped at a portrait hanging on the wall above the headboard of his bed. Standing on the bed he flipped a hidden latch and opened the painting like a cabinet door. He spun the dial code, waited until the green light came on and pulled the door open. Removing a small automatic in a shoulder holster, he checked the magazine. He also took a packet of assorted bills that he knew totaled one thousand dollars.

Next he went to the bathroom where he stripped and examined his bruised body. His face was still sore, but he carefully shaved, avoiding the three deep scratches on his cheek. After a hot shower, he lay on the bed and almost immediately fell asleep.

Later he awoke and dressed in chinos, a shirt and loafers. Then he called the office and left a message for Judy, saying he was back in town.

Taking the gun and money along with a leather jacket he left the condo. Stepping into the lobby, Barkow waved to the guard at the counter. "See you later, Hank." He entered the garage elevator. He slid behind the wheel of the black Mercedes and drove slowly out of the garage.

It was 9:30 p.m. when he arrived at a low bungalow with palm trees. He walked up to the front door. When the door opened a short man with blonde hair squinted into the darkness with narrowed eyes. "What do you want?"

"Take a good look, Tab."

The porch light flicked on. "Good Lord, is that you Barkow? My God, what happened to your face?"

"Hi Tab, I need a little favor if you and Julie are not too busy."

"Come on in." He turned away. "Hey Honey, look who showed up."

Julie met Barkow as he entered the living room. She stared at him with wide eyes. "Hello, stranger, haven't seen you for a while. You look horrible. What happened?"

"Long story, Jules. I'm kind of in a hurry, but I wonder if you guys could do me a favor?"

"Sure, anything," Julie said. "Do you want a doctor?"

"There's a blue Chevy coupe in the parking stall next to where I usually park at the condo." He fished in his pocket, then handed what he found to Julie. "Here's the remote. It belongs to Terry at the Blue Note. Would you please drive it back while Tab follows you and return the keys to Terry?" He looked at Tab. "Also please give her this." He handed Tab a hundred dollar bill. "And tell her I said thanks."

"No problem, we'll be glad to help out. Would you like to stay for a glass of wine?"

"I can't. I gotta get going. Another thing, Tab—when you pick up the car, tell the doorman—you remember Hank, right?

Tell him if anyone comes looking for me, to just say that I've left the country for a few weeks and that's all he knows. Okay?"

"Well, next time you're coming to dinner," Julie said. "Call me when you can make it."

"Sounds great, Jules. See you guys later." He left, and a few moments later the Mercedes roared away from the curb.

"He looked like he'd been hit by a truck," muttered Tab.

Nodding, Julie said, "I'll drive Terry's car; you follow, and if anyone asks us about Barkow, we haven't seen him for a couple of months. Last we heard he was out of the country."

NIGHT FLIGHT

MAY 22, 2012, TUESDAY, 5:20 P.M.

CAIN FOUND THE locked room. Trifle was waiting outside the door, sitting in a wooden chair tilted back against the wall. "Give me the key to the room and I'll take it from here."

"She was making a fuss for awhile, banging on the door. But she's been quiet the last fifteen or twenty minutes."

"No problem," Cain said, taking the key. "You can go now." He unlocked the door and pushed it inward. Mary was sitting in an overstuffed chair, her arms folded across her chest, staring at him.

"I'm sorry to have kept you waiting," Cain purred. "We had quite a time of it here lately and kept the door locked for your protection. All is ship-shape now and we've located your car. Please gather your things and come with me."

Mary picked up her purse and muttered, "It's about damn time." She followed Cain to the elevator. As they dropped to the parking level he hummed a tuneless melody.

"Your car is a few blocks away. I'll give you a ride over," he said as they approached a dusty black SUV with heavily tinted windows.

"Thank you." Mary climbed into the front passenger seat.

Cain went around the back of the car, stopping to remove from his pocket one of several preloaded hypodermic needles in transport tubes. He slipped into the driver's seat. "See that button on the armrest?"

When Mary looked at the armrest, Cain plunged the needle into her upper arm and pushed the plunger down.

"What are you doing?" she gasped, then sank into uncon-sciousness.

⏱ SOMETIME LATER, FROM far away a blur of light crossed her eyelids. The drone of engines slowly increased in volume as she fought to regain consciousness. Hardly aware of a second injec-tion, she returned to the blackness of drug induced sleep.

Mary awoke in darkness. Trying to get her thoughts into some sense of order, she stared at the ceiling fan lazily revolving above her bed. Her mouth was dry and her tongue swollen. She turned the coverlet back and discovered she was still wearing the same clothes she had worn to Axelwood Labs. She slipped her legs out and sat upon the edge of the bed, then snapped on the small lamp on the nightstand. The suite looked upper class motel. Heavy drapes were drawn and cool air filled the room.

Feeling light headed, she walked slowly to the bathroom. A sealed drinking glass was among the various shampoos and lotions. She filled the glass and drank deeply. Her head was begin-ning to clear; she remembered being drugged. The bathroom boasted a shower, a tub and a commode. In the bedroom, a comfortable chair was beside the bed with an armoire standing against the wall.

Mary opened the only other door and entered a tastefully decorated living room. A small kitchenette was partially visible in a side nook.

Am I in a hotel suite? There was no telephone. Her purse was there but her cell phone was missing. She tried the entrance door and realized she was locked in. Feeling dizzy, she returned to the bed and lay down.

Mary began to reconstruct her movements of the past day. She had arrived in Phoenix by plane. She'd traveled by cab to a hotel and checked in. As her mind cleared she remembered going to the Blue Note Bar by taxi; then getting a rental car and driving to Axelwood Labs. Her car was missing and she had been locked in a room for a time and then was taken to get the car. *Yes... that's when I was drugged... when I got in his damn car.* The next thing she recalled was waking up. Unconsciously, she rubbed an aching shoulder.

BARKOW THE HUNTER

DRIVING THROUGH THE night Barkow pulled over at an all-night café and ordered a cup of coffee. Sitting at the back of the room he made a call to Judy.

"Hello."

"Hello, Judy. This is Barkow. Sorry if I woke you."

"Hi Barkow. No problem, I'm still up. It's good to hear your voice again. I've been wondering when you would come back to work."

"I'm in town, but I might be away for a while yet. I wanted to see whether anything important has happened."

"Not really. The other adjusters are covering for you and it's not been busy lately. Hey! I got some news for you. Remember Mary Cruthers?"

"Yeah, in fact I think of her on a daily basis."

"Well, good news. She's in town and I'm having dinner with her tomorrow night at seven."

"Mary's in town? You mean she's here, in Phoenix?"

"Yes and she's looking for you. She called me from Axelwood Labs and we made arrangements to meet for dinner."

"Good Lord, Judy, you say she was at Axelwood Labs when she called?"

"Yup, she said she was trying to find information about you. She had heard that Carrie Axelwood might know where you were."

"Okay, where's dinner taking place? I'll meet you there."

"It's at the Four Seasons downtown, at seven."

"Tomorrow night at seven, great. Listen, Judy, don't mention this to anyone. I'll be there for dinner and fill you both in at that time. Thanks for the information and I'll see you later."

"Okay."

Barkow was silent in amazement. He had never expected Mary to come looking for him. He wondered what she was up to. She had made it clear that she had no affection for him. He'd honored her feelings, leaving with a broken heart. Now here she was again, four years later.

He ordered more coffee and a sandwich. As he ate, he turned over his feelings for Mary Cruthers. Since they had parted, he'd never had a relationship with another woman that lasted more than a weekend. He still loved Mary. And back when he was groggy, coming out of the drugs he realized the woman who had gotten in bed with him was definitely not Mary. Something was tugging at his mind. Something important was missing that he should be able to remember.

Barkow paid for his meal and walked slowly back to his car. He began driving toward his condo. He kept running over and over the day's events, trying to pull everything into focus.

He wheeled into the parking garage and noted Terry's car was no longer by his parking space. *Tab and Julie picked it up,* he thought as he locked the Mercedes and took the elevator up to the lobby. "Hi again, Hank!" He said as he walked up to the doorman.

"Hey Barkow, you still don't look so good. How you doin'?"

"I'll be fine in a day or two. Anything happening?"

"Nope, quiet as a church."

"Good. I'll see you later." Barkow walked to the elevator. When he arrived at his door, he checked the tiny, half toothpick, which he'd wedged between the door and jamb about knee high. It fell to the floor as he gently pushed the door open.

He entered and relocked the door, undressed, then put on slippers and robe. He filled a glass with ice and poured two fingers of bourbon, then sauntered into the den and sat on a leather desk chair in the dark. He thought about each event, from the time he'd come out from under the influence to present. He considered, in detail, every word and action. He touched the three deep scratches on his left cheek as he thought of the woman who had put them there while babbling about FalseLife and claiming to be Marie. He remembered being dizzy, weak and confused. The fight played in his mind as a mental video. *I defeated those two familiar stumble-bums in that room where I had been locked up. I snuck downstairs and went around behind the building; I checked the delivery trucks backed in to the dock. Then I found* the Lexus with the keys in it and—

He thought about the trucks again. *They had the name and logo of Axelwood Labs on their sides! That's it!* The feeling of doubt and the recurring sense that he was forgetting something important vanished. Then, *Wait— Judy said Mary was at Axelwood Labs. My God! She was right there in the same building with me!*

Without warning, exhaustion settled over him like a shroud. He finished his bourbon, went to the bathroom, and went to bed, where he fell asleep with a vision of Mary clouding his mind.

Barkow awoke early the next morning and decided on his next move. He dressed in a black suit and nested his pistol in a shoulder holster.

Just before leaving, he took a red colored toothpick from the bar, snapping it in half as he walked through the room. He discarded one half in a waste basket, then opened the door and stepped into the hall. He bent and carefully pushed the broken end of the toothpick between the door and jamb so it would be perceptible only to someone who was looking for it.

He drove to Great Metro office and went to his office. Various messages were stacked neatly in the center of the desktop. He sat down and went through them. Only one aroused his curiosity, from Hernando J. Mendoza, Attorney at Law. It was on a Great Metro message slip like the rest and had been phoned in asking Barkow to call him back as soon as possible concerning an urgent matter of his health. Only the name and phone number was printed on the slip, but along the side in longhand it read, *May 22—Barkow, this call came through Axelwood Lab. Judy.*

A quick look through the yellow pages showed no Hernando J. Mendoza as an attorney. Barkow went to Judy's office and knocked on the door.

"Come in."

He opened her door and stepped inside.

"Hey, I was getting worried about you!" She stood up and gave Barkow a hug, then stepped back and looked at him. "Damn it, Barkow, you look like you've been in a fistfight. Where've you been these past few weeks?"

"It's a long story. I'm extremely concerned about Mary Cruthers. Tell me, Judy, about this call from the attorney." He showed her the message slip.

"When Mary told me on the phone she was at Axelwood Labs I didn't think much about it. Then you called, sounding somewhat upset and talking about Axelwood Labs. You also said you would meet us for dinner tonight at her hotel restaurant. Later that message came in from the attorney. I noticed the caller ID flagged the message as coming from Axelwood Lab and thought you should know."

He spoke quietly. "I'm damn well upset about it. Keep all this under your hat for a while, Judy. I'll explain in detail tonight when we get together for dinner."

"I need a cup of coffee, you want one?"

He nodded. "Sounds good."

Together they walked out of her office and down the hall to a small room with a copier, coffee pot and office supplies. They each filled a cup.

Barkow said, "I'll be at my desk for a while and then out to take care of some business. Thanks for all your help."

"You just be careful and I'll see you tonight at seven.'

They went to their respective desks and Barkow called the number of Adelita Ramos.

"Hello. Ramos, Attorney at Law. "

"*Hola, mi buena amiga Adela. ¿Cómo estás hoy?*"

"Barrkow, do no try to fool me *con su gringo hablar español.*" Barkow laughed.

"Of course, amigo," she said. "I'd be happy to help you. What's up?"

"Will you check out the name Hernando J. Mendoza? Supposed to be an attorney. Let me know if you find out anything interesting about him. Keep this between you and me and send me a bill for your time."

"I don't have to look up that ambulance chasing scumbag. He's a low-life Mexican lawyer all right. He got his certificate on the Internet in Mexico. He's no one you want to know, and he's been mixed up in several shady deals that I've heard of."

"Okay, that's all I needed to know. Thanks again. How about lunch today?"

"Sounds good. Meet me at La Cholla at noon?"

"I'll be there. Adios, mi amiga."

Barkow hung up, then called Harold H. Goodfellow, CEO of Great Metro Insurance in New York.

"Hello Harry, Barkow here. Got a few minutes?"

"Hello Barkow, what's up?"

"I'm loaded down with some personal matters. I need to take a few months off work. My accounts are all up to date, nothing pressing that can't be covered easily by the other claims agents."

"Tell you what—take ninety days off with pay. Call it your vacation. I'll call the Phoenix office and inform them."

"Thanks Harry, I knew you would understand. I'll see you when I get back." He hung up the phone. He stopped by Judy's office and said, "I'll see you and Mary later this evening," then left for his lunch meeting with Adela. After lunch, he drove to the Blue Note. Stepping through the beaded curtain into the lounge, he went to the bar, took a stool and ordered Blanton's on ice.

"Tell Bert I'd like to talk to him. Barkow's the name."

"Sorry Mr. Barkow. Bert is the night-shift bartender. I'm Bobby, the day fill in until Bert comes in around six."

"Is there a phone number where I can reach him?"

"Nope, it's company policy not to give out employee numbers."

"No problem. I'll catch him later."

They got to talking about the habits of customers as Barkow sipped on his drink. Bobby said it was odd that he'd had customers come in both yesterday and today. "She was a real looker yesterday. Came here in a cab that left her stranded, so then she called a rental company to bring a car for her to lease for a few days. While she was waiting, we talked and she ordered a lemon drop. She was very particular about the car too. It had to be a Lexus, late model club coupe."

"What? What color was the car?

"I don't know, but she was going to Axelwood Labs"

"Thanks Bobby!"

Barkow downed his drink and laid a twenty on the counter, then rushed out of the bar to the Mercedes. "Damn," he muttered, "but at least I know where she's staying."

He started the Mercedes, peeled out of the parking lot, and made his way to the Four Seasons Hotel. He went directly to the hotel front desk. "Do you have Mary Cruthers as a guest here?"

"One moment, Sir. Yes Sir, we have a guest by that name."

"Good! Her room number please."

"Oh Sir, we can't give out room numbers."

"Then can you call and tell her that Barkow is here and wishes to speak to her?"

"I can leave a message to that effect if that will do."

"Please do, and say it's urgent that I speak with her."

"Of course, Sir, at once."

"Tell her I'll be waiting in the bar."

Barkow left the counter and found the bar. He took a small table for two in the back corner of the dimly lit room and ordered Blanton's on the rocks.

While waiting, he sipped the mellow drink. After nursing it for fifteen minutes, he ordered a second. Twenty minutes later he finished the second drink and went back to the front desk.

"Did you leave my message?"

"Yes Sir, and since you seemed so concerned, I also did a bit of checking. It appears that Miss Cruthers took a cab yesterday and has not returned. Her room was made up and it hasn't been disturbed."

"Okay. Please put in a note for her to call Judy Moreno at Great Metro Insurance."

"Yes Sir."

Barkow returned to the Mercedes and on the car phone called the number on the message slip.

"Hernando J. Mendoza, Attorney at Law."

"Hello Hernando. This is Barkow. You wished to speak with me?"

"Si señor. It is important to your health that you do not search for Ms. Cruthers."

"And why do you say that, Hernando?" Barkow questioned.

"Because Señor, you could accidently have an accident."

"I doubt that," Barkow said quietly.

"Would you like to meet and discuss the situation?" Mendoza said.

"Yes, I would." The old familiar background music began welling up in his mind.

"Meet me at El Toro Cantina in one hour," Mendoza said and hung up.

Barkow smiled as he started the engine and wheeled out of the parking lot. He drove straight to the El Toro Cantina and parked. Inside he took a chair at a back table and ordered tequila, lime and salt. From the dark corner, he watched the patrons as they arrived and departed. The place was obviously a hangout for a tough Hispanic crowd. When two heavyset men with cutoffs, tattoos and pigtails entered the tavern, Barkow pegged them at once. They took stools at the bar and ordered tequila. Barkow stepped up behind them, put a hand on each one's shoulder and leaned in between them. "Perdón," he said. "You waiting for Mendoza?"

"Si señor," one said as they nodded. Both of Barkow's hands left their respective shoulder and grabbed the outer ear of each head, slamming them together with enough force to stun. He pushed one man forward and pulled the other back to meet a bone crushing jab by his right fist while he still held on to the fellow's ear with his left. The other patrons were scuttling out the door. Pulling the head by the attached ear toward him, he stepped back and as the man came off the barstool, once more Barkow's right fist slammed into his jaw. He fell like a dead weight to the dirty concrete floor. The other man had spun around on his barstool only to meet a left jab straight to his nose and upper lip. He dropped on top of his unconscious friend. The bartender, raising a club from behind the bar, suddenly stopped all movement as he looked into the barrel of the small automatic in Barkow's hand. The hard, cold chips of steel in Barkow's eyes caused him to lose all interest in retaliation. He let the club clatter to the floor and stepped back.

Barkow smiled. "When Hernando arrives, tell him I would be pleased to discuss the arrangements for his funeral. All he has to do is give me a call." With that, he walked out the door and drove away.

🕐 AT SEVEN, HE was waiting near the entrance to the restaurant and when Judy entered he motioned her over. "Hi Judy. Have you heard from Mary?"

"Nope, not a peep."

They chose a table where they could watch the entrance and ordered drinks as they waited. Barkow filled her in on his strange adventures from the time he had been gone from the office until today. "So you see, Marie Moringgale, who is actually Carrie Axelwood, was behind the whole thing. At the hotel, I found out Mary went to Axelwood Labs yesterday when she called you before going in. As it turns out, I unwittingly stole her rental car to get away. Something very strange is happening and I want to get to the bottom of it." He glanced at his watch.

After deciding Mary was running late, they ordered. In a hushed voice, Judy said, "That's some story. When I spoke to Mary she said you and Carrie had some sort of connection. I remember Carrie was suing Great Metro for four million dollars and you handled the case."

"Yeah, she spent a lot of time trying to get close to me. Beautiful as she is, there's something about her that just isn't right. I wouldn't become socially engaged with her at all. The cloying fondness she displayed was actually what drove me away." He glanced at his watch. "Damn, look at the time. Nine forty-five and she hasn't shown up. I don't like the looks of this."

They left at ten o'clock, each to their own destinations. Barkow drove to the Phoenix Police Department, Violent Crimes Bureau on West Washington. Parking the Mercedes close by, he walked across the street and entered the stucco building. "Is Detective James Greenwell available?"

The Desk Sergeant picked up a phone and pushed a button. "Someone at the desk wants to see Greenwell." He replaced the phone and started to sort some papers.

"Is he coming?"

"Take a seat."

As Barkow turned around to find a chair, a short man with thinning hair and wearing a dark blue suit approached. Barkow said. "Are you Greenwell?"

"That's me," said the man. They shook hands.

"My name is Barkow. I was told by Adelita Ramos if I ever needed a good cop to look you up."

"Come with me," Greenwell said, and led the way back in the

direction he had come. He stopped at an old scarred desk littered with papers, photos and a beer can with the top cut out holding an assortment of pens and pencils. "Okay Mr. Barkow, call me Jim. Are you a client of Adelita's?"

"No, just a good friend. And just Barkow is fine."

James Greenwell smiled at the serious looking man and nodded. "What's on your mind, Barkow? Coffee?"

"Yes, coffee sounds good. Listen, I have a rather long story to tell you. Do you have some time or do I need to come back?"

"I have the time." He stepped over to a coffee pot on the counter. "Cream or sugar?"

"No thanks, black's fine."

As the two men settled themselves, the detective shoved everything on his desk to one side, then took a yellow lined tablet from his desk drawer.

"I can take notes as you talk, or I can record your voice and pick out the important points later. What'll it be?"

"The recording would be easier because it is a rather long and strange story."

"Okay, and I'll keep it to myself." He removed a recorder from a desk drawer and set it on the desk with the red light facing Barkow. "I'm ready for you to begin."

Barkow started from the time he was discharged from the Army. He told the Detective everything that had happened to him right up to the time he entered the police department that evening.

Along the way, Greenwell wrote down a few words here and there. When Barkow was finished talking, Jim leaned back in his chair. "I see your concern. The crux of the case is you want to find out what happened to Mary Cruthers. Anything I tell you from here on is to be kept between just us two, understand?

"Yes, I understand."

"Okay, the Phoenix Police already has an interest in Axelwood Labs. We've noticed a gathering of some known gangsters at that location. We also know that a well-connected hit man out of

Chicago was in and out of the place during the latter part of your story. He departed in an ambulance from the Labs and went to the Phoenix Airport. The ambulance driver delivered a patient to an Axelwood private jet, then returned to his home base without Cain Martin."

"Do you think Mary was the patient?"

"I don't know, but it wouldn't be a surprise. Look, if you'll swear out a statement to the effect that your cell phone was stolen while you were there and let me take a few pictures to show you suffered physical injury, we can go in with a search warrant."

KOJO

AXELWOOD RETREAT WAS set well back from the Highway, nine miles north of the fishing village of Dennery on the island of St. Lucia. Lush tropical plants, growing in wild confusion, form a living wall to within fifty feet of the long, low Spanish-style building. The entrance road from the highway plunges into the shadowed depths of the jungle, where broad leaves brush the sides of cars as they pass on the curving roadway. Branches and tangled vines arch over the crushed-shell surface of the road, which curves like a snake, working its way through the profusion of dense jungle until it breaks out into the sun-drenched gardens surrounding the Retreat.

A glass of rum punch in one hand and a white handkerchief in the other, Kojo was sitting on the veranda with a paddle-fan slowly revolving above. He took a mouthful of the drink, savored it for a moment and swallowed, than wiped the sweat beads from his bald head. Kojo was a giant of a man of Haitian decent, subordinate of a supreme being called Bondye, who does not intercede in human affairs. Being fearful of all gods, he also practiced a form of the Roman Catholic faith. He was ultimately controlled by religion. He also sent prayers and offerings to lesser entities, the spirits of Loa. Kojo had learned the art of survival in the slums of Haiti. Although his command of English was not particularly good, he had a quick and devious mind. He stood seven feet and three inches in height and weighed three hundred and forty-eight pounds. By using connections with Haitian crime syndicates, he had managed to make his escape from Haiti to St. Lucia. He thought of how fortunate he was to have this position at Axelwood Retreat. He was well-paid and seldom left the property, his only day off being the first Sunday of each month, when he enjoyed his little recreation. Today was Wednesday, May 23rd; he had tired of pestering Delsie and was taking a break.

He thought of the young woman locked in the back bedroom. She was drugged when she arrived, having been brought to him last night in a car by Martin. He remembered the softness of her body as he had carried her in. He also remembered the violent confrontation with Martin. The car had rolled up the driveway and slid to a stop just outside the front door. Cain Martin, hatless but still wearing his signature trench coat, had jumped from the driver's door of the car and slammed it hard.

"Good evening Mr. Martin," Kojo had said as he'd walked up to him.

"Good evening my ass!" Cain had snapped, his hands jammed deep in the coat pockets. "Why in the hell didn't you come to the damn airport and pick her up yourself, you lazy piece of crap!"

"Madam say Kojo get package from Mr. Martin. That all she say. Kojo not know when or how Mr. Martin bring package. Kojo no lazy."

"Your kind are always lazy, fat and stupid."

Kojo was two feet taller than Martin and outweighed him by a hundred and fifty pounds. His eyes were large, round and white in a coal-black face. He balanced on feet spread wide apart as he flexed his hands from fists to open palms, breathing deep, knowing from the bulge in Martin's coat pocket he could be seconds away from death.

Martin said, "Well, stupid, get her out of the car so I can get the hell outta here!"

Kojo had wrenched the car door open, nearly tearing it off the hinges. He stooped, ducked inside and lifted the uncon-scious girl from the seat. As he stood up, he turned and walked directly to Cain Martin and stopped, towering over him. "Some day Mr. Martin no talk bad to Kojo. Some day, Kojo put Martin in bloody pieces." Then he turned and walked toward the front door of the retreat.

"Fuck you, fat boy!" Cain had shouted, and then turned back to the car. He'd violently slammed the back door shut, then slipped into the driver's seat. He gunned the engine, expertly spinning the car around, the wheels spewing dirt and shell fragments as he fishtailed out of the yard and down the driveway, heading back to the airport.

KOJO'S PASSIONS

As Kojo sipped his rum on the veranda, he thought of the day he would carry out his plan to leave the Retreat once and for all. He smiled as he mulled over how he would kill Cain Martin, and the things he would perhaps do with Madam. He just needed time to get enough money to live comfortably. His thoughts turned back to the captive young woman again. She would be so nice to take deep in the bowels of the Retreat, a place he wasn't supposed to even know about. Once there he could do many things to her with great pleasure until she was dead. Tomorrow would be June third, the first Sunday of the month. Another girl would be brought in from some other island for his private pleasure. That was why he couldn't save much cash. The girls cost a lot of money and he could not bring them here, but had to rely on the old stone monastery, which lay in ruins far back in the jungle from the rocky coastline of St. Lucia.

Kojo stood up. He finished his drink and placed the glass toward the back of a vase of flowers on a side table. He smiled as he thought of how he would chastise the serving girl for not cleaning it up if it was still there in the morning. He went into the building and through the entrance hall, which led to a huge living room. Threading his way across a thick carpet he unlocked and entered Madam's private den. Walking across the room, he went directly to the floor-to-ceiling bookcases of polished cherry. At one section of bookcase, he took down a thick book with red leather cover. Behind where it had been, he slid a small panel aside to reveal a recess. He pressed a button in the wood and stepped back as a section of bookcase slid outward and moved over, leaving a wide enough space to enter the hidden room.

Even though he was not supposed to know this secret room existed, he was fully aware of every nook and cranny of the Retreat. He sat down at the bank of monitors and pulled out the control panel. Tiny hidden cameras were built into the walls and concealed in room décor throughout the Retreat. They enabled him to peer into virtually every corner of each room in the building. He turned on the power and the many monitors blinked on. The girl was sitting in one of the overstuffed chairs. She was still wearing the clothes she had been wearing when she'd arrived. He turned on a running video, recording of the interior rooms where she had been placed, then sat back and waited.

Kojo watched the prerecorded video as she slowly awakened and stood up; still fully dressed, she searched the small apartment. He hoped she would take a shower or bath so he could see her naked body. He zoomed in and brought her face up, so it filled the entire screen. She had a somewhat haunted, vacant look in her features. Two tiny crinkles of doubt lay between her eyes. Her lips were compressed, slightly pulled back causing small curved creases to appear in the cheeks. Kojo smiled. She was worried and concerned about where she was and what had happened to her.

It no matter, he thought. *When Madam done wid her, maybe then I gets her for my own self.*

The next morning on Sunday, June 3rd at 8:30 a.m., dressed in black and carrying a red satchel, Kojo stepped outside from his private room to greet the day. The sun was rising above the jungles of St. Lucia. As he approached the veranda, he spied the glass he had left yesterday. In a loud, angry tone he called, "Delcie?"

She hurried out of the building onto the veranda. "Yas, Mr. Kojo?"

"Delcie, you a sloppy slut of a cleaning maid. You know

you is to have used dishes and glassware picked up, washed and replaced where they belong, ain't dat right?"

Concern filled her face. "Yas Suh, Delcie know she do dat."

"Look!" he thundered as he pointed at the glass. "Do dat look like you pick it up and clean it?"

Her concern melted into fear. "No Suh, it doan look like it."

"I could let it go since this be Sunday. First Sunday of da month, my special day. But no, you does no show respect when you talks to me. Go to da the pantry an' get my quirt, and be quick about it."

"Oh no, Mr. Kojo Suh. Doan use that thang on me. I clean it right away."

Kojo reached out and caught her by the arm as she started to leave. He held her with one huge black hand as he slapped her. Pulling her with him, he backed up and sat in the chair, then yanked her face-down across his lap while she blubbered for him to stop. Pulling her dress up revealed she was wearing nothing beneath. Holding her down with an arm across her back, he began to slap her backside, pleased as the dark brown skin turned a reddish glow. Then he pushed her off onto the veranda floor. He smiled as he watched her struggle to cover herself. "Delsie very lucky today," he said cheerfully as she began to rise. He stopped her from getting up. "Stay on your knees, Delsie," he growled, then smiled as he leaned forward with forearms resting on his thighs. She started to sob again. "You is a lucky girl, because you don't got no panties on. Delsie 'members what Kojo say and now she don't wear no panties when she work in de big house. Now child, you go on and wash dat glass and put it away. You got spanked 'cause you no show Kojo respect when he talk to you. You is to always answer me and add Mr. Kojo on the end. Remember?"

"Yas Suh, Delsie gonna 'member always. Mr. Kojo." Tears streamed down her face.

"Go on. girl, get de glass and clean it."

He watched as she stood up and grabbed the glass. then ran

into the building. Kojo was happy. He had given Delsie a good scare and that delighted him. She was young, only sixteen, unable to read or write and he was training her as his private slave. He was unconcerned that anyone would hear the ruckus she had put up because this was Sunday. The workers were away and there were no guests other than the white woman locked in the back bedroom.

Taking his bag, he went through the Retreat and into the built-in garage at the back. He got into a gray van, backed out, drove around the building and into the winding driveway. Eventually he turned onto the paved highway, where he attempted to dodge the potholes as he made his way to Dennery.

Leaving the small settlement behind, he drove a few miles and then turned onto a dirt road that veered toward the ocean. The route ran alongside a rocky beach by the roaring Atlantic where the surf at times washed into small sandy areas among the rocks. The dirt road began to climb until it was perhaps a hundred feet higher than sea level. It eventually became a grassy byway rather than a road, winding along the eastern edge of the island.

He stopped high above a small bay that washed into the mouth of a box canyon with jungle growing down to the edge of the water. He stepped from the van and walked to the sloping edge of the canyon. Two rocky hooks reached out like arms, one on either side of the partially submerged canyon, extending to a point within fifty feet of meeting, where one turned in and the other out, leaving a narrow space between them. From a boat offshore, no break whatsoever appeared in the coastline. It looked impossible to land a boat anywhere in the vicinity.

There was a girl in a rowboat that was held between two chains. One stretched from the inner arm of the bay to the prow of the boat. Another ran from the stern to the small sandy beach and disappeared between two huge boulders. Her hands were shackled. "Ah, my little flower."

Carrying the bag, Kojo began to make his way down the treacherous, rocky path that wove back and forth in switchbacks from the top down to the tiny beach. He eventually came out of the trees onto the small sandy plot and followed the chain from into the recess between the two boulders. There, he found the mechanism for drawing in the boat. When he'd beached the boat on the small stretch of sand, he opened his red satchel and removed the black headgear with red eye patches. An evil looking face had been carefully sewn into the hood, giving him the look of Satan. He slipped it over his head and fitted the black gloves onto his hands.

As Kojo stepped away from the hidden area, the girl in the boat gasped, then began to sob and shake, thinking she was about to die.

Kojo never allowed his victims to see his face. Somewhere in his warped mind he thought, if they could not see his face, he could treat them as inhumanly as he wished without affecting his soul. He was very much afraid his soul could be corrupted and he would not be able to get into the Catholic heaven.

The thought flashed across his mind that he would have to wear his black outfit when he killed Martin. *Aint no point in taking chance of no gettin' into heaven when de time come.* He reached for the terrified girl.

"No! Doan touch me!" Her eyes blazed on the verge of madness.

Kojo looked her over. The girl was wearing the remains of a dress with dried blood spattered here and there on it. She had a wild, insane look in her eyes. Her appearance spoke of the serious disaster which had fallen upon her. He took the water-tight payment package from his bag and opened it. From the three thousand, five hundred dollars, he removed all but two hundred, then resealed the package and dropped it on the bottom of the boat. He swore a black oath at the henchmen he dealt with to obtain women for his use. They had used the woman for themselves and ruined her. "No pay top dollar for used trash!" he muttered.

Tying the red satchel to his belt, he lifted the screaming

woman out of the boat and flung her over his shoulder and began the slow climb back up the steep trail.

Kojo was unhappy. This one was so far gone that he would not have much fun with her. The body lay limp on his shoulder and her breathing was very hoarse. He arrived at the top of the hill and began threading his way through the thick, tropical foliage.

Eventually Kojo and his burden came upon the ancient monastery. The jungle had reclaimed most of it. The only complete rooms were across the back on the opposite side against the perimeter wall. Kojo entered the room on the back corner. The woman had stopped her foolish, ragged breathing. It had been getting on his nerves. He placed her, face down, on the stone slab of an ancient altar. It had a half-melted, large white candle and a crystal vase partly filled with water sitting on one end, items he used for his personal ceremonies. As he began removing the shackles from her wrists, he fitted the key into the locking bracelets and suddenly stopped. "She die, damn to hell! Da bitch die 'fore I could use her. Damn all de bitches in de whole damn world!" He pulled her body from the stone slab and carried it to a gaping window, having lost its frames and shutters centuries ago. There, he dropped the body outside onto the pile of human bones. In a month, her remnants would only be yellowed bones like the rest and he would have a new prize to play with.

As he drove the van back to the Retreat, he thought again about the men who found women for him. "By all dat's holy I gonna teach dem bastards to no fuck with Kojo." He slowed only for the sharp switchbacks in the ancient road that wound along the edge of the jungle covered mountain. When he pulled onto the paved highway, he switched on the radio. During a break in the music, the local news of the island came on, ending with the weather forecast. *Now I gots to wait a whole month 'fore I gets another one!* he thought, as the weather man was talking about a building storm along the South American coast. Kojo yelled at the radio. "Why I give a damn 'bout your stupid storm, when I lose my woman!" He jabbed the radio into silence and thought about his bad luck and how Delsie was going to have to make up for it.

DETECTIVE AT WORK

MAY 28, 2012, MONDAY, 9:00 A.M.

DETECTIVE JIM GREENWELL, Phoenix Police Department, drove his unmarked car out of the city heading southeast. As he passed the Flying J truck stop and thought about how Barkow had duped the biker into getting the stolen Lexus out of the area, a smile crossed his face. He eventually came to the turnoff. As he rolled up to the barrier arm, a uniformed guard came to the driver's side window.

Jim flashed his badge and ID. "Hello. I'm a detective with the Phoenix Police. I'd like to talk to whoever's in charge of this complex."

"Yes Sir. Please sign in." He handed Greenwell a clipboard with a roster under the clip.

After signing in, Greenwell handed it back. The guard thanked him and returned to the guardhouse. When the barrier arm lifted he drove to the visitor's lot, parked and went inside.

A well-dressed woman was at the reception desk. "May I help you?"

He handed her his card. "I'm Detective James Greenwell of the Phoenix Police Department. I'd like to speak with whoever's in charge of this complex."

"Certainly, Officer. Please have a seat and Mr. Hansen will be with you in a moment." She returned to the papers she had been working on.

Within a few minutes, a tall man appeared before him. "Hello, Detective Greenwell. I'm Mark Hansen, Director of R & D. Please follow me to my office." He turned and led the way through a hallway and into a well-furnished office with a huge walnut desk. He gestured toward a comfortable chair and then sat behind his desk. "What can I do for you?"

"I'm here regarding a visit by a woman named Mary Cruthers. We know she was here recently and had her rental car stolen. Nobody's seen her since she came here."

"Yes, I know whom you are talking about." Hansen said. "She just appeared out of the blue wanting an interview regarding information for implanting some sort of device into a person's body and controlling them with it."

The detective nodded while jotting in his note pad. "What did you tell her?"

"It was a strange request and something I had never heard of except perhaps in a science fiction movie. I said I knew of nothing of that sort happening here at Axelwood Labs. She thanked me and left the building only to find her car had been stolen. Made quite a scene about it."

"What happened then?"

"We had our Security Force conduct a quick search and questioned the gate guards. It appears that someone simply drove her car out the gate. She had left her keys and papers in the car."

"What did you do?"

"We notified the Maricopa County Sheriff's Department, explained what had happened and gave them a description of the car. Then we drove Miss Cruthers back to her hotel in Phoenix. That was the last we saw of her."

"Which hotel?"

"The Four Seasons."

"Who drove her?"

Hansen looked down at his desktop, nibbling at his lower lip. A look of concentration crossed his face. "One of the guards, I believe."

"I want to speak with that guard. Please call him in now."

"Certainly." He picked up his phone and punched the button for the Personnel Department. "Hello, Larry. Take a look in the files and find out who drove that woman whose car was stolen back into town." He nodded, glancing at Greenwell. "Call me as soon as you get the name and where he is right now." He hung up. "He'll call back in a minute or two."

Six minutes passed before the phone rang. "Hansen," said the director. He listened a few moments. "Why?" After a short pause, he jotted down a note, listened a bit more and hung up. "It seems, Detective, that particular guard was let go directly after the incident occurred. He was the one who allowed Ms. Cruthers car to drive out of the gate. His name is Charles Dumont, and this is his home address." He handed Greenwell a note.

"Thank you," the detective said. "By the way, is Ms. Axelwood here today?"

"No Sir, she is not."

"I want to see the guard log for the day in question. Please arrange that right now."

"Of course. Stop by the guard shack on the way out and they will show it to you. I'll call and let them know you're coming."

Greenwell thanked the Director and left the office.

Mark Hansen picked up his phone and punched in a private number.

"Axelwood," Carrie said.

Hansen explained all that had happened and how he handled it.

"You did well, Mark," Carrie said quietly. She thought, *We must get rid of Mr. Dumont.* She cut Hansen off and punched in a new number.

"Martin," he answered in an oily voice.

"I have another job for you. A Mr. Charles Dumont of Phoenix has been the cause of a severe problem. This is urgent. Take care of the matter tonight. Contact me in the usual way when the job is accomplished. Here's the address."

"It will be handled," Cain said softly and hung up. He began to contemplate what he'd have to do to accomplish Carrie's orders. He began ticking off the facts. *Today is May 28 and I'm in Chicago after knocking off those two bums in Phoenix on the 22nd. I would be stupid to go back and snuff Dumont tonight. That could tie me to both murders.* He picked up the phone and punched in a number.

"Caesar's Place."

"This is Cain Martin. Let me talk with Willie."

"Hi Cain, what's up?"

"Listen, Willie, I got a job that needs handled right now, tonight in Phoenix. The tab is fifty G's. Can you get that blonde ape of yours to do it?"

"I'll have his ass on the next flight out."

"Thanks. Here's the address."

⊙ AFTER SHE HUNG up with Cain Martin, Carrie called a new number. The call didn't connect. She hung up and retried with the same result. Then she punched in a different number and waited. After several rings, someone said, "Blue Note."

"I wish to speak with Bert, the bartender."

"Just a moment." The receiver clattered as it hit the counter and someone called, "Bert, phone!"

After a short wait he came to the phone. "Bert."

"Why doesn't your private cell phone work?" Carrie said. "With the salary you're paid, you need to have it on you at all times."

"Sorry, Ms. Axelwood. It's not working and I haven't gotten to the phone store to have it fixed."

Carrie exploded. "For the sweet love of Jesus H Christ! Can't anyone do a goddamned thing without me telling them as if they're ten fucking years old? How in the hell do people like you manage to dress yourself? I want you to keep an eye on Barkow. Hire someone and have him checked out: where he lives, whom he sees and what he does. Make sure it's someone you can trust, and you'd better know your goddamned job depends on doing this right!"

"Yes Ma'am," Bert said, surprised at her attitude.

"Now get your lazy ass to a store this *minute*! Buy yourself a goddamned phone!" Her voice rose to an insane screech. "If you can't get the same number, call me and give me the new one! And Bert, if I don't hear from you in twenty minutes, you're fucking *fired*!" She slammed the phone down on the desk.

⊙ Meanwhile at the guard shack, Greenwell parked and went inside.

"Mr. Hansen just called," the guard said as he handed him a log book, open to May 22, 2012.

Greenwell scanned the entries. In a note pad, he jotted down the following:

Company limo, left 1:10 p.m., returned, 2:35 p.m.
Company bus, left, 1:32 p.m., returned, 2:55 p.m.
Private car, left, 2:59 p.m.
Company SUV, (Martin) left, 3:12 p.m., returned 4:43 p.m.
Vehicle and driver's legs coated with dust and white powder.
Three men left earlier in this car, only one returned.
2 company patrol cars left, 4:15 p.m., returned 4:49 p.m.
Private ambulance left, 6:51 p.m., returned 8:20 p.m.

Interesting. He handed the log book back to the guard. "Thanks for the info."

⊙ Back in Phoenix at his desk, he made a phone call. "Hi Wally, it's me. You got five minutes?"

"Hi Jim, what's up?"

"I need a favor. Can you line up a helicopter ride of about a hundred miles round trip? This would be official Phoenix Police business and I think the Sherriff's Department will also be interested. Looks like I might have uncovered a rat's nest today."

"Sure thing, Jim, I'll work it out. Let's meet for lunch at La Placita at noon tomorrow and you can fill me in on the details. I'll have the bird ready."

"Great! See you then."

Sergeant Walter E. Manning, the traffic control helicopter pilot of the Maricopa County Sheriff's Department, hung up and scribbled a note: *Greenwell, noon, 29th*.

On the evening of May 28, 2012 at 11:35 p.m., in an unlighted alleyway behind a row of cheap track houses, a dark form gripping a length of iron and a pair of pruning shears slipped through the back gate of a particular residence. He cut the electrical power to the home, then kicked in the back door and entered. The sleeping ex-guard of the Axelwood Patrol died from crushing blows of a tire iron that mangled his face beyond recognition. The assailant then snipped off all ten digits from his hands and flushed them down the toilet. The assailant, swift and silent, exited the house and returned to the alley.

EYES IN THE SKIES

MAY 29, 2012, TUESDAY, 11:45 A.M.

JIM CROSSED THE asphalt street; heat waves rose from the concrete sidewalk as he entered the La Placita Café. Removing his sunglasses he looked around while his eyes adjusted to the dim interior. Seeing Wally at a table for two, he crossed the room and dropped onto the empty chair. "It'll get hot today," he said as he poured coffee into his cup from a container on the table.

"According to the paper, a hundred and eight in the shade. What's going on?"

"Another murder happened last night, on the south side. Someone, probably a crack-head, beat a guy to death with an iron bar. CSI is there now, getting the details," Jim said. "I need an air tour over Axelwood Labs. I'm investigating what appears to be murder and kidnapping."

Lunch completed, Wally said, "Follow me to the copter pad and we can take a look-see. You won't need a camera because we'll be using a traffic bird and it's equipped with a mounted camera. We can zoom in for whatever shots you want."

Once in the air, it took only a few minutes to cover the distance between the city and Axelwood Laboratories. "I'll control the camera and you can tell me when to zoom in and out as needed," Wally said over the helmet mike as he began a banking turn that took them in a wide circle of the buildings below.

Jim's voice crackled over the mike. "Get both long and zoomed-in shots of the layout of buildings." The copter circled twice while Jim watched the monitor.

"Now let's follow the fence with the concertina wire on top, all the way around the property."

"You got it!" Wally banked to follow the metal fence that went entirely around the hundred and fifty acre plot, then to a location where Jim had spotted faint tire tracks, where a vehicle had turned onto the property through a gate in the fence. The tracks ran southwest across the desert floor. At about half the distance to the southwest property corner, the tracks stopped. Jim, watching the monitor showing the tracks, suddenly blurted into the helmet mike, "Wally, get a close up of that red thing sitting in the foliage." The camera zoomed in on a bright red, construction wheelbarrow under a mesquite tree. The tire tracks had reversed back to the gate.

On the monitor, Jim could have counted the stitches on a baseball as Wally flew in a tight circle around the wheelbarrow. Scuffed footprints and an obviously disturbed patch of ground showed near the wheelbarrow with the stenciled word on the side: *AXELWOOD*. "Get a lat-long for this location, Wally," he said and received a thumbs-up.

Later, in the hangar office with the mission completed, Wally handed Jim a DVD containing both audio and video of the flight.

"Thanks a lot, Wally."

The two men parted company, and Jim drove back to his office, with its littered desk to develop the case with the new information. He leaned back in his chair, holding a coffee cup without drinking. *I hope Mary Cruthers isn't in that patch of disturbed earth. But if she is, then who rode with Martin in the ambulance on the afternoon of May twenty-second? The flight plan had been filed for New York City, but the plane had never arrived. Cain Martin, a known hit man, had obviously killed someone and buried them in the desert, but who?*

CARRIE GOES SHOPPING

MAY 29, 2012, TUESDAY, 12:15 P.M.

IN ANSWER TO a soft knock at her office door, Carrie quickly slipped a folder under some computer printouts on the desktop. "Come in." With a grave look on her face she sat back in the leather executive chair and waited.

Jacques entered and shut the door, then came to stand in front of the desk. "It's taken care of, Ms. Axelwood."

"Well done, Jacques. You may call me Carrie, and stop acting like a scolded dog; you have no reason to hang your head. Those two bumbling clowns that you set such store by caused all the troubles between you and me."

She waited while Jacques tried to decide whether she had finished talking.

"We got no troubles, Carrie. I knew those two guys a long time and I really thought they would do better than they did."

"We have no further use for them." She smiled. "We are taking a vacation, just you and me. You will like that, won't you, Jacques?"

"Yes Ms. Axe— uh, I mean Carrie. Yes, I'd like that a lot."

"Good. Go and pack what you need for a trip. No! Just put on your best suit and tie. We can buy anything in the way of clothing you may need. We leave in twenty minutes." Then with a sweet smile, she said, "Run along like a good boy!"

"Thanks, Carrie." Jacques growled as he stepped back. "I'll get ready right away." He turned and left the office.

Carrie watched the door as it closed. She tapped the highly polished nails of her right hand on the desktop. *Did I detect a glimmer of hatred in those brutish eyes? Greed... envy... or perhaps not understanding? Something flashed across his face. I'll have to keep a close eye on him for a while. He knows way too much to be allowed off the leash for any length of time.*

Her desk phone jangled. She picked it up. "Axelwood."

"Captain of the guard here. Just thought you should know, a Sheriff's Helicopter buzzed the Lab buildings and now it's flying over the back acreage."

Carrie's eyes flashed. "Thank you." She hung up.

Pulling out the folder and printouts, she checked her carefully tended and dated, common to-do lists and various self-reminder notes. She jotted a new note referencing Cain Martin asking her for a favor: *Have the Axelwood plane, when in Chicago, pick up Martin so he may take care of some urgent business in Arizona.* In other, previously dated papers she had made references of a decision to send Howard Billings to Chicago to check on the bookkeeping of some Axelwood properties. Another scrawled note read, *Tell Simmons he will fly Billings to Chicago and he is to pick up Mr. Martin on the way back, allowing a free flight for him to Phoenix as a friendly gesture.*

She also tore off a piece of lined tablet and scribbled on it: *In Chicago look up a man named Trifle. Martin mentioned him as a personal bodyguard.*

She smiled as she crumpled up that note, like it had been thrust into a pocket, then placed it several pages farther back in the file. Another notation stated her concern and distrust of Cain Martin: *I sometimes think Martin is trying to set me up. I cannot trust him.*

In other files and notes were references to other contacts. Mark Hansen, the Director of R&D at Axelwood Labs, was mentioned many times. Several notes hinted that he did not always give Carrie complete reports on things that happened; it appeared to her that he had intentionally withheld some things.

She quickly gathered up the folder and then computer printouts and placed them in the safe, shut the door and spun the dial. Once again the strange little smile crossed her face as she thought of the upcoming trip.

They rode in the limo, arriving at a private entrance for owners who kept their planes at the airport. Once they were aboard Axelwood's company jet, the pilot contacted the tower for permission to depart. A flight plan, already filed for LaGuardia Airport, allowed them to take off at once.

Later, in the private cabin, Carrie and Jacques sat opposite each other with a small table between them. They played backgammon, killing time.

"I'm bored!" Carrie exclaimed as she closed the game board. She stared into Jacques face and reached across the table. "Give me your hands." Jacques held his hands out and she took them into her own, then began gently rubbing her fingers over the callused palms. As she felt the hard, thickened skin, she gazed into the small black pupils beneath his overhung brow. "Are your feet, just as hard skinned as your hands?"

"Probably. What is it with you about a man's hands and feet?"

"You wouldn't have the slightest idea, would you Jacques?"

He looked at her without answering. He remembered how she had begged him to punish her in the basement of the laboratory building. *I know she likes to be roughed up. Crazy bitch is probably thinking about it right now.*

She dropped his hands. "Remove your shoes and stockings." She watched as he bent down and untied his shoe laces while his suit jacket almost split down the back. A look of disgust crossed her face. She slipped from her chair and crawled to his feet, now bare. She sat cross-legged on the carpeted floor, took a foot in her lap and began to rub her hands over the sole. She felt along the edge of the callused pad of his heel and up the Achilles tendon. She looked up at him, as he stared down. Her hands roamed over his foot, feeling each toe in turn, with their thick, square cut nails. "Do you have any other hard skin?" She murmured as she looked up at him with bright, snake-like eyes.

"Nope!" he muttered as he tried in vain to think of something else to say.

Carrie suddenly dropped the foot and spun around, twisting her skirt high up her thighs. She got to her hands and knees, leaned on the table and stood up. "Get me a drink!" She walked across the cabin to a built-in recliner and sat down.

Jacques, dumbstruck at how her tone had changed so quickly, spoke sharply. "What kind you want?" He started for the liquor cabinet.

"Don't use that tone of voice with me! You're paid to do whatever the hell I tell you to do. Dark rum with cola on the side, and be quick about it!"

He poured the rum into a glass filled with ice cubes. Taking a can of cola he popped the top open and set the two drinks on the built-in side shelf of her lounge chair. As he turned to leave, she shouted, "What in hell's name is this? You expect me to drink from a goddamned can?"

He quickly got a glass and took it to her.

"*Ice*, Jacques! Put some fucking ice in the damned glass!"

He brought the ice bucket and tongs over and filled her glass.

"That's a good boy. Now run along and let Mama calm down."

Barefooted, he returned to his seat, his thoughts blurred with anger. *Just wait until you need some punishment. I'll punish the hell out of you then, you little bitch, and I'll enjoy doing it.*

⊙ THEY DEPLANED AND rode in a hired limousine to The Arlington, a luxury hotel. The next day, May 30, in the hotel restaurant they had a late breakfast. Carrie called the dispatcher and requested the same limousine.

In the passenger compartment, Jacques sat beside Carrie in his brown suit. A thin orange stripe outlined a plaid pattern on the jacket. His orange tie and cordovan brown shoes completed the outfit. They made an odd looking pair. Carrie looked chic in a high-necked white blouse, a fitted black jacket and a knee-length skirt, her hair severely pulled back into a bun, earlobes centered with black onyx studs. Impeccable makeup set off her fair skin to perfection. A faint perfume lent the final touch of wealth.

Arriving at a brownstone building, they went inside and through a door marked *Tailored Perfection*.

"Ah, good afternoon Ms. Axelwood. How nice to see you again."

"Good afternoon, Mr. Grummins. I wish you to tailor a suit of black wool for Mr. Trifle. Please show us your fabric samples."

"Of course, Madam," he said. "Please take a seat while I get them. Would you care for coffee, water or tea?"

"Thank you, no."

"Sir?" he said as he looked at the man.

"Nothing for me," muttered Jacques.

After picking out five of the fabrics, Carrie said. "Make five suites of these fabrics. The pant legs should have a proper break where they touch the shoes. The style is to be whatever is in vogue at present. I also want a dozen fitted shirts with French cuffs that go well with the suits, along with coordinated silk ties in conservative colors. When can they be delivered?"

"I have all the fabrics in stock. It will take approximately thirty days from today, around the end of June, if that is satisfactory?"

"That will be sufficient. We are staying at the Arlington Hotel. I shall expect them to arrive within thirty days. Thank you, Mr. Grummins. It is always a pleasure doing business at your shop."

"Thank you, Madam. I appreciate your business." Turning toward Jacques, he said, "This way Sir, for measuring and fitting."

After two hours of taping, chalking and fitting, with Carrie offering suggestions and demands, they left by limousine to an upscale men's store. Carrie chose five pair of black dress-shoes for Jacques, a black suit of clothes from off the rack and a white dress shirt. In addition, she purchased an oriental silk robe and other accessories, plus cufflinks and a gold ID bracelet.

"You may have these things sent to the Arlington Hotel under the name of Carrie Axelwood," she said as she handed over a credit card.

"Thank you, Ms. Axelwood. We'll send them over at once."

Carrie and Jacques left the store and found the limo. The driver was sitting at the wheel, reading a paperback book. As they approached the car he quickly got out and opened the rear door for Carrie. Jacques went around and got in on the other side.

Back in their suite of rooms, Carrie turned on Jacques as soon as they entered. "Since when do you have to open the goddamned door to get into a rented limousine? I pay that company plenty of money to do their bloody job. You make me look like a fool!"

Jacques was taken totally by surprise. "Huh? What did I do wrong now?"

"Not only the fact you have no common manners, you also do not have a clue how to dress like a gentleman. When your new clothes arrive, I do not want to see you dressed in any other way than in a suit, tie and dress shoes. Do you understand that simple concept?"

"Okay Carrie, whatever you say."

She looked at him with disgust. "Throw those cheap rags in the trash and wear the suit I bought off the rack today. Use that suit until your proper clothes arrive."

"Okay Carrie."

"And stop saying, 'Okay Carrie.' You sound like a magpie."

"O... uh... all right, Ms. Axelwood."

"Draw me a bath." With a sigh, Carrie walked out of the room and into the bedroom, slamming the door behind her. She kicked off her shoes and began undressing as Jacques came into the bedroom, re-closed the door softly and crossed to the marble-covered walls of the bathroom. She heard the water splashing into the oversized bathing spa, ringed with water jets.

She finished undressing as Jacques came out. "Your bath is ready. Bubble bath, soap, perfume and oils are on the ledge by the tub. Do you want anything else done?"

Standing naked, she looked small. Her perfectly crowned breasts stood out from her chest above an hourglass figure that curved inward, then flared at the hips. Her long, dyed-black hair was piled and pinned on top her head. She seemed innocent and unaware of the hungry look on Trifle's face.

"Yes. Get undressed and join me," she murmured as she walked past him and stepped into the bath water.

BARKOW THE HUNTED

JUNE 1, 2012, FRIDAY, 9:04 A.M.

THE PHONE ON the polished mahogany desk jangled. Barkow reached across the keyboard of his computer and picked it up. "Barkow."

"This is Hank at the front desk. A guy just came in here looking for you. If I ever saw a phony hood, he was one. Had a cheesy New York accent and was wearing a long coat. I told him you were out and would return later."

"Thanks Hank. Did he say anything else?"

"Yeah, he asked me what kind of car you had and I said I had no idea because the cars come and go from the basement parking."

"You did the right thing, Hank. Anything else?"

"Nope, he just turned around and walked back outside. I bet he's out there waiting for you though."

"Good job. I'll be down and take a look at the security tape. Maybe I'll know who he is."

"Okay. See you then."

Barkow put on a shoulder harness and tucked a small black automatic into the holster. In the lobby of the building, he waved to Hank, then followed him into his office behind the counter. On the tape, a thin man of average build came through the door and approached the counter. He looked out of place for Phoenix. No one wore a felt business hat and trench coat in Arizona. The man had a sallow face. His eyes shifted back and forth as he made his request to the doorman.

There was no sound on the video tape and Barkow had no recollection of the man.

"I've never seen him before. He's trying to look like from out of town, as you said. If he comes back, call me and use the words, *Mr. Barkow.* That way I'll know it's him."

"You bet. I could tell he was trouble. I'll keep an eye out for that one."

With a wave of his hand, Barkow stepped into the elevator to the parking garage. As he walked to the Mercedes he kept a sharp lookout, but failed to see anyone at all.

Getting into the car he turned the ignition. The engine roared into life. He backed out of the space and made his way to the exit, turned right and sped down the roadway, aware of the tan Ford that pulled out from the curb shortly after he passed it.

He increased the Mercedes' speed above the posted speed limit and made a screeching right turn onto a side street. He gunned the engine and roaring for one block, then negotiated a howling left around the corner. Then he made a U-turn and pulled over to the curb. In a moment. the tan Ford shot past the street where he was waiting. He called Detective Jim Greenwell as he pulled away from the curb heading back the way he had come.

"Greenwell." He sounded tired.

"Hi Jim, Barkow here. You find anything interesting about my case?"

"Yeah, I did. You busy now?"

"No, I was just heading out for lunch. You want to join me?"

"Sure thing, let's meet at Hernando's. Tex-Mex and good food."

"Okay, see you there."

They met at the Mexican restaurant and selected a corner table. Barkow said, "So, catching any criminals lately?"

"Haven't lately, but I'm on to something."

The waitress stopped by and they each ordered a beer.

Barkow smiled. "Me too. I got some guy from out of town,

looking for me. He's dressed up like a cheap hood from Chicago and drives a tan Ford."

The detective grinned. "I got more than that." He told Barkow of his visit to Axelwood Labs and the copter ride. "So the way I see it, somebody is buried out in the desert and somebody took a plane ride with Cain Martin." Greenwell watched Barkow as he related his news. "I also found out that Carrie Axelwood and that stooge with long arms have taken a flight by private plane to New York City. I have a few spotters who keep track of who comes and goes around Axelwood Labs."

Barkow quietly said, "We've got to dig up that grave." he stated in a flat voice.

"Yeah, I've been working on that. Now listen, we don't know yet what's going on. For one thing, all we found was some tracks out to the desert and back."

The waitress took their orders. As she walked away, Barkow leaned over and said, "I want that grave dug up. How soon can you do it?"

The detective shrugged. "Soon as I can get a court order, but not until then."

"Okay. When do you think you'll get it?" Barkow said as the waitress delivered their salads.

"Probably in a week or so," Greenwell said while he added salad dressing. "You can't be involved with the search. It's a police matter and better that you're not there."

Barkow nodded. "Understood."

Jim said, "Another thing—three men left the Lab complex for that trip into the desert and only one returned. That seems to point to the fact that Mary probably was not been invited to go along. However, she may have been the one to leave in the ambulance."

"Sounds reasonable," Barkow said. "I hope so anyway."

JIM GREENWELL AT WORK

JUNE 12, 2012, TUESDAY, 8:06 A.M.

A CONVOY OF PHOENIX Police, County Sheriff, and Arizona DPS cruisers roared down the highway in bright, morning sunshine. A police pickup towing a flatbed trailer with a small backhoe chained down, brought up the rear. With lights flashing blue and red warnings, they turned off the state highway onto a paved road that led to the entrance of the Axelwood Laboratories complex. The lead vehicle, a police cruiser, presented the court order to the gate guard and demanded to see whoever was in charge of the compound. The guard called Mark Hansen, Director of Research and Development at Axelwood Labs.

"Hansen."

"This is the main gate security. We have a number of vehicles here, from the Sheriff's Department with a court order. They want to speak with whoever is in charge."

"Have them drive in and park in the delivery area in the back of the buildings. I'll meet them there."

"Yes Sir."

The chain of vehicles drove through the gate and around the building where they parked. The law enforcement officers all gathered in a group below the two men in business suits, standing on the empty loading dock. Officers of the Arizona DPS, Maricopa County Sheriff's Department and Phoenix Police task force, including Detective Jim Greenwell, went up the steps to the loading dock platform.

"Hello Mr. Hansen," Greenwell said as he presented the court order to search the premises both inside and out. Hansen looked at it briefly, then passed it to the man who stood by his side.

"This is Howard Billings, our company controller at this complex," Hansen said.

Greenwell nodded. Billings looked the court order over, then handed it back to Greenwell.

Greenwell handed the controller a clipboard with a paper under the clip. "Sign this acceptance slip and inform your employees we will be searching the premises." Billings signed the paper and Greenwell turned away to address the group of people standing below the loading platform.

"Okay men, listen up. I'm Jim Greenwell, Phoenix Police detective in charge of this task force. You have all received assigned locations to search. Each group has a leader who is in charge of your group and will be in radio contact with me at all times. I expect you to be courteous and thorough. You are not to interrogate any employees of this establishment. Now get to it, and when you finish your section or find anything you deem suspicious, you are to contact me. The driver of the pickup pulling the tractor, come see me."

As the men broke up into groups and began to spread out, Jim turned to the driver of the pickup. "Hi Harry. We'll go out in the desert first thing. Are you the backhoe operator as well?"

"Yes, I run the equipment and I have Tom with me as a helper if needed."

"Good. I'll lead in the squad car."

The cruiser, with the pickup following, pulled up to the guard gate. Greenwell asked for the key to the side gate padlock.

After several minutes the guard returned and said.

"Sorry, the key seems to have been misplaced. I called security and they don't have it on their keyboard either."

"No problem. We have bolt cutters with us," Greenwell said.

The exit arm went up and both vehicles drove out. After arriving at the gateway in the north section of the fence Jim stopped; leaving the motor running, he retrieved the bolt cutters from the trunk of the cruiser. He found the chain was not locked and the padlock was hanging closed, on a link in the gate. He cut the padlock and it fell apart. Jim opened the gate, then tossed the cutters in the trunk. He put the padlock in a labeled evidence bag and placed it in the back seat.

They arrived at the GPS location and found the red wheelbarrow. Both vehicles parked a small distance away. Harry and his helper began unloading the backhoe; Jim started taking video of the wheelbarrow and the surrounding area.

Careful to stay clear of the wheelbarrow until it was checked for fingerprints, Harry maneuvered the backhoe into position at the edge of the depression with the shovel poised above two small cacti. He began to expertly direct movements of backhoe arm and bucket, digging up the sand and rocks. About three feet down he came upon a layer of larger rocks. While Jim videoed the action, Harry carefully scraped together the rocks. Scooping them up with the bucket, he deposited them beside the hole. As the shovel-teeth raked through the material in the hole it snagged the edge of a bag. The helper jumped down in the hole and pulled the plastic-lined paper bag out of the sand. Broad printing on the side identified it as Construction Lime and cautioned the use of a breathing mask.

Harry raised the backhoe shovel and swung it to one side. "I'll get the hand shovels," he said as he turned off the power to the backhoe. He walked back to the trailer and pulled two shovels and a pair of leather gloves from a rack of tools along the front. He handed one shovel to Tom, his helper, then pulled on the gloves, slipped down into the hole and began to dig away the loose sand and small rocks. A few minutes later he came up with a man's shirt; almost at the same time Tom found another one. These were laid aside with the lime sack. In the hole there was now in evidence, a mixture of lime, sand, rocks and a putrid smell.

Jim said, "Okay boys, take it easy. It's getting close."

The two men went to their knees and began to scoop away

the loose material with their hands. They quickly came upon the first decomposing body.

"This one was shot between the eyes," Harry muttered as he scraped away sand from around the decaying face of a large man with no shirt. Some remains of a bandage were clinging to what remained of his nose.

After Jim took a few photos, Harry said, "Get hold of his feet, Tommy." They heaved the body out of the hole and rolled it to one side. They could make out the rough shape of another individual littered with lime and sand in the hole vacated by the corpse.

"Found the gun," Harry said. "Still has the silencer on the barrel."

Jim took a few more pictures, then pointed to something behind Tom's feet. "Tom, what's that?"

Tom reached down and pulled up a pair of black leather driving gloves. He tossed them up with the other things.

They cleaned the sand away from the head of the second body, which lay face down on the rock bottom of the hole. Harry looked up at Jim. "It's not the girl. He was shot through the back of the head." After Jim took a few pictures, Harry knelt and inspected the man's head. "Looks like his jaws were wired shut, what there is left of them. And it looks like there's a shovel and a pick under the body."

"Okay men," Jim said. "That's enough." They tossed their shovels out and climbed from the hole.

"Leave everything as-is and wait here until the corner arrives. You can reload the backhoe, but don't touch anything else." Jim turned off the camera and walked a little ways off. Taking a cell phone from his inside pocket, he punched in a number.

"Barkow."

"It's not Mary in the hole."

"Thank God," Barkow muttered with a sigh of relief. "What did you find?"

"A couple of men, both shot through the head."

"Is one of them oversized, the other one smaller?"

"Yes. I'm sure it's the two guys you were fighting with to escape. Obviously they were executed."

"They were in the wrong business. Not cut out to do the job they were hired for."

"Yeah, I just wanted to let you know. Take care, Barkow. I got work to do."

"Thanks Jim."

Greenwell cut the connection on his cell phone, then called the Sheriff to let him know what they'd found. He told him to get both the coroner and CSI on the way to investigate the crime scene and pick up the bodies.

BARKOW ON THE LOOSE

BARKOW, WITH NARROWED eyes, stared at the unopened bottle of bourbon in his hand. With his lips clamped in a tight line he replayed in his mind, the conversation he had finished with Jim Greenwell.

The two clowns were paid off and sent to hell. He thought. *Apparently Mary was either held captive, or she was taken on the plane to God only knows where. If I can somehow get hold of that pilot, I'll know in a very few minutes where he took Martin and whoever it was in the ambulance with him. Flight plan was for New York, according to the police, but the plane did not land there."*

As these conscious thoughts were running through his mind, on another level a plan of action was forming. Jim Greenwell could not be of help to him if the destination were out of the United States. He suddenly set the bottle down, snapped open his cell phone and called Greenwell.

"Greenwell." the detective answered.

"It's me again—listen, Jim, do you happen to have that copter pilot's number?"

"Yes. What you need him for?"

"Just a thought. Maybe he knows something about the private jet that Axelwood owns. I know it's kept at the Phoenix airport."

"What good is that for us?"

"Well, for starters it seems like that plane is coming and going a lot, bringing people in and out of Axelwood Labs. With

Mary missing and possibly taken out on that plane, I want to learn all I can about it."

"It wouldn't hurt to check it out. His name is Walter Manning and the number is 440-5461. Keep me informed and tell Wally I said hello."

Thanks. I'll see you later." Barkow said as he hung up.

He immediately called Walter Manning's number.

"Manning."

"Hi! My name is Barkow. I'm working on a case with Jim Manning. He gave me your number and said to say hello. Can we talk for a minute or two?"

"Sure thing, if you can hear me."

"Yes, it's okay. You hang around with private pilots at the airport, don't you?"

"Not so much. I know some of them, is all."

"Do you know who pilots the Axelwood jet?"

"It's a guy named Simmons, Bob Simmons, but I don't know him. I just heard his name mentioned a time or two."

"That's all I needed. Are you on the clock now?"

"Yes, until rush hour is over around seven. What's up?"

"Tying up loose ends."

"Bye Barkow."

Barkow snapped his phone shut and returned to his thoughts. *If they took her in an ambulance to the plane, was she hurt? Maybe she was drugged to keep her quiet. If she were dead, it would more or less stand to reason she would have ended up in the hole with the others.*

He began mentally cataloging facts and placing them in order on a timeline. He thought about the men he'd fought to escape, and then about fighting them earlier at the Blue Note. *But something else happened. I fought with the two men, the cops came and left, I was drinking coffee and then I was at the piano with Laura.* Suddenly, recollection clicked. *A woman! And that long armed guy!* A moving picture formed in his mind. *They were leaving as the cops were coming in. She stopped at the exit... stared at me.* "It was Carrie Axelwood with her hair dyed black." He said aloud while his fingertips gently rubbed the three scratches... causing intellection: *These also, were made by Carrie—only then she was called Marie.* Snatches of foggy conversations swirled in his brain, then understanding, clearing away cobwebs of doubt. The details fell into order one by one.

He took the elevator to the lobby. "Hi Hank, how's it going?"

"Hi guy." Hank answered. "Nothing new here. I haven't seen that stranger again."

Barkow smiled. "He drives a tan Ford. When I catch up with him, we're going to have a little chat. I'll be back later." He headed for the garage.

"Take care." Hank returned to his paperback.

He peeled out of the garage and turned right, roared to the end of the block and squealed through a left turn, then pulled over to the curb and stopped. He got out, walked back to the corner and looked toward the garage. He smiled when the tan Ford pulled into the entrance.

GETTING THE FACTS

BARKOW DROVE TO the private entrance gate for owners who lease space from Sky Harbor Airport. Parking the Mercedes across the street, he left the car and walked to the personnel entry gate.

"Hi," he said in a friendly voice as he approached the tiny admittance booth and handed the attendant his card. "I want to find Bob Simmons, a pilot for Axelwood. Any ideas?"

"The plane landed a while ago," the guard said, "but he hasn't come through this gate yet."

"Does he always leave by this exit?"

"Yeah, this one is closest to the parking lot."

Barkow took a fifty dollar bill from his wallet and stepped closer. "If I give you this bill, will you give me the high-sign when he goes through the gate? I'll be right over there in my car and I don't know what he looks like."

The guard's eyes lit up. "For fifty bucks, you bet I will."

"Thanks Mack!" He handed over the bill. "I'll be watching and don't tell Mr. Simmons how you made an easy fifty today."

Barkow sat in his car, monitoring the exit gate. The car radio produced low music. A half-hour had passed when a short, balding man in chinos and a black leather jacket arrived. The guard stopped him and said something inaudible. The man laughed and as he walked through the gate, the guard pointed at him while looking at Barkow.

Raising his hand in response, Barkow turned the radio off and watched Simmons walk through the parking lot. He went

160

straight to a motorcycle and pulled on a helmet as he straddled the bike. In a few minutes he rode out of the lot and made a right turn.

Barkow started his car and watched the rearview mirror long enough to let the rider get a block away, then made a u-turn and trailed after him.

Eventually, the man turned into the driveway of a sleazy strip-club and pulled around in back. Barkow did not follow, but drove on and turned at the next corner, where he passed Simmons parking the Harley near the back door. He circled the block and parked the Mercedes on the street, several doors from the club.

Taking his time, Barkow got out of the car and walked toward the tavern. Once his eyes grew accustomed to the dim light inside the darkened building, Barkow spotted the pilot at the bar with a glass of beer. He made his way to the bar and stopped behind the man. "Bob," he said, speaking close to his ear, "I just came in and noticed a guy messing with your bike. I thought you'd like to know."

Simmons quickly spun around. "Thanks, I'll check it out." He headed for the back door.

Barkow followed him out.

Bob turned and looked at Barkow. "There's no one here."

"Yeah, I know. I need to have a little talk with you in private. I want you to tell me about a patient you took on a flight a few days ago. You filed a flight plan for New York, but never arrived there and I want to know where you went and who the patient was."

"That's something I can't do for you," Simmons said. "It's Axelwood's business and— hey, whatcha doing?"

Barkow grasped Simmons by the front of his leather jacket and slammed him against the stucco building. He put his face up close. "Talk, or I'll beat the living shit out of you!"

"It... it was a woman on a stretcher. I think she was drugged. The guy with her was Cain Martin. He only said one thing to me. He… he told me to fly to George Charles Airport on Saint Lucia but not leave any trace of where we went or he'd come back and kill me."

"Who's Cain Martin?" Barkow snapped.

"Someone you don't want to cross. A tough guy from Chicago is all I know. I sent in a flight plan for New York but flew to Saint Lucia."

"And where can I find Carrie Axelwood?"

"All… all I know is, later I flew her and Jacques to New York, La Guardia Airport."

"Where was she going?"

"I… I don't know," Bob said. "On the way in, she had me call for Top Hat Limousine Service to have a car be available with Jeremy as the driver. She also said to get the plane in for service because they would be away for an extended period of time. That's all I know."

Barkow released the man, and walked away. *Mary was taken to St. Lucia in the Caribbean Islands.* Moments later the black Mercedes sounded a greeting chirp as he pressed the remote button. Still deep in thought he drove back to his condo. At the entrance door, he discovered the half-toothpick was inserted a bit higher than he had put it at knee height and it was pushed in point first. Haunting, musical notes began to build in volume somewhere in the depths of his mind. He slipped the small automatic from its holster and carefully checked the door. It was locked, so he inserted the key, gently turned it and eased the door open. The oiled hinges silently rotated, revealing nothing out of the ordinary within. Barkow methodically went through each room, making mental notes: *Here a pillow slightly turned; there a shoe moved aside; an unopened bottle of Blanton's Single Barrel Bourbon on the mantel with the label half-turned to the wall.* He knew without a doubt that someone had gone through his place. The dial of the wall safe behind the framed portrait had not been turned as the tiny smear of rubber-cement over the bottom edge of the dial was still intact, although the center pillow had been nudged a bit out of place, perhaps by a toe.

"Whoever went through here was damn good at it."

ALMOST A NORMAL COUPLE

JACQUES UNDRESSED AND stepped into the huge marble bath with Carrie. He sat at the far end, so their feet touched. He peered at her as he tried to ascertain what temperament she was in. He knew how quickly she could change from an easy-going friendly person into a screeching, evil-tempered bitch, descending on anyone who happened to have done something to set her off.

Carrie began to caress the sole of his foot with her toes beneath the fragrant clusters of bubbles floating on the bathwater. She looked small in the huge bath with the bubbles coming halfway across the globes of her breast. Jacques was reminded of a scolded little girl in an ordinary bathtub. The similarity was most evident in her facial features. All her makeup had been washed away, giving her the natural look of a child. Her hair was racked high on her head and as he watched, she slowly pulled it apart, letting it hang free in the water.

"Jacques, have I been mean to you?" she said quietly. "Everything has become so difficult in my life lately, all because of that damned claims adjuster."

"It's all right, Carrie. I understand and I'll stay with you as long as you'll have me. I ain't had nobody treat me as nice as you have."

"Aw, you big jerk, Trifle." She motioned him over to her. "Come over here and let Mama make up with you.

That evening after attending the Broadway show, *Chicago*, Carrie wanted to go bar hopping on the lower west side of town, a seedy, tough area known for gangs, hookers and crime. The first bar she chose seemed like the regular clientele was primarily made up of members of the plumber's trade. It was noisy, smoky and had a dirty concrete floor. Some sort of party was in progress because everyone had badges with names in bold letters. She and Jacques quickly left.

The second place was more upscale, with a bouncer on a stool at the door and a three-piece band playing loud jazz to the crowd of mixed customers. A trio of barely clad girls were dancing on a small stage. Carrie looked around for a table and found only one prospect; two large men were seated at a table for four. She walked straight to them and said. "Would you gentlemen mind if we sat at your table?"

"No problem, pretty lady," the larger of the two said. With his foot, he pushed out the chair closest to him. Nearly drooling, he looked her up and down as she seated herself. Although both men were wearing somewhat rumpled suits and ties, Carrie and Jacques were by far the best dressed people in the nightclub. She was wearing a flimsy, black, sleeveless dress with v-neckline that ended somewhere below her cleavage, with charcoal nylons, patent leather heels and a diamond-encrusted collar. Jacques was wearing the suit Carrie had picked from the rack earlier in the day. White French cuffs extended from the sleeves, allowing the gold cufflinks to glitter from the darkened interior of the jacket sleeve. A colonial red tie in a flawless Windsor knot, set off the white shirt perfectly.

A barmaid came by to take their drink order. "Two drink minimum," she said. Carrie ordered martinis, straight up.

"Porter," Jacques said. When the drinks were delivered, two martinis, a chilled glass and two bottles of dark ale, Jacques laid a fifty on the table. The barmaid quickly snatched it up.

"What did you think of the show, Jacques?" Carrie said.

One of the men across the table said, "Jacques! Yes Sir. Now that's what I call a real superior name. Right JB?"

"Oh, yeah Eddie; that's a fine name, for sure."

Jacques ignored them and answered Carrie. "I thought the

songs were pretty good, but kind of old fashioned." He looked directly into Carrie's eyes.

"Well, the genre was set in the twenties, so they would seem old fashioned."

"What's a genre?"

The two men broke out in loud, obnoxious, laughter.

The bouncer looked across the room and smiled.

"Jacques wants to know what a genre is," one howled as he pounded the table. The other man rocked back and forth on his seat.

"It's an expressive style of music, Jacques," Carrie said as she turned an icy stare on the man who had spoken. "You, Sir, have the manners of a pig," she said with a sneer. "In fact, I believe the pig superior." With that, she picked up a martini and drained it, her eyes never leaving the face of her antagonist.

"Aw, come on, honey, I didn't mean anything. Just struck me funny is all. I'll buy us a bottle of champagne and we can make up. Okay?"

"First of all, I'm not your honey," Carrie said. "Second, I don't think it's a damn bit funny, and third I don't want you to buy me anything."

"Rich bitch," he snarled. "Just 'cause you got money don't mean you come down to this part of town and treat us like trash." A switch blade appeared in his hand as he stood up, shoving his chair back.

The bouncer watched from his stool but made no move.

Two things happened in two seconds. Jacques stood up and slammed a full bottle of ale against the forehead of the man with the knife, which Jacques retrieved as the fellow collapsed. He turned on the still-seated man across the table, grabbed his necktie and pulled with such force the fellow was folded across the table at the beltline. Putting his face close to his opponent, Jacques said in a low growl, "Get your fucking friend out of here before I shove this pig-sticker up your ass!"

Unable to get his breath with the necktie pulled tight around his neck, the man's eyes bulged out of his face, which was turning a shade of purple. One hand was flat down on the table among the spilled drinks and the other was frantically trying to pull the tie out of Jacques' hand.

The manager rushed up. "Gentlemen, gentlemen! Please calm down!"

Jacques grabbed his lapel and snarled, "You in charge?"

"Yes... yes, I am."

"These two monkeys—who are they?"

"Part-time employees."

The bouncer strolled up and stood on the balls of his feet with his legs apart.

Jacques dropped the tie, letting the black-cherry face fall on the table.

Carrie stood up and nodded sideways at the bouncer. "What position does he hold?"

"He used to be my bouncer. Now he's fired."

"Very well, fire these two slobs also; should they happen to be here if or when I return, I will see to it that you are fired also. Come, Jacques, let us leave so this man may put out the trash." She walked out of the room with Jacques trailing behind.

Back in the limousine, Carrie told Jeremy to take them to a tavern named Caesar's Place by the waterfront.

"Are you certain, Madam? I only ask because it's a notorious hangout for a very tough crowd."

"Yes, Jeremy, I am certain."

As the sleek, black limo sped through the dark streets, Carrie sat close to Jacques, holding one of his hands in both of hers.

"I love the feel of your hands," she said in a softer voice than normal as she felt over the scarred knuckles of his thick fingers and gently brushed the hair growing on the back of his hand.

"I'm glad you like them."

"I want to check out Caesar's Place." Carrie spoke more to herself than to Jacques. She'd heard from Cain Martin that it might be up for sale and from time to time she needed the ties, for certain business connections that could only be found in such a place. She smiled. *It will be much like the place where I found you, Jacques.* The driver pulled up before the tavern and set the brake. He got out, opened the door for Carrie and offered his hand as she stepped out onto the sidewalk. Walking around the back of the car, he opened the other door.

Jacques stepped out and handed the driver a fifty dollar bill. Quietly, he said, "Stick close, Jeremy. We might come out in a hurry."

"I'll be diagonally across the street, backed into that alley. Just raise your hand when you come out, if you want me to come over real quick."

Jacques nodded, then turned and followed Carrie into the tavern. Eyes followed them as they walked behind the row of customers seated on stools at the bar. Most had their collars turned up as if not wanting to show any more of their features than absolutely necessary. The place reeked of stale cigarette smoke and unwashed bodies. As they neared the end of the row, the bar made a sharp left turn to the wall of the building. On the last stool, with his back against the wall, was a well-built man with a red bandana folded into a strip tied around his forehead. He was watching them from across the room; a cigarette hung from his lips. Smoke curled upwards, along the side of his face. They were being scrutinized.

Carrie had also recognized that he would be the one to talk with. He had broad shoulders with thickly muscled arms hanging from the openings of his sweatshirt, where the sleeves had been cut away at the shoulder seams. His blonde hair, a tangled mass, was held in place by the bandana above a week-old growth of beard. He had a strongly featured face with a pink scar running from the inside of his left eye in a sweeping curve to just below the corner of his mouth. She walked directly to him and stopped. "Hello, big boy."

"Hello, yourself; what's a sweet piece like you doing in here? Looking for a little action?"

His left hand lay in his lap. The right was folded around a beer can, almost hidden from sight in his oversized fist. Carrie's eyes locked on the fist holding the beer.

"Maybe, maybe not. What else do you use those hands for?"

"I make naughty girls behave," he said as his eyes flicked over to Jacques, then back to her. "I also throw punks like him out on their ass."

"Do I look like a naughty girl?" Carrie said as she began to slowly reach toward his massive fist. Jacques' lips pulled back into what passed as a smile. He was not concerned about Carrie's attitude or her flirting with this guy. She could eat him up and spit out the bones while looking for the next victim.

Jacques stepped around Carrie and up close to the man with the blonde hair. With a sharp click the point of a stiletto pricked the big man's side. "Okay, Blondie," Jacques growled, "that's enough of the happy talk. Unless you want me to carve a chunk out of your liver, you're going to put your fucking *hands*... in your fucking *lap*... and shut your fucking *mouth*." His gaze still locked on the big man's eyes, he said quietly to Carrie, "Are we finished here?"

"No. I would like to speak with the owner if he is here."

A sharp little jab of the blade brought an intake of breath, along with a trickle of blood from the seated man. "Speak up, Stupid. I don't have all fucking night."

"Yeah... he's... he's upstairs," the man said.

As he kept the tip of the blade a quarter-inch deep in the man's side, Jacques slid his empty hand up along the man's back and grabbed a fistful of yellow hair, then twisted and yanked, jerking him off the stool. "Show us the way, or I'll gut you right here."

Carrie turned and looked at the row of faces watching them. She smiled sweetly and then strutted along behind Jacques and the muscle-bound giant, who seemed to be walking on tiptoes. They marched up the stairs and stopped in the hallway.

The blonde man gestured with his head. "This is the door."

"Well, dickhead, knock on the fucking door!" Another sharp dig with the knife brought instant results.

Inside, someone said, "Whaddya want?"

"A gentleman and a lady want to see you. It is extremely urgent."

"Okay, okay. I'll see them in a few minutes."

Jacques growled, "Open the damn door!" and pushed the blade deeper.

Blondie opened the door and Jacques shoved him inside. A girl was straightening her dress as she moved away from the desk, behind which sat a weasel of a man. He was ferret-faced, his thin, greasy hair in disarray; his shirt was unbuttoned almost to the waist.

Blondie said, "Willie, these two—"

"Jesus Christ! What the fuck do you want?"

Carrie stepped forward. "Cain Martin told me to look you up." Then she turned and said, "Take the boy out, Jacques. I'll be finished in a minute or two." She glanced at the girl. "You too, sister. Get out."

The girl fled without a sound and the door slammed shut.

Looking straight at the weasel, Carrie said, "Cain said you're connected."

An oily smile appeared on the owner's face as he removed a cigar from a teak box on the desk. "So how's Cain doing?"

"Whatever the hell I tell him to do. I'm in the market for someone in the Big Apple to put on the payroll. You interested?"

"That depends on the wages. A man of my abilities don't come cheap."

"You'll get paid what you're worth starting with a ten thousand dollar retainer. You will be available 24/7 for whatever service I may require of you."

A slow smile began to form around the cigar crammed into the corner of his mouth. "Like I said, I don't come cheap."

"Listen to me, you snotty little, two-bit piece of shit." Her gaze bored into him. "I can shut down your operation within six hours and have your slimy carcass gutted and on the city dump in six and a half. I'm only here on Cain's recommendation. You want the fucking job or not?" She opened her purse and brought out a thick, neatly banded packet of new, one hundred dollar bills. "You got three seconds." She turned and walked to the door, but before she reached it, in a high-pitched voice he squeaked, "I'm in!"

"Smart move, Willie." She turned back and dropped the packet of money on his desk along with her business card. "I'll be in touch."

"Wait! Here's my card and my private number."

As Carrie walked away, she laughed. "You've been checked out. I know more about you and your dirty little habits than you know about yourself."

"But—" The office door slammed shut.

BARKOW TALKS BUSINESS

BARKOW, DRESSED FOR travel, packed the last few items in a small, leather carry-on. The automatic would be left behind because he could not take it on the plane. In a phone call to Judy, he informed her Mary had been drugged and taken to St. Lucia. He was going there to bring her back. Taking his carry-on and a lightweight jacket, he placed his usual toothpick check in the door jamb and then took the elevator down to the lobby.

Hank said, "Hi Barkow, looks as if you're on your way out."

"Yes and I plan to be away for a while. Did you know someone went through my place? Maybe the tan Ford guy."

"No shit? I've been keeping an eye out for him too. Damn it!"

"No problem," Barkow said. "I'm going to have a little talk with him; I don't think he will come back. I'll return in a week or so. Take care."

"Be careful, Barkow. See you later." Hank returned to his ever-present paperback.

Once in his car, Barkow donned a gray, snap-bill cap and pulled it low so the bill was resting on the top of his sunglasses. He reached under the driver's seat, removed a twin to the black automatic in his condo and shoved it into his jacket pocket. He backed the Mercedes out of the parking slot, pulled the gear shift into drive and squealed through the parking garage, drove up the ramp and out the exit onto the paved thoroughfare. He glanced in the rearview mirror and grinned as the tan Ford pulled away from the curb, hot on his trail.

He drove fast, through the streets, eventually taking an on-ramp to a divided avenue that led out of the city. He sped along, changing lanes to pass cars and occasionally checking behind him. The tan Ford also weaved in and out of traffic.

Coming out of the suburbs and into the desert he gunned the engine up to eighty-five. The Ford was slowly creeping up on him. He boosted the speed to ninety-five and the Tan Ford hung with him. The road made a wide, banking curve; the Mercedes shot around it at a hundred and five miles an hour, leaving the Ford behind. He swerved around another curve, slowed to sixty and rolled down an off ramp. Barkow entered a rock-strewn canyon and eventually turned onto a dirt side road. After cutting through a thicket of mesquite trees, he drove into the yard of an old line shack that was falling apart.

Getting out of the Mercedes, Barkow quickly entered the opening that once held a door to the dilapidated building. He went straight through and out a side window. The tan Ford roared out of the mesquite thicket and slid to a stop in a cloud of dust behind the Mercedes. The driver unfolded his lanky body out from the car, drew a revolver and hurried to the entrance. As he peered into the shaded interior of the building, Barkow, who had slipped around the building, stepped up behind him and placed the barrel of the automatic against the back of the man's head. "Don't move or I'll blow your fucking head off," he said quietly. The man froze in position, his revolver still pointed into the shack.

"Can I turn around?" he asked without moving.

"Only if you want to die. Now, take your gun by the barrel, with your left hand and hand it over your right shoulder to me."

The man reached toward his hand holding the gun.

Barkow jabbed the automatic hard against his head. "Slow, damn it!" This thing's got a hair trigger and I'm on a thin edge."

The gangly man, with exaggerated slowness took the gun barrel-first and handed it back to Barkow. "Now can I turn around?"

"You can step sideways and put your nose and both hands on the wall, then step back, feet apart.

Without taking his eyes off the man against the wall, Barkow jammed the revolver into his waist band and quickly frisked the guy. All he found was a package of chewing gum.

"Okay, tough guy," Barkow said, "you keep your nose on the wall and answer my questions."

The man said, "I just wanted to—"

Barkow shoved the man's face hard against the wall. A small trickle of blood ran from the thin hawk-beak nose down the sun bleached plywood wall. Barkow slipped his automatic into a side pocket and took the purloined revolver from his waist. He pointed it at the back of the man's head. "Listen, you stupid bastard, I'm fed up with your ignorance. Who hired you to follow me?" He pulled the hammer back with a sharp, metallic click.

"Bert… Bert hired me."

"Bert who?"

"Bert the bartender. That's all I know." Seconds slowly ticked by as Barkow stared at the back of the tall, skinny kid.

"You talking about the bartender at the Blue Note?"

"Yeah, that's Bert."

"Who the hell are you?"

"I'm Larry. Larry the Fitz."

"Larry the what? Are you jerking me around, you little turd?"

"No, no. I'm Larry the Fitz… Larry Fitzsimmons.

"What are you supposed to find out about me?"

Larry's voice rose in pitch. "Well, Mr. Barkow, I'm supposed to find out where you go and who you see."

"What's Bert paying you?"

"I don't know, Mr. Barkow. I just got in the spy business. I'm an actor."

"Okay, Mr. Larry the Fitz Fitzsimmons, you can turn around now."

As the skinny fellow turned around, he was looking directly into the barrel of his own revolver.

"You the one who frisked my place?" Barkow snarled.

"Oh, no Sir... I stood lookout in the hall while Bert went in."

Barkow held Larry's revolver out and flipped open the cylinder. He shook his head in amazement. Larry's eyes grew large and wide; he began to tremble.

"You got no fucking bullets in your gun!"

"It was... it was only for show... Mr. Barkow... Sir."

"Look Kid," Barkow said, handing the empty gun to Larry. "As of right now you are out of the spy business. You damn near got your head shot off because you're mixed up in a game of life and death. I want you to go home now and under no circumstances are you to call Bert. I will be talking with him very soon on your behalf, I will see that you get paid for the work you did for him. I do not want you to ever see, speak with or have any other communication with Bert. Not ever again. Do I make myself clear?"

"Yes Sir, Mr. Barkow. You got my word on it."

"You are to return to acting as a career. Is that understood?"

"Yes Sir, Mr. Barkow, Sir. Thank you, Sir."

"And stop calling me Sir."

"No, Sir, I mean yes Sir, absolutely Mr. Barkow.

Shaking his head, Barkow walked back to the Mercedes and left.

Barkow drove directly to the Blue Note and pulled into the employees' parking lot.

His eyes took in the empty expanse of the lounge. A dust cloth covered both the piano and the bench. The small, barren dance floor was surrounded by tables with chairs turned upside down on their tops. The only light was at the back bar, whence came the unmistakable sounds of someone moving things around. Barkow walked around the bar and found Bert, on hands and knees, rummaging under the bar. He grabbed him by the belt and pulled him backward. Barkow stopped as he looked into the frightened face of Bobby, the day fill-in barkeep. "Sorry, Bobby. I thought you were Bert. Where is that son of a bitch?"

Bobby got to his feet and recognized the man in the snap brim cap. "Hey, Barkow, you about scared the pants off me. He hasn't come in yet. Can I help you?"

"No, but Bert can. When is he due in?"

"In about half an hour. What did he do?"

"He's messing in my business. Have you noticed anything different about him lately?"

"Only that he asked me to fill in for him a few times, which he never has before. Also, he was coming on to Laura, but she would have none of it. About a week ago they had some hard words and then Terry got into the act and was yelling at him, so he up and walked out of the bar. The girls called me to come in and finish out Bert's shift.

"Thanks, Bobby. Maybe you better stick around, because I got a feeling Bert won't be working tonight. By the way, do you know who owns this bar?"

"Yeah, it's some old guy who lives in San Francisco. The bar is being handled by a management company here in Phoenix. The money is deposited in a bank every night when the place closes. Laura's doing the books and she meets with one of the company men at the end of each month. That's about all I know except there were some rumors a while back that the place may be up for sale, but I think those were just rumors."

"All right. Thanks for the info. I'll wait for Bert to come in." He slouched on a bar stool at the darkened end of the bar, in brooding silence broken only by a faint mental melody that intermingled with partial memories of old Army raids in the back of his mind.

Twenty minutes later, Bert made his entrance, coming through the back door and walking toward the bar. "Who the hell owns that black car out back?"

Barkow left his stool as the mental music rose in tempo; he moved up behind Bert without making a sound. He locked his left fist on the collar of the man's shirt, stopping him in mid-stride. With his right hand he grabbed the belt in the middle of Bert's back, and with a spin and a great heave, Barkow threw him into the nearest table stacked with chairs. The table tipped over and its chairs went flying, leaving Bert face-down among the furniture.

Barkow knelt and placed a knee in the small of Bert's back. He grasped the necktie as the legato passage upgraded to a roar in his skull. Pulling back on the tie, he leaned close to the man's head and said in a grating voice, "What the fuck you doing going through my place?"

In a convulsive voice, Bert choked out, "Barkow?"

"Just who the hell do you think it is, you goddamned piece of trash?"

"I can't breathe!"

Barkow put more weight on his knee, centered on the spine as he pulled harder at the tie, causing an unpleasant gargling wheeze to come from the eye-bulging red face. "I can break your back and hang you with this fucking tie, and I will unless you tell me everything I want to know, starting right fucking now." He released the tie, letting the man's face fall on the floor. Getting up, purposely putting more pressure on Bert's spine, he righted a chair and sat on it. Bert was clawing at the necktie, finally getting it loose enough to take short, gasping breaths.

Barkow watched as the man tried to sit up, only to grit his teeth at the pain in his back. "You're playing in a high-stakes game, Bert, and you're *way* outmatched. Now tell me who you work for."

"My back! You broke my damn back!"

He nudged the man's back with his boot, bringing forth another agonized grunt of pain "Not yet, but if I don't get a fucking answer, I can take care of that right now."

"Axelwood... Carrie Axelwood."

"How long?" Barkow said, eyes narrowed.

"Couple of months."

"Why are you checking me out?"

"I'm supposed to keep tabs on you... just business." Bert moaned the words.

"Yeah? Well let me tell you about this particular business: if you ever come within shouting distance of me again, I'll kill you. Do you understand that?"

"Yes."

Barkow growled, "Say it like you mean it, Bertie boy."

"Yes Sir, Mr. Barkow. I understand you."

"Now, this bar, for example. This is *my* hang out. That means you gotta get your skinny ass out of the Blue Note—I'd recommend out of Arizona—and keep it out. If you see Carrie Axelwood before I do, you tell her I'm coming for her. Do you understand that?"

"Yes Sir, I understand."

"Repeat it, you miserable bag of shit."

The phone on the bar clamored.

Bert choked out the words. "Tell Carrie you're coming for her."

"And know this—you had a kid named Larry working for you. As of right now, he no longer works for you. You are going to send him a thousand dollars, and after that you are never going to be in contact with him again. If you do, I will make it my personal business to talk with you again. And Bert, if I have to come back I won't be nearly as polite as I was this time. Got it?"

"Yes Sir, Mr. Barkow. I got it."

The phone was clanging away and Bobby picked it up. "Blue Note." After a few seconds of silence, he said, "I locked the back door. We have a private conversation going on right now. I think we'll be finished in about ten minutes."

Barkow snarled, "Now, you do understand everything I've said to you, right, Asshole?"

"Yes Sir, I understood every word Sir."

Barkow stood up and the music in his mind gradually faded in volume. In a seeming trance, he rolled his shoulders.

Bobby said, "Both Terry and Laura are at the back door, Barkow, ready to go to work... if you're finished talking with Bert."

" Better get the trash out first." He nudged Bert with a boot. "If this jerk ever gives trouble to anyone here, let me know."

"Sure will, Barkow. You gonna stick around?"

"No, I have unfinished business on the East Coast. I'll see you when I get back. I'll let the girls in and tell them to lock the door after me and you can open when you're ready."

He walked across the room and turned the lock on the back door. When he opened it, both Laura and Terry were waiting. "Hi, girls. Bobby will be the bartender tonight; Bert has quit the position." He turned to Terry. "Will you go in and help Bobby get ready to open? I need to talk with Laura for a minute."

"Sure thing," Terry said as she slipped inside, closing the door behind her.

"Laura, I understand you're doing the books for the Blue Note and are in touch with management. Is that correct?"

"Yes, I am."

"I also understand the place may be up for sale. Have you heard anything about that?"

"There was some idle talk about the owner maybe wanting to sell. He's in his eighties and lives in San Francisco."

"I might be interested in buying him out. Would you consider inquiring into it for me? Just feel him out a bit, but don't spread the word that I'm interested. I'm leaving for the East Coast on business. When I come back, we can discuss it."

"Sure thing, can do," Laura said. "How long will you be gone?"

"Maybe a couple of weeks. I'll be in touch and thanks, Laura."

After telling her to lock the door when she got inside, he went to the Mercedes and was soon driving on the freeway to the airport. The mellow notes of "The Chains of Love," almost inaudible, were soothing his mind. On arrival, he put his car in the extended parking, placed the automatic under the seat and went to the ticket desk. "One way to LaGuardia."

CAIN MARTIN SKIPS TOWN

June 17, 2012, Sunday, 1:12 P.M.

CAIN MARTIN WAS a guarded and calculating man. He had made a lot of money working for Carrie Axelwood. His bank account was loaded because he was good at his job.

As he sat in his modest, three room apartment shining his shoes, no one would suspect he had more than a few hundred dollars in savings. His appearance was that of a nondescript, rather bookish man. He had the kind of face that was easily forgotten. He bought inexpensive suits off the rack. His ties were dowdy and cheap. He habitually wore creased trousers and polished shoes. He routinely wore a frayed trench coat and wide-brimmed, felt hat. Devoid of concern, he also lacked sympathy of any sort.

As he applied a spit-shine to the shoes, his mind was completely blank. He could go into a near-trance at times, leaving him staring without expression at nothing. The phone brought just such a stupor to an end as he became aware it was jangling. A look of disgust crossed his features; he set the shoe down and reached for the phone.

"Yeah, who is it?" he said softly.

"It's Willie the Wimp. How ya doin', Cain?"

"Doin' okay, Willie. What's up?"

"I'm callin' to thank you for tipping me off to Axelwood."

"No problem. Did she give you a call?"

"Hell no—she came to see me in person."

Cain Martin became alert. Without changing voice inflection, he said, "What did she have to say?"

"She hired me on the spot. Gave me a ten grand cash retainer and said she would be in touch. She's quite a looker too." He giggled. "Have you been getting any of that stuff?"

Cain's eyes narrowed, he gripped the phone like a vise. Keeping his voice calm, he said, "What's the ten G's for?"

"She had one hell of a tough guy with her," Willie said. "He handled my bouncer like he was a high school kid."

"Yeah, that would be Trifle, her whipping boy," Cain said. "He follows her around like a goddamned puppy. What's the ten grand for?"

"Just a minute, hang on." Willie's voice became muffled as he held the phone against his breast. "Hi honey, just sit over there and I'll get rid of this guy." Coming back in a clear voice Willie said, "I gotta go Cain, talk to ya later."

Cain looked at the phone. "What the hell?" He opened his address book and found Willie the Wimp's phone number. He punched in the numbers, viciously jabbing each one with the point of a finger. He fumed as the phone rang—once... twice... three times—and then Willie's recorded voice said "Busy now, leave a number and I'll call back."

Cain slammed down the receiver and began to turn over the conversation he and Willie just had. He thought of the fact he had recently killed two people at the Labs for Carrie and two more in Chicago. *Carrie mentioned things have gotten hot in Phoenix, told me to lay low and not call her.* A lawsuit was in the works because the police had found the grave in the desert. *She said I'd bungled the job and she was going to take a long trip.*

He put the facts together and came up with an unavoidable answer. She was dumping him and Willie the Wimp would do her dirty work. He picked up the shoe and began methodically polishing the black leather, periodically spitting on it. It had been a lucrative arrangement between him and Carrie, but it looked as if everything was going down the tubes. His thoughts jumped from one fact to another, progressing along a line of depressed reasoning. *She had me take that girl down to Saint Lucia... She's so obsessed with Barkow she seems to be going insane…. Could she somehow put it all on me? It was me who forced the pilot to fly the girl to the Caribbean after filing a false flight plan. And someone tipped off the police that I was in Phoenix during the time of the murder.*

In a mechanical action, his right hand kept applying polish to the toe of the shoe, working the polish into the leather. *A leading homicide detective, James Greenwell, is heading up the case of the double murder.* A random thought crossed his mind. *At times, Carrie has a thing for Trifle and yet at other times, she treats him almost with hatred. He's a hardened street fighter and can be a mean one.* "Could he be taking my place? Or could Willie? Am I being played for a patsy?" The ringing phone startled him. He picked it up. "Yeah?"

"This is Detective Dan Wiggins of the Chicago Police Department. Is this Mr. Cain Martin?"

He was instantly on guard and by somewhat changing his speech pattern, his voice sounded smooth as silk and at ease.

"No, Mr. Martin is out of the country. Would you care to leave a message?"

"When do you expect him back in town?"

"I really can't say when that may be. He frequently travels, you see."

"And you are?"

"I am Conrad Williams. He hired me to paint the kitchen while he's away."

"Thank you, Mr. Williams. I'll check back later." The line went dead after a click.

Cain Martin, being a cautious man, added the fact that the Chicago police were taking an interest in him. He immediately called his personal banker and arranged for a wire transfer of all remaining funds to an account in Jamaica.

Cain, being very alert, changed into a special suit of clothes. He pulled an old wheeled trunk from a closet and began packing. He also removed his emergency stash of fifty thousand dollars from inside a wall and divided it into four packets. One in his breast pocket, two in the special pockets sewn at the inseam area inside his trouser legs, at thigh level, and one in the trunk. He called his landlord to say he would be out of the country for several months.

Rolling the trunk, he went into the parking garage and walked to a battered old pick-up. Putting on gloves, Cain loaded the trunk, then got behind the wheel. Driving the sputtering old truck he headed for a certain bridge over the river. He couldn't be traced through the truck as he had never touched it without wearing gloves. The title had never been changed after he bought it for cash from an individual who needed some quick money. At the river he parked, then walked along the walkway over the slow moving water. Slipping the guns from his inner coat pocket, he let all three drop into the murky water below.

Back in the pick-up he headed to the airport. *Have to take out the pilot, the girl and Kojo,* he thought as he drove, keeping close to the posted speed limit. Near the airport he left the truck in a long-term lot and took a shuttle to the airport where he purchased a ticket to San Juan, Puerto Rico. Arrangements were made for his suitcase to be flown ahead and held in storage until he picked it up.

☺ WHEN CAIN ARRIVED in San Juan, he took a taxi to a waterfront bar he had heard about from others of his ilk. Telling the cab driver to wait, he went inside and walked directly to the bartender.

"I'm looking for Clip Henderson."

"Wait here." The bartender picked up the phone. After a few hushed words, he turned back to Cain. "Sit tight." He returned to washing bar glasses.

Soon a Hispanic man wearing a tee shirt with blue jeans approached. "You are to follow me, Señor." Cain trailed the man across the barroom and out a side door. Once outside the man grabbed him by the front of the coat and pushed him up against the wall. "What you want Clip for, gringo?"

"Just tell him I'm a friend of Willie the Wimp and Jose Garcia, among others. My name is Cain Martin, from Chicago."

"Wait here, gringo." The man went back through the door while Cain, with a scowl on his face, began to pace back and forth. Ten minutes had passed before the Latino opened the door and motioned Cain back into the bar. They walked to a corner where Cain followed him up a darkened staircase.

"In here," the man said as he opened a door and shoved Cain inside.

"What the hell?" Cain muttered as he automatically tipped his head down, using the hat brim to shield his eyes from the bright light. He reached behind him for the door knob only to find it locked. Standing before a glaring white light, blinded, he could see nothing.

Someone spoke from the darkness beyond. "What do you want to see me about Mr. Martin?"

"Are you Clip Henderson?" asked Cain.

"Yes, I am. I apologize for the light, but it's the way I do business. I understand you know Jose Garcia and that he mentioned my name to you. Is that correct?"

"Yes. That is correct."

"Where did you meet Jose?"

"I met him through Willie the Wimp. They are connected in a business venture in Cleveland. They wanted me to come in on it with them; I refused for various reasons. If you'd like to check, give Jose or Willie a call and ask them about me. Otherwise, let's do business so I can be on my way."

"I know all about you, Mr. Cain Martin. What is it that you want?"

"I want a .357 semi-automatic pistol and a box of hollow-point ammunition."

"The price is seventeen hundred dollars US."

Cain slowly removed his wallet and counted out seventeen one hundred dollar bills. Head down, he groped behind the light and lay the money on the desk top.

"Chico, give Mr. Martin his merchandise."

The lock clicked behind Cain and he was yanked back into

the hall. A brown paper sack was shoved into his hands as the door slammed shut. It took several seconds for his eyes to become accustomed to the dim light in the hallway, and he discovered he was alone. He opened the bag feeling the cold steel of the gun and a box of bullets. He quickly opened the carton of ammunition and loaded the weapon. Cain shoved the .357 Desert Eagle into one pocket and the remaining bullets in another. From the base of the stairs, he made his way to the door and went to his taxi, thankful the driver had waited.

He had the cab take him to a booking agency. There, he bought a ticket on a small passenger ship leaving San Juan for the Virgin Islands.

The ship departed Puerto Rico on time and during the cruise, Cain spent most of his time talking with a Jamaican bartender in the ship's only bar. With a layout of cash it was revealed Cain should look up a bar called The Sailor's Home.

The ship eventually arrived at the Islands. Cain began checking the sleazy dives and strip joints along the waterfront until he came to The Sailor's Home. Finding the owner, he mentioned the bartender's name as a way of introduction.

After paying a hundred dollar bribe, he got the name of a boat for the type of trip he had in mind. He walked the marina docks until he found the fishing boat named *The Captain's Gig*, which looked both dirty and unkempt. Cain hailed the skipper and offered him a considerable sum of money to take him to St. Lucia. On arrival, he was to land him on a deserted coastline near the village of Dennery.

"Well now," the skipper said, "I think that can be arranged, but it's going to cost you a bit more than that."

"How much more?"

"Just about twice as much." The skipper said.

"No. The sum I mentioned was adequate." Cain turned and began walking away.

The skipper was a greedy man. It so happened he would be making a trip exactly as Cain wanted. Perhaps he could combine the two. He quickly made up his mind. "Hey Buddy, maybe we can work something out."

"I ain't your buddy and you got my price," Cain said—he kept walking.

"Okay. We got a deal. Be here at daylight tomorrow when we depart."

"I need to leave right now," Cain said. "I have another captain who will take me for a few dollars more."

"Okay, okay," the skipper said, "come aboard, but we have to fuel up first and get some supplies. There's going to be some rough weather ahead because a storm is moving up the South American coast."

Cain walked back and boarded *The Captain's Gig*. The skipper fired up the engines while the deckhand untied the boat lines. The boat backed away from the finger pier, then moved slowly toward the fuel dock.

"You can start by paying for fuel and supplies," the skipper said.

"You must think I'm a rube, eh Captain?"

"Hell man, it's your trip. The least you can do is pay for the fuel out of what you owe me."

"I don't owe you shit until you put me ashore close to Dennery," Cain said. "At that time I will pay you the agreed-upon amount. "I'm going to be sitting right here on the flying bridge beside you all the way. Your man can stay below."

CARRIE'S VEXATION

JACQUES RELAXED, SITTING in an easy chair, reading the *New York Times* sports section. He skimmed through the pages skipping over a small news item that concerned severe weather causing a soccer game cancelation on the east coast of South America.

Carrie was across the room making a phone call. The connection to Bert's special number began to ring.

"Hello?"

"Who in the hell are you?" Carrie blurted out.

"It's me, Bert. I can't talk so good right now."

"What happened to you?"

"That son of a bitch, Barkow, beat the hell out of me," he said in a strange, high-pitched tone. "He almost killed me Carrie. I'm leaving town."

"No Bert, you are not leaving town!" Carrie snapped. "You work for me, remember?"

"I ain't stayin' in Arizona no more, Carrie. He told me to get out or he would kill me, and I believe him."

"You will remain in position at the Blue Note until I call you. Understand?"

"He left a message," Bert said. "Said to tell you, he's coming for you."

"Now you listen to me Bert, I'm going to—"She glared at the phone. *How dare that little shit hang up on me?* She fumed for a few moments, then redialed the number. The line was no longer in service. "Damn him!"

"What's wrong?" Jacques said as he crossed the room.

"We're going back to Phoenix. I'll call Bob to bring the plane right away." Carrie said—she began punching in the number for the pilot.

"Hello?"

"Bob, this is Carrie. I need you to fly to New York and pick us up right away."

"No can do, Carrie. Plane's in the shop being serviced. Can it wait for another day?"

"No, it can't wait another day. I have to get back and take care of Barkow. It seems no one can do a damned thing without me there holding their hand."

Bob suddenly felt sick to his stomach. "Carrie...." He hesitated. "I had to tell Barkow about the flight to New York with you and Trifle."

"What?" Carrie screamed. "Why did you tell him that?"

"I thought he was going to kill me, Carrie. I really did. That man is insane. He made me tell him about Cain and the drugged girl too."

"What? God *damn* it, Bob! What else did you tell him?"

"I told him anything he wanted to know. He's a killer Carrie. Those granite eyes looked right into my soul. And by the way, I think he's trying to find *you*."

Carrie slammed down the phone and stalked to the middle of the room. "I think we need to take a little trip to St. Lucia." Her eyes appeared hard as glass marbles; she seemed on the edge of a mental rampage.

"This entire scam with Barkow is falling apart. Apparently he's the cause of the police finding those bodies and now he's looking for me."

"Relax Carrie," Jacques growled. "I can take care of Barkow if he comes around bothering you." He wrapped his long arms around her. "He just thinks he's a tough guy, that's all."

"Jacques, he actually *is* a tough guy. He's probably the toughest man you will ever come across. If the best in the business couldn't put him under, by pumping him full of drugs, he must be something close to unstoppable when he has a clear head."

"Don't worry, Babe. Nobody's gonna touch you as long as I'm at your side."

"Okay," Carrie said. "Get our stuff picked up and packed. I have a couple more phone calls to make; then we can be on our way."

She returned to the desk and phoned another of her employees. "Hello Willie, this is your employer."

"Hello, Ms. Axelwood. What can I do for you?"

"I have information that a person named G. B. Barkow searching for me. If that man comes smelling around you, I want you to handle him very roughly. Do you understand me?"

"Sure thing, Boss. Just how rough do you want it done?"

"As rough as you know how. You understand me, right?"

"I get your drift. Trust me, Boss, it will not be a problem."

"And Willie," said Carrie, "you'll need more muscle than that sweet boy we saw when we were there. Barkow is not a pussy cat. He needs to be handled by experts, and with great care."

"All right, Boss. I can handle it, no problem."

"And make him suffer... make it slow." Carrie spoke softly into the mouthpiece before she laid the phone in its cradle.

She called Cain Martin and received a recorded message saying the phone had been temporarily disconnected. Next she called Axelwood Retreat. When Kojo answered, Carrie said, "Kojo, this is Madam. Is everything under control?"

"Yes, Madam. All under control."

"The girl is all right?"

"Yes, Madam, girl all right."

"Listen, Kojo. Cain Martin could be coming to the Retreat. He may be in a vile mood, so I want you to be ready if trouble starts. I am also coming to see that certain plans I have will be carried out."

"Yes, Madam. Kojo be ready. Kojo no take shit from Mr. Martin like last time."

"All right, I will be there tonight or tomorrow morning."

"Kojo thanks Madam."

Carrie hung up, then called and chartered a seaplane to take them to St. Lucia. She also called to make sure the ship for their Around the World Cruise would be in San Juan, Puerto Rico on July 3rd and ready to depart for a year-long voyage on the 4th.

After a bellboy had taken their luggage down to the lobby, Jacques and Carrie took their final ride in the limousine to an air-service company on the waterfront where they found their chartered flight, a Lake LA-4-200 Buccaneer with single prop above the fuselage, tied up to a floating platform, engine running at idle.

While their luggage was being loaded aboard the plane, Jacques handed the Limo driver a three hundred dollar tip. He paid the service bill for the use of the car and driver with a credit card. The driver printed out a billing receipt, showing every address they had visited, including the mileage accumulated and the charge per mile, plus the driver's time and rate of pay. Jacques handed Carrie the billing ticket and they climbed aboard.

The pilot, standing on the floating dock, threw off the mooring lines, shoved the plane away and scrambled aboard. He slow-taxied the plane away from the docking platform and radioed the tower for departure information. When he received the go-ahead, he pushed the throttle forward, revving the engine for takeoff. The plane shot forward, skimming over the water, gaining speed until it became airborne. The roar of the prop driven engine made talking difficult, so they did not talk much.

In a loud voice to Jacques, Carrie said, "This is the best plane I could get on such short notice."

He nodded, then looked out the window, watching the shoreline slip away. They flew south to Miami where they refueled, then headed southwest toward St. Lucia.

Leaving Miami in darkness, the engine's roar had a hypnotizing effect on the passengers as they dozed, broken only by the occasional lurches and sudden drops as the plane encountered pockets of instability in the atmosphere. They were startled by the pilot's voice as it crackled, crisp and clear over a speaker in the cabin.

"Attention folks. Sorry for the inconvenience caused by turbulence. A storm is working its way northward along the eastern coast of South America and is presently between Rio and Salvador. This storm is affecting an area approximately fifteen hundred miles in diameter causing some serious air turbulence ahead of it. We shouldn't be very much affected, but the ride will be bumpy all the way to our destination. I'm planning to set down in Dennery Bay which is just south of the village, near the cemetery. Keep your seat belts fastened at all times. I'll keep you advised of any change in plans."

"Looks like it'll be rough all the way," Jacques said.

"No sleep for us until we get there." Carrie answered.

They turned off the cabin light and sat in darkness, reasonably comfortable in the soft leather seats. Suddenly the plane dropped, evoking a screech of alarm from Carrie.

Jacques said, "Make sure you keep your seat belt fastened snug." He took her hand.

"I hate this," Carrie muttered, as she squeezed the hard, calloused hand.

Soon they flew through an eerie formation of reflected light into a huge mass of dark, cloudy canyons. The speaker startled them with the pilot's voice. "Folks, the storm has rounded the eastern point of Brazil and is crossing the equator. It has intensified and may become a hurricane. I have checked by radio; both Fon d'Or and Dennery Bay are in high-wind conditions with heavy chop on the water. It won't be possible to touch down near Dennery Village. I'll have to take you to Point Seraphone, in the bay at Castries. It's on the opposite side of the island. If you must get to Dennery, you'll have to hire a car and drive across the north end of St. Lucia to get there. They've suspended all bus service on the island until this blows over."

Carrie yelled to be heard over the engine. "That is not acceptable!"

"I understand your concern, Ma'am, but there's nothing else I can do. The weather is getting worse all the time. I'll probably not get out of Castries once I land there. I could set you down at San Juan, Puerto Rico, but that just puts you farther away. I suggest you take Castries and wait out the storm there, then drive to Dennery as soon as it passes."

"How long do you think that may be?"

"It all depends on the speed of the storm." The pilot answered. "Right now it's moving northwest at a sustained speed of eighteen miles an hour. It could speed up, slow down, or go in a different direction altogether."

"Very well, we shall take the Castries option."

After much jarring through the turbulence, they eventually broke out of the thick, gray clouds on an approach to the Bay of Castries. The plane touched down in heavy chop, making loud thumping noises as the fuselage encountered the tops of pitching waves. Once it forced its way into solid water, the plane decelerated and began a slow, bouncy journey toward a floating platform.

"Watch your step, Ma'am." The pilot said as he handed Carrie down from the cabin door onto the floating dock.

He helped Trifle with a hand down. "Take her up to the waiting room and I'll get the luggage."

A strong wind blew in scattered drops of rain, peppering them as they hurried up the gangway from the dock to a small building. Throwing the door open, they quickly slipped inside and pushed it closed against the roaring wind. Two workers went out to help the pilot bring in the luggage.

The pilot spoke to the agent after getting the gear inside. "Where can I tie down until the weather lets me take off again?"

"Better do it right where you are. It's going to get a lot worse than this."

The pilot nodded and went out into the wind-driven rain

as Carrie stepped up to the desk. "We need to rent a car. Where can we get one?"

"There's a rental agency about a mile from here. I can call them to bring a car over if you like."

"Do so," Carrie said. "And tell them to bring the best and the largest one they have."

As they waited for the car, their pilot came back from tying down his plane.

"We are getting a rental car," Trifle said. "You want a lift someplace?"

"No thanks. I want to watch the plane for a while. I need to make sure it'll be safe enough in this weather."

"Well, I appreciate all your effort." He handed the man a hundred dollar bill and walked back to where Carrie was sitting.

Eventually the car arrived, a compact Toyota with a bad cough. The young driver hurried inside.

"Is that the best you have?" Carrie demanded, as she looked out the window.

"It's not only the best, but it's the last one available."

Carrie marched over to the desk. "Can you call another car rental?" she said.

The clerk looked at Carrie and shook her head. "There are no others open, Ma'am. They've shut down until after the storm passes."

Jacques came over and took Carrie by the arm. "This one will get us there. I'll load our things and we can get on the way." With some double hooked bungee cords, Jacques got enough luggage tied down on top to make room for the delivery boy in the jump seat.

They took the boy back to the rental agency in a rundown building on a dirty lot while slanting rain skidded across the pavement. While Carrie waited in the car, Jacques took care of the paperwork. He asked which road they should take to go to Dennery.

"That's over the mountains on the other side of the island," the woman at the desk said. "I wouldn't start out now. There's a big storm coming in from the southeast."

"Yeah, I know," Jacques said. "What road should I take to get to Dennery?"

"Mon Repos is the road that takes you to that village."

"You got a map?"

She handed him one.

"How far is it to Dennery?"

"In a straight line it's around thirty miles, but you have to drive over crooked, winding roads, so it's more like fifty."

"Thanks," Jacques said as he walked out of the building. He opened the car door on the driver's side and crammed the luggage from the top into the small jump seat area, then pushed the seat all the way back allowed a bit more leg room. His broad shoulders extended past the backrest. His long, thick arms were folded like a bird's wings. With calloused hands gripping the steering wheel and both knees pressed against the dashboard, he looked like an orangutan in a child's toy car. Carrie, being a much smaller person, fit the car's interior reasonably well, although she could not get the seat back to recline, so it remained nearly straight up.

Jacques started the engine and jammed the manual gear shift into low for a lurching start, grinding it into second and eventually third. He had attained a speed of thirty miles an hour when the car hit the first jarring pothole with enough force to pitch them forward. It pushed Jacques hard against the steering wheel and flung Carrie into the dashboard. She found her seatbelt and snapped it into place.

Wind-driven rain slanted out of the dark sky at a thirty-five degree angle; the wiper blades slammed back and forth in a vain effort to keep enough water off the windshield so Jacques could make out the road. The roadside gutters were simply square concrete troughs running full.

Out of town, the paved, narrow road seemed to have larger, deeper chuckholes. They crept along at twenty miles an hour, dodging this way and that. Every so often a wheel would drop into a sharp edged pit with a bone jarring thump as the tire hit the opposite side. The little Toyota wheezed and coughed, as it bumped and banged its way forward, on a mountain road to Dennery.

BARKOW IS COMING

BARKOW, SELF-ABSORBED IN his own interests, waited in the Sky Harbor Airport for his flight to LaGuardia. His ruminations concerned Mary Cruthers. *She came to find me in Phoenix near the time I came out of being drugged. Somehow they connected her to me; that's why they took her to St. Lucia.*

He had taken it for granted that after years of being alone, Mary had finally come to her senses, realizing he loved her and she loved him. His thoughts leapt from one suggestive scenario to another. *She probably quit her job and was coming to make amends.* Now she was dangerously tangled up with Carrie Axelwood.

He would go get her from St. Lucia after stopping long enough in New York for a final talk with Carrie. *If Mary has been harmed, I'll kill Cain Martin and anyone else involved.*

⊙ BARKOW AWOKE WITH a sense of something happening. No outward indication of awakening showed; his eyelids barely cracked open to reveal a mere slit of view. The plane was decelerating and suddenly the captain's voice came loud and crisp over the speakers, "This is the captain speaking. We are descending to LaGuardia Airport. Cabin personnel, prepare for landing."

Then came the sounds of seat adjustments being made and lights over various banks of seats blinked on as passengers gathered their belongings in preparation for landing.

"Thank you for flying the friendly skies of United and

welcome to the Big Apple. The current time in New York City is 8:46 a.m. Have a great day."

Deplaning, Barkow went directly to the land transportation booth. "I am searching for information on the Top Hat Limousine Service."

"Yes Sir, in the card rack, top row."

Picking out the white card with top hat and cane logo, he read *Top Hat Limousine Service, for distinctive people*. Barkow took the brochure and walked over to a bank of seats as he drew out his cell phone and dialed the number.

"Top Hat Service," said a male voice.

"Hello. My name is Barkow. I need some information regarding two clients you picked up a few weeks ago."

"I'm sorry, Sir, but we do not reveal any information about anyone who uses our services. It is the policy of our company."

"I understand," Barkow said politely. "Goodbye." He rented a car with a GPS and plugged in the address for the Top Hat Limo office. He arrived within a half-hour.

"Welcome to Top Hat," said the man behind the counter. "May I be of service?"

"I hope so," Barkow said as he handed his card to the man. "Carrie Axelwood was raving about the incredible service she received from your company. She recently used you again and told me to look up your firm when I needed a limousine. She even declared I should use the same driver."

"Ah yes. Ms. Axelwood is one of our premier customers. We have never received a complaint. May I arrange an accommodation for you?"

"Can you give me her same driver?" Barkow smiled. "I believe she said his name was Jeremy."

"Ah yes." The service manager beamed. "Jeremy is off duty the next three days. Do you need a car right away?"

"Not for four days," Barkow said. "But I need to make some special arrangements and I have a couple of questions for the driver. Can you have him call me as soon as possible?"

"When would be a good time for him to call?"

"I am short on time, but I will be available at any time before 3:00 p.m. today." Barkow replied. "Use the cell number on my card. I must be off now, but I will be sure to tell Carrie it was a pleasure to do business with you."

"Thank you, Mr. Barkow. I will be certain a car is available in four days."

Barkow quickly walked out of the office and drove to the nearest restaurant. He bought a newspaper, took a booth in the back and ordered. He had barely begun the sports page when his cell phone rang.

"Barkow."

"Mr. Barkow, this is Jeremy Jorgenson, driver for Top Hat."

"Hello Jeremy," Barkow. "I hear you know how to keep your mouth shut. Is that correct?"

"Yes Sir. I most certainly do."

"Okay. I have one thousand dollars for you if you can tell me where you took Ms. Axelwood when she hired you recently. Are you interested?"

"Yes Sir."

"Very well. I am at Sherri's Diner on Piedmont near LaGuardia. Be here in twenty and don't tell your boss, understand?"

"I'll be there. How do I know you?"

"Green shirt, snap-bill cap, booth in the back," Barkow said.

"See you in twenty." The line went dead with a click.

Barkow snapped his cell phone shut and went back to the sports page. Finishing the section, he noticed on the back page, a weather report about a storm that was raging in the Caribbean Island chain. *Maybe I can get in without being noticed.*

Jeremy entered the restaurant and looked around. Spotting Barkow in the back booth he walked over and offered his hand. "I'm Jeremy. What would you like to know?"

"I need to know where you took Carrie Axelwood when she was here recently."

"I can get fired for revealing that kind of information."

Barkow stared at him. "I've already offered you a thousand dollars specifically *not* to let anyone know what you've revealed, so how's anyone going to know?"

"You're right, of course," Jeremy said. "In fact, I figured you might want this." He handed Barkow the billing copy, showing the list of places and addresses of each stop he had taken Carrie and Jacques.

"Did you pick up any idle conversation along the way?"

"No, Sir, but I got an idea her bodyguard is one tough son of a bitch."

"It's been a pleasure doing business with you," Barkow said as he handed Jeremy ten new, one hundred dollar bills folded in half. Still gripping the money as the driver took hold of it, he said, "Jeremy, Mr. Trifle is a goddamned pussy compared to me. Just something to remember if you should decide to go back on your word."

Jeremy swallowed hard and nodded as Barkow released the cash. The driver left. Barkow laid a five dollar tip on the table, walked up to the cash register, paid his meal ticket and returned to the car.

First place on his list was the Arlington Hotel. On arrival, he asked to leave a message for Carrie Axelwood.

"I'm sorry, Sir. Ms. Axelwood has checked out and left the hotel."

As Barkow followed the list he picked up information from bellboys, waiters, luggage handlers and doormen. He was beginning to know a lot about the habits of Carrie and Jacques. He had spent the entire day traveling from one place to another. He visited an upscale tailor, a dozen overpriced restaurants, even a Broadway Theater.

At seven in the evening, he arrived at a sleazy club on the lower west side. As he stepped through the door the reek of stale beer and smoke seemed thick as the air in a steam bath. After ten minutes with the bartender, he went back to his car, glad he was not in the plumber's union of NYC. At the next stop he paid a ten-dollar cover charge to get into a cocktail lounge featuring a jazz trio and dancing girls. The place was packed. Customers were milling around laughing, talking and drinking. The strong smell of cannabis lingered among the sweating bodies. Barkow drifted back to the bouncer sitting at the entrance door.

"Damn crowded in here," he said. "Where's the action?"

"Depends on the kind of action."

"I'm looking for an uptown couple, dressed to the max, they were here a few days ago." Barkow held up a fifty dollar bill. "The guy would have looked like a gorilla in a tux, the babe a knock-out with dark hair. Does that description ring a bell?"

The bouncer said, "I'm new here, but I think I know about who you're looking for. The two bozos I replaced had the shit kicked out of them by the guy you're talking about. From what the barmaid told me, the woman really chewed out the manager and she was wearing a diamond choker worth two-fifty large."

Barkow handed the bill to the bouncer. "Anything else?"

"Nope," he said, taking the bill. "After they left, the manager fired the two guys along with the door bouncer and hired me."

Barkow nodded and as he started for the door, the bouncer said, "One other thing—I heard they were riding in a black limo."

"Yeah, I know." Barkow stepped out into the night.

His next stop was at Caesar's Place, a dirty little tavern close to the waterfront. He entered and stopped a moment, scanning the long, narrow room. Two men were standing by the wall to Barkow's right. At the final barstool, where the bar turned and attached to the wall, sat a man with red bandana tied around his head that held back a shock of blondish hair. He was looking directly at Barkow.

As he began walking down the length of the bar, no one on the stools turned around, but the two men who had been standing near the wall were now following him. He reached the end of the bar and with two quick steps, grabbed the man with the bandana and jettisoned him directly into the oncoming men, creating a sprawling tangle of bodies.

A swift kick to the blonde's kidney put him out of commission. One of the other two had risen to one knee. A punch to the throat dropped him like a sack of flour. The other man was up and moving toward him. Barkow spun once and landed a kick to the side of the man's face, knocking him unconsciousness.

The blonde man was up, although bent sideways, holding a knife in one hand while pressing his damaged side with the other.

Barkow growled, "Give me that blade and get your ass out of here!" The man dropped the knife and limped toward the door. Barkow turned to glare at the bartender, who was holding a baseball bat. "Who owns this dump?"

"Willie... Willie the Wimp," the man said.

"Where?"

"Up the stairs, on the right."

"Be smart," Barkow said, cold eyes leveled at the bartender, "and you'll live to see sunrise. Otherwise, I have two men outside with sawed-off shotguns."

The bartender nodded, put the bat down and walked back to the center of the bar. The customers' heads turned as one to look at the entrance, and no one moved. The only sound was a soft gurgle from a man trying to get his throat working.

Barkow folded the knife blade into the handle and walked quietly up the stairs. One hard kick against the spot next to the knob caused the splintered door to fly back, carrying away parts of the lock and jamb as it banged against a wall. On the couch, wearing only a white shirt and a pair of black sox, Willie the Wimp was between the legs of a woman with her knees up by her ears.

Barkow growled, "Get rid of the broad."

Willie, with the sudden departure of passion, slipped back and said to the woman, "Go on, get out of here." She quickly got up and bolted through the demolished doorway.

"Carrie Axelwood was here with a long-armed ape in a monkey suit," Barkow said, tapping the folded knife on the palm of his hand. "What did she want and where did she go?"

"She—" Willie swallowed hard. "She hired me and left. Are you Mr. Barkow?"

"Who the hell do you *think* I am, you little piece of shit? What did she hire you to do?"

"I don't know Mr. Barkow, she just laid ten large on me and said she'd be in touch. I'd never seen her before and I haven't seen her since. I swear to God, that's how it went down."

In his mind, a low, haunting melody rose in volume. Barkow took a step closer to where Willie was cowering on the couch. "Tell me Willie," Barkow said quietly as the knife blade sprang open with a snick. "How does it happen to be that you know my name?"

"She... she called me and said you may... may be in touch."

Stepping close to Willie as the music roared in his brain, Barkow touched Willie on the cheek with the razor-sharp tip of the blade. Willie cringed, shaking with fear as Barkow drew a line in a two inch, comma-shaped curve, welling blood.

"Well, you be sure to tell her, the next time she calls, I'm coming for her." He spoke in a flat, dead voice, devoid of emotion. He lowered the knife, wiped the bloody tip on Willie's white shirt and snapped it shut. The volume of the "Chains" melody slowly receded. "You got that?"

"Yes Sir, Mr. Barkow. I got it and I won't forget to tell her." Drops of blood slowly formed and ran from the curved cut.

"If you send anyone after me, Willie, I'll come back here, and I *will* kill you."

"Yes Sir, Mr. Barkow. I understand."

Barkow turned, walked through the dismantled door and down the stairs.

Eventually, Willie's hammering heart calmed down. He pulled on his pants and staggered to the doorway, peering out.

The place was deserted except for the barkeep and two seriously damaged men. "What the fuck happened?"

The bartender shook his head. "Barkow happened."

Driving back to the airport, Barkow returned the rental car and taxied to the same seaplane company Carrie had used.

"I was told by Carrie Axelwood I could hire a plane from here to take me to St. Lucia. Is that correct?"

"Yes Sir," the clerk said. "In fact, she recently flew out. There's quite a storm in that area and her plane is now stranded there until the weather clears, which may be tomorrow."

"Do you have other planes here can do that same trip?"

"Yes Sir. We have several planes available at present."

Barkow purchased a one-way ticket to Dennery. He waited at the loading area for a shuttle to the seaplane dock. At midnight, he discarded the knife into the sea and boarded the plane. Buckled in, he was soon lifting through the blackness of night.

CAIN MARTIN'S BOAT RIDE

CAIN MARTIN PULLED the collar of his trench coat up and his hat brim low. He sat on the flying bridge behind the captain. The boat's hull was on plane as it skimmed across the water in the darkness. Only the port and starboard running lights, plus a small instrument panel were turned on. The wind howled across a two-foot chop on the water's surface forming into deeper waves. Rain spattered them as the hull knifed through building seas.

Cain could not make out anything ahead or behind them in the darkness. Only the faint glow of the instrument panel offered any indication where the captain was. As the weather intensified, the captain shouted, "That's it. We have to get off the bridge and run her from below." He started down the ladder, Cain following. The fury of wind increased and the boat began bucking hard as it smashed through the tops of running waves.

Entering the cabin, Cain pushed the hatch closed against the storm. The tall helmsman chair crashed over backward. The captain grabbed the wheel and wrestled control of the boat, putting it on course to hit the waves at a three-quarter angle. Cain held onto the overhead safety rails in the cabin with both hands. The deckhand steadied himself against the galley table, which was built like a cafeteria booth into the side of the cabin. Assorted charts, coffee cups and tools were sliding back and forth against the low rail circling the tabletop as the boat violently lurched through heavy seas. The helm chair, now on its side, was driven back and forth as the violence of the pitching boat increased. A carton of canned food slid across the deck, crashing into a bulkhead and splitting apart. Cans of soup, beans and brown bread, rolled back and forth adding to the chaos. The captain yelled over the storm noise to the deckhand. "Get that gear secured, for Christ's sake and lash the cabin drawers shut! We still have a ways to go before we can get into the lee of an island."

Cain's stomach began to slosh, threatening to come up; he could taste the bile in his throat. "Are we going to make it?" he shouted at the captain

"Just get someplace and hang on," the skipper yelled. "We need to get into a lee; then it won't be so bad."

Cain's stomach suddenly revolted, the contents spewing out through his mouth and nose onto the salon deck. As the boat slid sideways Cain staggered and stepped into the mess, then slid across the deck and collided with the deck hand. They both went down among the cans of food and assorted boat gear clattering back and forth across the cabin floor.

The deck hand shrugged into a life preserver, then threw one at Cain and another near the captain. Then he began crawling back and forth, picking up loose items and stowing them in containers, which he secured to the cabin bulkheads.

After two and a half hours of buffeting through rough water, the wild pitching and yawing gradually began to lessen as the boat slipped into the sheltering waters of an island on the opposite side from the wind-driven storm. The deckhand lashed down all moveable objects.

The boat churned its way through choppy water until it passed the large island of Guadeloupe and moved again out into the full force of the storm. Cain, green-faced and once more gripping the overhead rails, fell into a series of dry heaves. The boat, quartering into three-foot waves, would rise on the side of a running wave, ride it for a moment as the keel was driven over the top, then crash into the next wave with a loud thump that shivered the fiberglass hull.

After an eternity of being slammed this way and that, *The Captain's Gig* at last slipped into the protective waters of Dominica.

Too sick to care, Cain climbed into a bottom bunk and began to moan as if he were going to die.

The skipper set the Global Positioning System to a small inlet along the coast of Dominica. As the boat came about to the proper course on autopilot, he motioned the deck hand to follow him up to the flying bridge.

"We gotta get into Snail Cove," he yelled above the roar of the wind. "They damn well better have her ready."

"Another package to pick up?" The deckhand hollered back.

The skipper nodded in the windswept storm. "Make sure that old bastard has the cash for payment. If he doesn't have it, we can dump him on the way in."

Giving a thumbs-up sign, the hand turned and went below. He made his way to the bunk where Cain lay in agony. "Captain wants to see the cash before he takes you in."

Cain, so seasick he could not speak, simply groaned.

The hand grabbed him by the front of his life jacket and shook hard. "Show me the goddamned cash or I'll rip your fuckin' clothes off."

Cain, thinking he was on his deathbed anyway, mumbled, "Breast pocket." The hand quickly unhooked the life jacket belt and opened it. He pulled Cain's coat apart and found a packet of cash. He fanned it open, scanned it, and shoved it back into the man's pocket.

"Good boy." He muttered and left the cabin. Back on the flying bridge, he told the skipper, "He's got the cash. We ought to take the dough and dump his ass in the drink anyway. Who's to know?"

"Nope. I made a deal with him and I'm going through with it," the captain said.

"Okay. Here's the gun I took off him." He offered Cain's gun to the captain.

"Put it in a safe place for now," the skipper said as the boat approached an inlet with a small dock.

Two men in hooded rain slickers were waiting on the wooden dock, holding an individual between them. She was wearing the same yellow slicker although it was three sizes too large. As *The Captain's Gig* slid up to the dock and backed water to a standstill, the hand secured the boat lines to rusty deck cleats.

"Get her on board and into the top bunk," the skipper yelled down at the two men as he turned off the engines. He climbed down and met them on the dock when they returned from below. "Here's the cash," he said, handing over a package. "You got fuel for me?"

"Yeah, got enough to fill your tanks. I'll get the hose." He scurried up the boat ramp and began pulling a reeled hose from the back of a pickup, dragging it down the boat ramp to the old wooden dock. The wind was beginning to pick up again as the skipper unscrewed the fuel tank access plug from the starboard gunwale.

"Make sure she's secured to the top bunk," he instructed the deckhand. "I want this one in good shape when we give her to Kojo. After the last time, he threatened to bail on us."

"I checked her out," the hand said. "Still groggy, but she looks in good condition."

After fueling was complete, the boat began plowing its way out of the protected inlet of Snail Cove, once more on a southwest course for Saint Lucia. Eventually, they emerged from Dominica's lee and began bucking the wallowing waves that slammed the boat around as the twin props pushed them toward Martinique, an island just north of Saint Lucia. The squawk of the radio was giving intermittent weather reports on the tropical storm.

"That doesn't sound good," the skipper yelled above the roar of the wind. "This thing could break into a hurricane at any time."

"Y'think we ought'a take cover in Martinique?" the deckhand said in a loud voice.

"No. It was just upgraded to a tropical storm. Maybe it'll hold until we can get in and out of Saint Lucia. But we better get below for the final run."

As they climbed down the ladder from the flying bridge, the deluge of wind driven rain pelted them like buckshot until they managed to get into the cabin. The hand wedged his body into the built-in seat at the galley table. The captain stood with feet wide apart, gripping the wheel, watching the instrument panel. Cain moaned from his bottom bunk and the girl, cuffed to the top bunk, remained silent.

Part Two

CONVERGENCE

JOURNEY'S END

July 1, 2012, Sunday, 5:37 a.m.

THE CAPTAIN'S GIG, tempest-tossed in the stormy seas, eventually hammered its way into the lee of Martinique. It shot across the comparative calm water until it rounded the island's southern end into the violence of the storm.

"We have to cut to the windward side of St. Lucia, and it's going to be damn rough," the captain said. "I figure we can be in and out in two hours."

The boat churned forward, smashing over three foot waves, directly into the teeth of the storm. Angling across the stretch between the islands, they eventually rounded the north end of St. Lucia and began a zigzag southern course to keep the seas from striking them directly on the beam, which could cause the boat to broach, roll on its side and sink. The skipper, knowing these islands well, brought them to a point just off a rocky shoreline, where a tiny bay with two arms reached into the sea as if preparing to hug. The wind was at fifty-two knots with the surf shooting thirty feet in the air as it crashed against the rocky outer arm. The inboard extension stretched on past the outer, leaving a channel between them, spanning a width of seventy feet. The water reformed itself into complex rollers that roared through the slotted opening like a writhing sea serpent, forcing its way through the rocky passage. It filled the bay, washed over the tiny sand beach and reached into the mouth of the canyon. The rowboat, normally chained at the inner arm, lay splintered and smashed on the rocks, but the chain still led from the winch into the agitated water.

The skipper, on the flying bridge, steered the boat directly between the protruding breakwaters of the bay. The boat rode high on the back of a roaring volume of surf-like water that ripped its way through the fearful trough and expelled them into the bay.

The deckhand, with a sigh of relief, relaxed his grip on the weather rails. "That was a close one. I never want to do that again," he said as he flexed his cramped hands.

"I'm going to nose her up to the beach," the captain said to the hand. "You have to go ashore and see if Kojo left us a payment. I don't want to put the hull up on the sand because we may never get her off again."

The deck hand dropped a rope ladder over the side off the starboard bow. As the boat edged through the wind-rippled surface close to the shore, he climbed down the makeshift ladder and dropped into water up to his knees.

"Look around and see if you find anything," the captain shouted from the bridge.

In the pouring rain, the hand walked around looking for some sort of payment. He followed the chain that had been formerly attached to the rowboat finding it led between two boulders to the hand-powered set of gears. He discovered a bright red, waterproof satchel, partially buried in the sand. Opening it, he found five thousand dollars in banded packets. He fanned several open to make sure it was real money all the way through, then took it back to the boat.

"I got it, Skipper. Take a look," he yelled and with an underhand toss, threw the satchel up to the captain.

"Looks good," the skipper shouted. "Wait there and I'll get the others." He went below and stowed the satchel, then bent down to the white-faced Cain Martin.

"Okay Martin," he said as he grabbed the man's life jacket and hauled him out of the bunk. "I have delivered you to within a couple miles of Dennery. Now pay up."

Cain could hardly stand. His legs were weak from lying in the bunk for so long.

The captain held him with one hand and stripped off the life jacket with the other. He pulled open the front of Cain's vomit-covered trench coat and reached in, taking out the packet of money. "Now get your skinny ass off my boat!"

He shoved Cain to the open cabin door. As Cain stumbled and went face down on the deck, the captain quickly picked him up and shoved him toward the boat's starboard gunwale. "Jump, Martin!"

"I can't," Cain mumbled as he leaned over the gunwale rail.

"Sure you can." The captain pulled Martin up by his ankles and let him tumble over the rail into the water. He went below and unlocked the girl's cuff from around the railing of the top bunk. He literally pulled her out of the bunk and half-dragged, half-carried her to the side. She too, with an open cuff dangling from her wrist, was pushed into the water. The skipper yelled to the hand, "Cuff them together and get aboard. We're pulling out."

As the hand was climbing the rope ladder at the bow, the boat slowly backed away from the beach.

Martin and the girl, cuffed together, were staggering in knee-deep water toward the edge of the jungle. The warm tropical rain relentlessly splattered down upon them. Cain's only thought was to get into the safety of the trees.

The boat, picking up speed, made a wide arc heading for the opening between the rocky protrusions protecting the bay. The skipper was at the helm laughing in the pouring rain, and the hand had clamped onto the bridge weather-rails in a death grip with his eyes tightly shut. The throttles were pushed all the way forward, and the boat had attained maximum speed when it entered the slot, meeting the incoming waves head-on. The captain gritted his teeth and yelled, "Come on baby, one more time!"

The boat buried its nose into the first wave and bulled its way forward. It suddenly broke onto the surface, shooting ahead like a wild animal. A rogue-wave from seaward rolled in like a mountain of water. At 6:15 a.m., *The Captain's Gig* was halfway through the slot when the enormous wave struck the outer arm and washed over. It hit the side of the boat, shoving it against the rocky side of the inboard arm. Both captain and hand were thrown off the bridge and onto the rocks as the boat heeled sideways and landed on top of them. The water held the shattered hull against the rocks as it washed over the inner arm and rolled into the mouth of the canyon.

The girl's left hand was cuffed to Cain's right. They were attempting to climb uphill from the beach when the boat had backed away. Both looked back when *The Captain's Gig* made its wide turn and headed full speed for the slot to the open sea. They watched the water roll over the outer barrier and capsize the boat, killing the two men who had just released them.

"Good riddance," Cain said. "Those two assholes got what they deserved."

As the massive wave rushed toward the beach the girl screamed. It filled the bay, washing up into the jungle, submerging plants and trees as it rose between the sides of the canyon.

Although Cain and the girl were climbing the sidewall of the jungle-covered canyon, they made only a few more steps before the water rose around their bodies, carrying them upwards. It quickly rose above their heads for what seemed like an eternity, then dropped, leaving them hanging fifteen feet above the ground, the handcuffs caught in the upper branches of a tree.

The outward flow, meeting ocean waves washing into the slot, destroyed what remained of *The Captain's Gig*, pummeling it between the rocky projections.

KOJO UNHINGED

JUNE 30, 2012, SATURDAY, 6:37 A.M.

KOJO, STILL INFURIATED at being denied a woman last month, sat inside by the window, watching the wind-driven rain as it deepened into a severe storm. He had been exceptionally cruel in the treatment of his apprentice slave.

"Delsie!" he yelled, as he threw his glass across the room where it shattered as it hit the tile floor. "Get you ass in here and clean up this mess."

"Yes Sir, Mr. Kojo, Sir. I is coming fast as I can," she cried as she limped into the room. Her arm hung at an odd angle and one eye was swollen almost shut with purple skin surrounding it. There was a cut on her left cheekbone and one side of her lower lip was badly bruised.

He glared as she knelt and brushed broken glass into a dustpan.

"Fix me another rum punch, girl," he snarled, "an' be quick about it."

"Yes Sir, Mr. Kojo. I be quick." She started to get up.

"Damn you, girl! Dump that glass in the trash first!"

"Yes Sir, Mr. Kojo. I dump it."

She hurriedly brought the drink, saying, "Here drink, Mr. Kojo, Sir."

"Good girl, Delsie," he said. "Now you sit on the floor over there while I drink."

Kojo was only half-drunk. Tomorrow would be his favorite day of the month. He thought about the pleasure he was going to have. It never occurred to him the storm might change all his plans. He had arranged to pay the procurer five thousand dollars to bring him a healthy, unharmed woman between twenty-five and thirty years old. *I am going to take my time with this one*, he thought, as he watched the wind-whipped palms outside thrashing in the increasing rain. "Delsie!"

"Yes Sir, Mr. Kojo," she said as she sprawled against the wall ten feet away.

"You go outside, girl, and get the storm shutters closed, then go directly to you room. I can feel it in my bones; we is in for a big old windy storm."

"Yes Sir, Mr. Kojo, Sir," the girl said as she painfully got to her feet and limped out of the room.

Kojo watched through the windows as she closed the storm shutters. The heavy rain, driven by howling wind, soon drenched her dress, making it adhere to her form. Kojo smiled at her discomfort as he finished his rum. When the last kitchen window was shuttered he got up and went into the living room where he unlocked the den door. He did not see Delsie outside closing the final shutter on the living room windows. She watched as he unlocked and entered Madam Carrie's private den.

Kojo was in a hurry. He went quickly through the secret bookcase-entrance to the monitor room. As had been his habit these past few days, he sat down and flicked on the monitors to the suite where Mary was held prisoner. She was at present reading, wearing a simple robe and lounging on a sofa before the fireplace.

Kojo stared, mouth agape, as her robe fell open to the loosely belted waist, revealing well-rounded breasts with erect nipples pointing slightly up and out from mounded areolas. She was leaning back on a pillow in the corner of the sofa, her legs bent at the knees. As Kojo watched, she wriggled and unbent one leg, extending it outward and down to the carpet, parting the robe further to reveal a dark thatch of black hair.

His mind began to form patterns of the secret room in the

basement. It was a unique room containing various implements for abusing people. He could picture this white-skinned beauty lashed to a cross or chained on a stretching table. His thoughts wandered through different scenarios in which he, taking his time, forced her to do grotesque things for his sexual pleasure. Compared to Delsie, she would be like champagne versus stale beer.

🕑 THE WINDSWEPT TORRENTS of rainwater raged against the roof and sides of the low, shuttered house. Delsie was in the process of closing the last shutter on the window. When she pulled it forward, her head was turned away from the onslaught of wind and rain, allowing her to see Kojo hurry through the room. *He not supposed to go into that room, but that not my business. Soon as he leave tomorrow I gonna run away.* She closed and locked the shutter, then crept back inside and quickly went to her room in the attached garage.

Delsie removed her rain-soaked dress, the only article of clothing she had on, and wrung it out over the chamber pot. She spread it to dry over the floor lamp shade and turned the light on to create some heat. She had another dress but it was only to be used when guests would see her. Shivering, she considered going to the kitchen and getting something hot to drink, but the thought of Kojo finding out caused her to remain in the unheated little room. She pulled her thin blanket around her shoulders. Sitting on the folding army cot where she slept, she put her simple mind to work.

Kojo spending a lot of time away lately. She thought. *When he do show up, he know exactly what happen while he gone. Could the den be where he go?* She took a deep breath for courage. *Mebbe I find out.* Wrapping the blanket more tightly around her, she slipped from her room and limped on bare feet into the dark house. In the living room, lighted by the muted glow of a small table lamp, she slowly edged toward the den door, which was slightly ajar. Kojo had been in a hurry and had not closed it. Delsie peered through the tiny opening, holding her breath.

It was quiet and dark except for a strange indirect light across the room. *Mebbe Kojo in there, sitting in the dark. He skin me alive if he catch me spying.* She cautiously pushed the door open another inch. Nothing happened. Eventually she opened the door enough to see into the entire room, finding it empty and dark, except for a bluish bar of light glowing from a shelf of books. The bookcase was at a strange angle, partially jutting from the wall. She crept into the room and peered through the secret opening into the monitoring room.

She gasped. Kojo was hunched forward, staring at the center screen in a curved bank of three luminous monitors. It was triple views of the same woman from different angles as she lay on a sofa reading a book. A fourth monitor over to one side cast a bluish light. It clearly showed a wide-angle view of the Retreat's dim living room.

Astonished, she stared at the monitors. The woman lay with her robe partially open, her arms in sleeves hidden from view. From time to time she crossed her legs, turned a page or slightly changed position.

Realization slowly built in Delsie's mind as she recognized the woman was the one Mr. Martin had brought to the house not long ago. Kojo had carried her into the house after an argument with Mr. Martin. The realization that he could also look into the living room clutched Delsie's heart, and she slipped away from the opening to the monitor room.

Thinking only to get out, she pushed the open bookcase-entrance back into place with a thump and limped quickly across the den toward the door to the living room. She collided with the edge of a desk in the darkness and fell. Kojo, roaring like an animal, crashed through the secret door to the den just as Delsie, naked in dim, bluish light, was trying to pick herself up.

Kojo caught Delsie by the hair as she gained her feet and savagely pulled her to him.

"What you do in den, Delsie?" he thundered. "You be spying on me, girl?"

"No, Sir. I hear a noise and I think it be spooks."

"Why is you naked?" Her shabby blanket was on the floor.

"My clothes is all wet. I couldn't wear my good dress while it dry off."

Kojo's mind was reeling. *What should I do? The girl has to be taught a lesson. She has to know my wrath. We are the only two people here, other than the white woman locked in the bedroom. A major storm is brewing outside.* A single result formed in his mind: *The basement special room.*

Holding her by the hair, he pushed her before him, back through the open secret bookcase entry. Inside, he marched her past the glowing monitors and down a short hall to a green glow, which proved to be a lighted combination safe dial. He had the numbers committed to memory and soon the door opened on a stairway. Pushing Delsie before him, they went down the stairs, through a door and into the special room.

Kojo flicked on a row of switches that turned on red flood bulbs suspended above the various BDSM fixtures. Still holding her by the hair before him, he pushed her toward a welded-iron cage. It had a head restraint built into the top, which could lock around the neck, leaving the head exposed for abuse. Using none of the special attachments, he simply shoved her into the cage and locked the door. With the attached chain hoist, he raised her above the floor.

That hold Delsie, he thought as he walked out of the room, slamming the door behind him. Kojo's mind was in turmoil. He mechanically climbed the stairs to the monitor room. Leaving the door open, he went past the monitors to the secret entrance back into the den and sat down. *Delsie know what I do in monitor room*, he thought. *Madam Carrie on her way and will arrive soon to see me. The white woman is locked up and will blab about being left alone.* His thoughts leapt ahead: *Tomorrow is first Sunday in July. I go make sure my woman delivered. I leave five large to buy her.*

Tomorrow, Kojo would take the van and go see if the girl was delivered so he could have his day with her. Maybe some solution would arrive on how to handle the rest of his problems. He was not aware Carrie and Jacques were, at that moment, driving the road to Dennery.

At the bar, he picked up a fresh bottle of rum and sat in his storm-battered room, drinking the night away.

WHEN CARRIE DEMANDS

July 1, 2012, Sunday, 4:12 a.m.

As the tropical storm lashed the jungle, its fury slowly beginning to wane, Carrie and Jacques, in the wheezing Toyota, were slowly closing the gap between them and Axelwood Retreat.

"I hope it's not much farther," Carrie said as she stared into the dim light of the headlamps.

"The rain is not as heavy as when we started," Jacques mumbled as he jerked the wheel to avoid potholes. "The wind and rain really slowed us down."

"We can ride out the storm in comfort once we get to the Retreat," Carrie said, trying to stretch her back. "This damn seatback will not recline and all I can think about is a comfortable bed." Her thoughts strayed to the Retreat where Mary Cruthers awaited her fate. *Cruthers*, she thought. *That good-looking piece holds the key to Barkow's heart. She will have to be eliminated. If he is searching for me, he will eventually come to the Retreat. Maybe I should give the girl to Kojo and have him take care of Barkow when he shows up.* A smile formed across her lips as she let that scenario marinate.

Jacques squinted through the slapping wiper blades. *The rain might be decreasing.* "It's getting lighter outside. I see a difference in the looks of the sky. The storm must be veering away, or it's moving past the island."

"Sunday can't come quick enough for me," Carrie said in a tight voice. She turned to face him. "I want this goddamned business finished. Then we can get aboard our ship. At least while here, we might be able to have a little fun. I have a very special

221

room for our use." Through half-lowered lashes, she saw the small, but telltale trace of a smile cross his lips. "You know how to please me, Jacques. I think you enjoy it as much as I do."

"I do what you want me to do," he said as he reached across and brushed her leg, pushing her skirt slightly higher.

"Don't start it now," she said in a small voice as she held his hand against her leg. "You know what I want can't be done in this rattletrap." Still holding his hand, she spread her knees apart and pushed it higher between her legs.

He glanced at her. Her head was turned to him, but tilted back, chin up, long lashes at half-mast. He squeezed her inner thigh.

"Damn it Jacques," she said weakly. "Don't start something we can't finish and—"

The front tire on the passenger side hit a pothole with a hard thump that slammed her against the seat belt and forced the steering wheel to jerk out of Jacques other hand. The front tire went off the blacktop, sinking into the mud while running along the sloping edge of the road. He quickly yanked his hand from between her thighs to get control of the car as it careened off the road, threatening to roll. Jacques turned the wheel to the extreme left and floor-boarded the gas pedal. The right front passenger tire, cramped in a hard turn, was now pushing a wall of mud before it. The rear tires, both off the road, were throwing rooster-tails of muck behind them with the car skidding sideways. The engine screamed as, inch by inch, the car crept toward the paved road. With a jerk, the front end gained the blacktop, followed in a heart-pounding second by the rear tires and fishtailing until Jacques regained control.

"God!" Carrie cried, wide eyed and obviously very excited. "I feel so alive! You have to take care of me pretty damn soon, or I'm going to turn into a real bitch."

"We're almost there Carrie, just hang on a while longer," he snarled.

"Hang on hell! Pull this damn car over!" Her intense blue eyes flashed cobalt fire. "I'm not accustomed to waiting for what I want."

"You want it in the rain, Carrie?" Jacques said, but stopped the car in the middle of the road and cut the engine.

"Just some sex," she said as she released the seat belt and opened her car door. "Hurry up, and make it rough." She toed her shoes off in the car and slipped out into the wind-swept curtains of falling rain, going to the front of the car. Standing back and leaning with one hand on the front of the engine-warmed hood, she stood on one foot, pulling sheer panties down and off, first one leg then the other. Jacques came from the driver's side, unzipping his trousers.

Carrie bent forward, laying her breasts on the low hood with feet apart and pulling the hem of her skirt up around her waist.

"Hurry honey!" Her voice cracked as driven rain hit the hood, forming wind-riffled pools before running off. He stood behind her watching the rain splatter on her white, bare skin, running in rivulets through the crease of her buttocks and streaming down her bare legs.

Swinging hard, he slapped one well-curved cheek, leaving a red handprint.

She wriggled in pain with a short, audible intake of breath as her skirt fell. She looked back at him. "You son of a bitch, that *hurt!*"

He moved closer with a stiff erection, pulled her skirt up one-handed to grip her left hip as he stepped between her legs. His other hand locked on the opposite hip. Using his knees, he forced her legs wider apart and with a single, bruising thrust buried the full length of his shaft between her swollen vulvas. In drenching rainfall, he began thrusting with hard, vicious jabs.

"My god you're killing me! Take it easy, you bastard!" Unconsciously she pushed back on each thrust. Wet hair hung on each side of her head, letting runnels of rainwater flow onto the hood.

Jacques knew exactly what she wanted and that she would become uncontrollable if he did not treat her as rough as she could take.

Carrie began to plead. "Stop it! Stop it, you son of a bitch or I'll kill you! You're hurting me!" Her voice changed to whimpering. "Goddamn it! Stop it! Stop it, please...." She began sobbing. "I can be good for you... I promise." She began to cry incoherently in the pounding downpour while continuing to match each thrust.

"Hurt me honey... hurt me.... Force me to please you...." Suddenly she screamed, "Harder Jacques! Faster! Harder!" She stopped pushing back.

He increased the pounding tempo, holding her pelvis in an iron grip on either side, vigorously pulling and pushing her back and forth like a sodden, rag doll. Her wet hair was whipping around her face in the same frantic, rhythmic movement of her torso. Suddenly she emitted a long, piercing wail, half-screaming, half-crying. He felt her cervix dip down to plunge into the semen as she spasmed. He pulled her roughly against him and held her with his shaft buried to its extremity, then allowed his climax to explode. Wind-swept veils of rain surged through the mountain valleys as a deluge of torrential rainwater blasted the interlocked couple. Exhausted, Carrie lay inert, collapsed on the hood of the car; Jacques, gasping for breath, leaned against the fleshy mounds of reddened buttocks as he bent across the hollow of her back, dominating her. Minutes later he stepped back, slowly pulling out. After several sobbing convulsions, she collected herself and pushed away from the hood. The wet skirt fell about her legs as she eased painfully around and got in the car. Jacques, his hair plastered flat by rain, sloshed to the driver's side, climbed in and started the engine. The red Toyota began moving down the twisting highway, leaving a pair of sheer, orchid-colored panties where they lay in a rain puddle on the highway. A reddish blush began to bleed through dark clouds. The time was 4:50 a.m.

BARKOW'S ARRIVAL

July 1, 2012, Sunday, 5:02 a.m.

THE SEAPLANE SHOT through the cloudy sky with an occasional glimpse of a rose-pink glow far in the east. Barkow sat in the co-pilot's seat, the only passenger on a flight to St. Lucia. The pilot looked over and said, "Good news. The storm is moving past the northern tip of Saint Lucia, so it looks as if we'll make the landing near Dennery."

"That's good," Barkow said as he stared at the enormous cloud formations. Eventually the plane began the descent and the northern end of the island appeared below. They banked and began a new course along the eastern coastline. Below them on a mountain road in a beat-up Toyota, Carrie and Jacques were also nearing his destination.

The plane began the long approach for Dennery Bay. "I'm going to set you down close to the cemetery. It's only a short way to the village from there," the pilot said.

Barkow nodded.

The plane landed with a minimum of instability as the boat-shaped fuselage cut through the low chop in the water and taxied toward a small wooden float tied to a finger pier. With the engine cut, the plane drifted slowly in perfect position alongside the float. The pilot stepped out with a line in hand, which he secured in a figure eight to a deck cleat.

Barkow deplaned in smattering rain, shook the pilot's hand and set off for the village. Pulling up his shirt collar and shoving his hands into his pockets, he trudged head-down against the rain toward the village of Dennery. From a previous Internet search, he knew that Axelwood Retreat was several miles north of Dennery on the Mon Repos highway. He was walking north on Mole road.

It was early morning, the first Sunday of the month, and all was quiet in the rain-soaked area. The sky was lighter, the rain had slackened, and ahead were the village buildings. It was early so he didn't expect to find anything open. He entered a section of beach homes as he continued along Mole road, which he knew eventually would cross Mon Repos highway. In due course, he came upon a restaurant. As he passed by, a side door opened and a man came out with a hinged sign, which he set up on the sidewalk announcing *Fresh Bread*.

"Good Morning," Barkow said.

"Good Morning, Mon," responded the fellow and turned to go back inside.

"You got any coffee?"

The man looked back over his shoulder. "Yeah Mon, please come in."

Inside the warm building were small round tables with two wire-backed chairs at each. The man gestured toward one of the chairs. "You sit, Mon. I bring coffee." He disappeared through a doorway.

Barkow was a big man. He carefully lowered himself onto the small wire chair. As he waited, the aroma of baking bread wafted across the room. The man came back with a tray which he set in the middle of the table. Two mugs, a coffeepot, cream and sugar were on the tray.

"We shall have our coffee, Mon, while I bake the bread," he said.

"Thank you," Barkow said. "I have not eaten for many hours."

"Ah, one moment. I will return. You may pour our coffee." The baker went into the back room again and returned with a sharp knife, a block of cheese and a round, golden loaf on a plate, which he set on the tray. He cut a few generous slices of mild cheddar and then cut the bread into thick wedges.

They each picked up a mug and saluted one another, then drank of the rich, strong coffee. With his teeth, Barkow ripped away portions of the chewy crust.

"This cheese goes well with the bread. The coffee is delicious."

"Thank you, Mon. I bake the bread for many shops in Dennery." They talked on about the island and the weather as time slipped by.

"It is a perfect breakfast," Barkow announced. "Do you happen to know how far it is to Axelwood Retreat?"

"About four and one half miles north, I believe. As for myself, I have never been to it. There have been stories about that place."

"Nor have I. However, I have some business there. What kind of stories have you heard?"

"Not good stories, my friend. Not good at all. It is rumored there is a giant black man there who practices the black arts. Mostly the place is empty, so I have heard, but especially well kept up."

Quietly, looking the man in the eyes, Barkow said, "I am going there to rescue someone. Where can I rent a car for the day?"

"Not around here, my friend. This is only a poor fishing village; those who come to Dennery already have their cars. There are some motor scooters about a block over for rent to tourists. Perhaps you could use one to get to your destination." A buzzer sounded. The baker excused himself and went to remove bread from the ovens.

Barkow felt refreshed. He stood and laid a fifty dollar bill on the table, then slipped out the side door still munching a piece of cheese. He walked over to the next block and found the building with a row of scooters and motorcycles. All were chained together, secured with a padlock. A sign on the door said the shop opened at 10:00 a.m. Barkow figured a four and one-half mile walk would take him perhaps an hour and a half, and it was only 8:30 a.m. Decision made, he returned to Mole road and before long came to Mon Repos highway, unaware that Carrie and Jacques had arrived at the retreat while he and the baker were eating breakfast.

KOJO'S REWARDS

July 1, 2012, Sunday, 6:15 a.m.

KOJO AWOKE AT six fifteen in the morning. He listened to the total silence. He could hear no rain, no wind. The storm had moved on. He felt irritable and grouchy. On the floor lay the empty rum bottle he had finished before going to sleep. Today was his special day, the first Sunday of the month. Since he had passed-out fully dressed, there was nothing to do but get up and go find out whether the girl had been delivered.

He thought about getting Delsie out of the cage to make him something to eat, but decided it might not stay down. He went to the bar and took a fresh bottle of rum, then to the secret monitoring room. Pulling the cork from the bottle he took a large swallow of rum and let it burn its way down his throat. The central monitor blinked on and there was the woman, just getting out of bed. He watched her walk naked to the bathroom and took another long swallow of rum, unaware she had become an addiction with him. He let his mind roam over things he could do with a beautiful woman like her. The rum hit his empty stomach, causing fire to spread through his veins. He watched as Mary leaned into the shower to turn on the water. She leaned farther, adjusting the temperature. Kojo let his eyes feast on the contours of her body that outlined a narrow waist before the curve of hips blended into her tightly rounded backside. He could feel his erection growing as he thought of how he would enjoy spanking her. She straightened up and turned around. Her slightly rounded swell of belly accentuated a triangular black thatch at the juncture of her thighs and torso.

Gazing at her figure on the screen Kojo let his mind soak in thoughts of sadistically dominating her as he lifted the bottle once more, but forgot to drink while he stared at the screen, slack-jawed. The naked woman put one foot on the toilet seat and leaned over to examine a toenail. Without conscious thought, he sat the bottle on the desktop, unzipped and began to massage himself.

Panting, he watched as she picked a bath mat from the shelf and bent forward to place it on the floor. Her breasts hung free like ripe fruit. She straightened the mat a moment before standing to lift her arms, causing both breasts to be pulled up and outwards as she enjoyed a long stretch. Kojo gasped, released the breath he had been holding and ejaculated. Mary stepped into the shower.

As she left his view, he picked up the bottle of rum again. He took a long, gurgling drink, almost emptying the bottle, and turned off the monitor. His blood was up. He thought of how he would use the new girl at the monastery.

In Kojo's alcohol-encumbered mind things were now as good as they could be. He left the room, picked up a fresh bottle of rum and went to the garage where he tossed the mask and the rum in the back seat. He put on his black suit, backed the gray van out at 6:54 a.m., and headed out the driveway. He was unaware that Jacques and Carrie were nearing the Retreat and would arrive in the next thirty minutes or that a very angry man in Dennery was eating bread and cheese for breakfast and would also be coming to the Retreat. Kojo drove south toward Dennery and the old, unused road along the coastline.

The storm had left palm fronds and branches scattered here and there on the roadway. His mind was on his upcoming pleasure as he dodged the potholes of Mon Repos highway and later passed through the village. Leaving the highway, he drove along a gravel beach and began the ascent up an ancient, rocky trail in four-wheel drive. Kojo encountered more signs of storm damage as the uphill climb entered thick jungle vegetation. A short while later he arrived at the hidden parking place atop the hill overlooking the small bay. He got out, retrieved the rum bottle and went to the edge of the steep bluff.

Two figures were standing at the edge of the jungle on the tiny strip of sand. They were looking toward the overlapping arms that made up the entrance to the bay.

"By all the gods," he uttered. "She be here, but why two peoples?"

Pulling the cork, he took a long pull from the bottle, resealed and returned it to the van. He quickly slipped the hood with red eye patches over his head and started down the steep, twisty path to the beach. At one switchback he had an excellent view of the inner arm, made up of enormous boulders dotted with sparse palms and other foliage. Intent on his mission, Kojo failed to notice the remains of the enormous outgoing wave or the stumps of broken palms and assorted debris. The remnants of two diesel engines, still yoked together on the rocks, lay in twisted wreckage. The sun glared off one bronze propeller, still attached to the end of its shaft and thrusting upwards at a low angle. Miscellaneous pieces of white fiberglass lay scattered about among palm fronds and driftwood.

Unseen by those on the beach, Kojo worked his way down through the precipitous jungle path. At the bottom, he slipped between two huge boulders. There, by the rusted winch, he searched for the red satchel he had placed in payment for the girl. It was nowhere to be found. He began walking toward the beach, a black demon with fire-eyes going for his rewards. It was Sunday, July 1, 7:10 a.m.

☺A HALF-HOUR AFTER Kojo had driven out, headed for Dennery, Jacques wheeled the Toyota onto the twisting, shell-encrusted entrance road and came to a stop before the Retreat building. Climbing out, stretching and stamping the kinks out of their legs, they entered the front door. Walking around the main floor, they found only silence.

"It's 7:30 in the morning on the first Sunday of the month," Carrie said. "This is the one day of each month that Kojo has off and can be away from the Retreat."

They went into the kitchen and Carrie showed Jacques where food supplies and tableware were kept. He could prepare some breakfast while she took a bath and changed clothes.

"Apparently all the help was sent home because of the storm," Carrie said. "It's a common practice in the tropics." She went to her private bedroom where everything seemed to be clean and ready for occupancy. Quickly stripping she soon lowered herself into the hot, oil-scented water of a large bathtub. A while later Jacques called from the dining nook in the kitchen, "Breakfast is ready, Carrie."

After eating Carrie said, "Come Jacques, let's take a look at our prisoner." She led him to the den and was surprised to find the door unlocked. Inside, where the bookcase stood ajar, she showed him the secret entrance to the monitoring room. Carrie's face clouded with anger as they stepped through. Jacques stared at the monitors mounted into a rounded wall above a half-circle desk. With the click of a switch the screens began to flicker to life. Carrie quickly found those that watched the apartment in which Mary Cruthers was secured. She was drinking coffee and reading a book. Used dishes and assorted pieces of clothing were scattered around the room.

"Messy, ain't she?" Jacques said. "Wonder who left this here?" He picked up an uncorked bottle of rum with a half-inch of liquid remaining and held it out so she could see.

Carrie's eyes flashed blue fire as she stared at the bottle. "God damn it! That's Kojo's brand. That oversized ape has been in here, probably gaping at the girl. I should have him horse-whipped. He knows this room is a restricted area." Suddenly she stopped. She was staring at the telltale, dried remains of semen on the seat cushion and the floor. "Damn his black ass! I give him a home, a job and all the benefits. A life of luxury compared to what he was used to and what do I get? Not a damned bit of common sense!"

Jacques went over to a round-topped trash container with a flip-top lid. "Here's a half-dozen empty rum bottles," he said, looking in. "Looks like Kojo had quite a party in here."

It was Sunday, July 1, 7:55 a.m.

⊘ Two HOURS LATER on the same morning, Barkow was walking the Mon Repos highway. He was wearing cargo pants, a tee shirt and boots. He'd discarded his shirt because of the heat. He continued walking; unaware the distance to his destination was not four and a half, but closer to nine miles. It was Sunday, July 1, 10:02 a.m.

A SWEET COUPLE

THE ROGUE WAVE had rushed in, capsizing the boat and taking both Cain and the girl by surprise. They were exhausted from the boat ride as well as being manhandled over the side into the shallow water by the captain.

The woman's left wrist cuffed to Cain's right, they balanced on a limb, facing each other. She had lost the bottom trousers of her rain suit but retained the long top jacket. The link between the cuffs had become wedged against the trunk by a small branch that grew at an angle close along the trunk before trending outward.

"Got to break the branch!" Cain said, still gasping for air. His hand was held above his head as far as his arm could extend. The woman was much taller than Cain, and her arm was bent at the elbow, but she was using it to maintain her balance on the limb.

"Get hold of that damned branch!" Cain demanded.

"I can't!" she screeched as she wobbled on the branch, causing the linked cuff on Cain's wrist to jerk his hand even tighter against the crotch between the branch and the tree trunk.

"Listen to me, y'dumb broad. If you don't grab that branch and pull it down so I can reach it, you and me are gonna die right here, hanging like two sides of beef on a hook."

"I can't do it!" she screamed.

Cain, on one foot, kicked at her knee with the other and suddenly both were frantically waving their free arms in an effort to regain their balance. Cain spoke in a quiet, reasonable voice. "Listen, girl, if you don't reach up and pull the branch down so I can get hold of it, we're going to hang here until we're too weak to keep our balance and one of us is going to fall off. Once that happens, there's absolutely no way to get free. Now don't panic. Just slowly raise your right hand as high up the small branch as you can and grasp it, then put all your weight on that arm without letting go of the branch."

Sobbing, she raised her hand to the branch.

"Atta girl," Cain said. "Now just reach as high as you can and get a real good grip. Slowly begin to transfer your weight from your legs to your grip on the branch. Keep your feet on the limb but bend your knees so you're pulling the branch down."

He held his breath as she started to lower herself and the branch bent. Cain held his left hand as high as he could reach, which was almost where his cuffed wrist was wedged against the tree. Eventually, he could touch the branch with his fingertips. He jumped the final inch and locked his hand around the slender branch.

With both their weight on the branch, it suddenly split where it was growing out of the trunk and dropped, peeling the thin bark with it. Both Cain and the girl were desperately trying to stay on the branch as their arms came down following the peeling bark.

"Straddle the limb!" Cain yelled as their bodies tried to follow the path of the peeling bark. "Hang on girl. Don't let go of this branch. I got to get some feeling worked back into my cuffed hand before I can climb down." After rubbing some circulation into his wrist and hand, Cain assessed the situation.

"I can't hang on any more," the girl whimpered.

"Just a little while longer," Cain said. "I got it figured. We have to begin to work our way farther out on this limb. As we do so it will bend with our weight and as it bends, we'll get closer to the ground. We have to do it now—right now—or we're both dead."

Very carefully and slowly, they began moving outward. They were spread out on the limb facing each other with Cain on the outer end of the limb, nine feet above the ground. The branch slowly began to bend as they squirmed farther out. Down one, two, three feet and with a crack the limb began breaking from the trunk of the tree. As it broke, it quickly dropped toward the trunk. The girl began sliding into Cain and he started slipping down the length of the limb until they fell the final four feet. Cain landed on his feet only to have his legs fold under him as the girl fell on top of him. They lay in a heap of tangled arms and legs in the soft sand.

They lay stunned, but alive, gasping for breath. After what seemed an eternity Cain fumbled himself into a sitting position. He checked the girl, who was quietly crying. "Are you hurt?" he said in a low, rasping voice.

"I don't think so." She groaned as she struggled to sit up.

They looked at their hands, scratched and bloody from gripping the limb as they slid down. The girl still had on her oversized raincoat.

Cain pulled his free arm from his trench coat and let it slip down his cuffed arm, so it hung like a wet blanket between them. "You better get that plastic raincoat off," he said.

"No. I have only a bra and panties beneath."

"Okay, but it must be like an oven in there. Let's see if we can work our way to the beach and find a way to get these cuffs off.

After a few minutes in the tropical heat, slipping and sliding between trees, over grass and jungle fern they moved down the canyon wall until the girl grabbed a branch and stopped their downward slide. Panting, she said. "I have to get out of this coat. Don't look."

"Sweet Jesus Christ!" Cain snapped, but turned his head as he searched his pocket for a penknife.

Eventually, they stumbled out of the jungle onto the small sandy beach where they had been when the rogue wave came in.

It was Sunday, July 1, 8.02 a.m.

☉ KOJO ROUNDED THE curve of the canyon wall and came face to face with Cain and the girl. They had ripped apart the seams and removed his trench coat and her plastic rain gear while still cuffed together. She was wearing only panties and bra, but had tied a part of the trench coat around her waist like a skirt. Their hands were scratched and bloody. They both stared at the giant of a man in a strange set of clothes.

"What in the hell are you supposed to be?" Cain snarled as he looked at the preposterous costume.

The girl, shackled to him, stared wide-eyed at Kojo.

"Why you chain together?" Kojo demanded. "Do Martin try steal Kojo's woman?"

Cain's only thought was to get rid of the handcuffs that held him and the girl together. The fact that Kojo had referenced his name, coupled with his size added up to his identity. *Stupid bastard's gonna blow his top.* "No problem, Kojo," Cain said in a calm voice. "I've been keeping her safe for you. Trouble is, I lost the key." Kojo's masked head cocked to one side as he tried to process what Cain was saying.

"Here she is, all safe and sound, just for you," Cain said in a matter-of-fact voice. "Do you happen to have a way to take these cuffs off?"

Comprehension dawned.

"Follow Kojo. I take off." He turned and started walking away.

To the girl, Cain whispered, "Come on and don't say anything." They walked around the shoulder of the canyon to the path and began the uphill climb. It was steep, narrow and full of switchbacks. The chained-together couple staggered and lurched their way upwards, breathing hard.

"Hey, slow down Kojo. We can't travel fast hooked together like this," Cain said in a panting voice.

Trudging up the path, Kojo's thoughts labored through the situation: *I have key in car. I kill Mr. Martin when I get him off my woman.* Arriving at the top of the hill, he went to the gray van and got the set of cuff keys. Cain and the girl were exhausted from climbing the steep path. They bent over, gasping, trying to get their breath back. Kojo, still wearing the hood, fumbled with the key, eventually removing the cuff from the girl's wrist.

"Wait by car," he demanded, pointing at the van.

Cain held his hand out with the empty cuff dangling from his wrist. Kojo slipped the keys into his pocket, grasped the hanging cuff and began to swing Cain around in a circle.

Cain ran, trying to stay on his feet. "Hey!"

The third time around, Kojo guided the running man directly into a tree trunk. He hit with such force it knocked the breath from his body and crushed his nose. Cain crumpled.

Kojo stepped forward and began to kick Cain Martin's body, which brought agonized grunts and groans from the injured man. The girl quickly crept into the jungle.

Kojo hated Cain and enjoyed kicking him. Each moan was a delight. Each solid connection of his foot with the body brought more ecstasy and rapture. Cain was coughing up blood and vomit, near death. Kojo kept kicking. He enjoyed the feeling of power until eventually, in a state of elation, he realized Cain was no longer alive. His head slowly cleared as reason returned. Now he would enjoy elaborately killing the girl. He looked at the van. There was no girl. He began to frantically search around the van and in the nearby jungle.

He screamed. "She gone! De damn bitch be gone!" *When I find her she gonna pay plenty!* Slipping and sliding, he hurried down the path to the beach.

After searching everywhere he could think of, Kojo decided she must have run downhill on the trail he had driven up. He climbed into the gray van, tossed his hood in back and drove recklessly down the trail in search of her. It was Sunday, July 1, 9:40 a.m.

🕐 HIGH IN THE vine-infested foliage of a gnarled tree the girl waited until the giant finally drove away, then climbed down. First she checked Martin and found he was dead. On an impulse, she searched his body. In secret pockets sewn inside a trouser leg, she found his bankrolls. She had been born in the islands and understood she must make her escape as soon as possible. Shrewdly, she left Cain's wallet on the body. She decided to wait for darkness, then make her way in the direction the van had driven to find a village. She would buy some clothing, then get off this godforsaken island.

It was Sunday, July 1, 9:47 a.m.

🕐 As BARKOW WALKED the road, he figured he had covered four miles. *The driveway to the Retreat should be coming up soon.* He had been told it was near a bend in the highway. As far ahead as he could see, there was no curve. Onward he trudged. He could walk all day if necessary, but the baker had told him four and a half miles. *He must have been mistaken.* The low drone of a car-engine came from behind and quickly increased as it approached. He turned and stuck his thumb out, but the gray van roared past, dodging potholes and broken asphalt. It was Sunday, July 1, 10:15 a.m.

UNDERSTANDING ACHIEVED

JULY 1, 2012, SUNDAY, 7:55 A.M.

STANDING IN THE monitor room Carrie looked at Jacques and said, "Kojo enjoys abusing people, women in particular. I never allowed myself to be alone with him."

"Some guys get pleasure from it," Jacques muttered.

Carrie's attitude changed. Her facial appearance became inflexible as rage and resentment intensified. She was furious with Barkow. He had failed to succumb to the drugs, and he was hunting her like common prey. The audacity of it goaded her anger to greater heights.

Her thoughts of Barkow reminded her again of her immediate problem and one possible answer. *Mary Cruthers... I'll give her to Kojo, let him take the fall if it ever becomes known what happened to her.* She turned the idea over, figuring the angles. *I hate that little bitch. Barkow's desire for her is the root cause of my failure to land him, and I want him so damn much it's driving me insane.*

Just visualizing Mary's suffering brought a twinge of sexual gratification. The memory of herself bending over the hood of the car flashed across her mind. She began to pant, slowly. "Jacques, follow me. There's a unique room I want to show you."

Jacques fell in behind her as she went down a short hall to a glowing green dial set into the wall. A door was open at the head of a stairway. She led the way down and into a dark room, where she activated a number of switches, some of which turned on muted red floodlights over several pieces of equipment.

"What the hell?" Jacques muttered. A cage was hung on chains that stretched from the darkness of the ceiling. It swayed in slight motion a few feet above the floor. He vaguely made out the shape of a person inside. "Carrie, come check this out."

Carrie flipped a few more switches and a cone of subdued, red radiance fell on the barred box. They both stared at the naked young woman. She lay on her side, weeping.

Carrie snapped, "What's your name?"

"Delsie!" She sobbed. "Please doan hurt me, Ma'am. I is a good girl."

"Who put you in this thing?"

"Mister Kojo lock me in, Ma'am." Her voice was rising in hysteria.

"Calm down, Delsie. We're not going to hurt you. Why did he do it?"

"I was out in the rain closin' de shutters like Mr. Kojo say to do, an' I see him go into the secret room an' look at the white lady on da TV.

"Do you work here at Axelwood Retreat?"

"Yes'm, I does." Delsie, now visibly trembling, stared at Carrie from one good eye.

"Jacques, bring this contraption down and get her out of it," Carrie commanded.

When Jacques lowered the cage and helped Delsie out, she stood with head bowed, one hand covering her private part, the other arm hung at an odd angle, her hair a tangled mass and her body covered with bruises and welts. One eye was swollen shut and discolored to greenish-yellow.

"Why are you naked, Delsie?" Carrie said.

"I had my blanket, but Mister Kojo tooked it away, Ma'am. My work dress was all wet from bein' in the rain. I only gots two dresses Ma'am, an' I dare not wear my white dress lessen' we gots company in de house."

"Did Kojo beat you, Delsie?" Carrie asked.

"Yes'm," Delsie whispered, almost inaudibly.

"He will not assault you anymore. Come upstairs and we'll get you some clothes," Carrie said as she turned for the stairway door. Delsie started to limp after her, but when putting weight on the bad knee she began to fall. Jacques swept her up in his arms and followed Carrie up the stairs.

In the living room, he placed her on the sofa. Carrie pulled a silk throw from a recliner and covered the girl. "Thankee kindly, Ma'am," Delsie said as a shiver brought a hard shudder.

"Jacques, go to the kitchen and heat up some soup," Carrie said. She turned back to Delsie. "When did you last eat?"

The girl had gone into shock and fainted.

They covered her with blankets and placed a pillow beneath her head. After Delsie roused, she managed to eat a bowl of soup and drink some tea.

They heard the roar of the engine as the gray van came charging up the shell-covered driveway and skidded sideways around the house. Kojo had the driver's door open, holding the remote. He jumped out as soon as it stopped. Half-running, he punched the button to raise the garage door.

Jacques growled, "What the hell is he trying to do, wreck the damn thing?" He glanced around for a weapon.

"Get ready for trouble," Carrie said. "Apparently he's pissed about something."

Jacques turned to a rack of billiard balls and accessories on the wall. He broke a cue in half, letting the tapered, leather-tipped end fall to the floor. Hefting the weighted butt like a club, he assumed a defensive position in front of Delsie.

They waited as the inside door to the garage opened and slammed shut. Kojo rushed into the room and slid to a stop, glaring at the three people.

"Why Delsie here? Delsie my slave. She be punished!" He stepped toward the sofa as Delsie pulled the covers over her head in an effort to hide herself.

"Stop, Kojo!" Carrie's sharp tone halted the giant in his tracks. "You do not *own* a slave. She is being sent home on my orders."

The spark of hatred appeared in the black man's eyes. He bared his teeth, turned in her direction and gathered himself to launch.

As he was about to spring, the weighted end of a billiard cue splintered across his forehead. He dropped to one knee, shaking his head as flashes of light exploded in the sudden brownout of vision.

Carrie stood before him, speaking in a loud voice. "Listen to me, Kojo. I have a gift for you. Something better than Delsie."

A throbbing pain filled Kojo's head, but the sound of authority cut through the pulsating bursts of anguish. He made out the Madam's face and turned to his assailant. Jacques was smiling. He held a pool ball in each hand, clicking them together, as he waited for Kojo to make his play.

Like a bull, Kojo propelled himself past Carrie and toward Jacques.

Jacques stepped back and swung his arms together, clapping a billiard ball against each of Kojo's temples with a dull thud. Kojo dropped like a hammered ox.

"Jacques!" Carrie gasped. "My God, you've probably killed him!"

Kojo lay face-down on the floor. Jacques bent and rolled the giant onto his back. A long, swollen bruise angled across his forehead from hairline to beneath one eye. Contusions were beginning to color each temple.

"He'll be all right," Jacques muttered. "Look at his eyes."

Only the whites were visible with the lower edge of the corneas showing. His eyelids batted up and down. "He'll have one hell of a headache though," Jacques chuckled.

"It's not funny, Jacques," Carrie said, trying to keep a smile from forming. "Put the girl outside in the van. Also, transfer our luggage from the Toyota. We're leaving as soon as Kojo understands what he must do."

"Anything else?" Jacques asked.

"Yes. Find out if she has any personal things she wants to take with her. She's going home and we're departing on our cruise."

Jacques helped Delsie to her feet and wrapped a blanket around her, and together they left the room. Carrie went to the kitchen and filled a large pot with water. She returned and poured part of it on Kojo's face, then set the remainder on the floor. He sputtered and with a drawn-out groan, put his hands to his head.

"Sit up, Kojo," Carrie commanded. He reeked of rum. "Do you want to die? You have to sit up or you *will* die."

He turned on his side and, after making several attempts, managed to achieve a sitting position. He grabbed the pot and gulped huge mouthfuls of water from the rim, then poured the rest on his head.

She spoke sharply. "Do you understand me, Kojo?"

"Kojo hear," he mumbled.

"We have taken Delsie away."

Kojo nodded.

"I am closing the Retreat in three days, understand?"

Kojo, now thoroughly aroused, said, "Why close?"

"You must leave by Thursday. You will get a severance payment."

"Kojo want stay!" he uttered fiercely.

"You cannot stay! I will give you twenty thousand dollars and the girl locked in the room.

"Why three day?"

"At that time a crew will come to destroy this retreat. By then you must be gone."

"Kojo stay here. Please, Madam," he said as tears rolled down his disfigured face.

"No! You must be gone in three days."

He held his hands over his temples and slowly began to rock side to side. "Kojo no leave, Madam."

She crouched beside him and spoke in a flat monotone. "You cannot remain in this building, Kojo, but after you deal with the woman in the bedroom, go to the town of Castries."

"Go Castries?"

"Find the bar named The Home Port. Talk to Billy Caruso."

"Billy Caruso… Home Port."

He'll give you ten thousand American dollars." She leaned closer, so her lips were next to Kojo's ear. "Billy will find a ship to take you to Jamaica. From there go to the town of Ocho Rios."

"Go Ocho Rios." Kojo nodded.

"Find the bar called The Bahamas Beauty. Ask for Benito. Tell him your name." She spoke in a stage-whisper. "He will give you the other ten grand and a place to stay until I call for you."

"Yes, Madam," Kojo whispered. "Kojo go Jamaica."

"Never say to anyone that you know me. Understand?"

"No tell," Kojo uttered.

"Repeat it Kojo," Carrie ordered in a baleful voice.

"Go Castries Home Port, ask Billy Caruso. He give money and ship Kingston. Go Ocho Rios, Bahamas Beauty, talk Benito."

"And?" Carrie demanded

"Leave in three day. No speak know Madam."

"Good boy." Carrie rose from her crouch, walked out of the building and got into the van.

Jacques started the engine. Carrie sat beside him and Delsie was curled on the back seat under a blanket. Dropping the shift into drive, Jacques gunned through the driveway curves and careened onto the highway. As they drove down Mon Repos, they passed a tall man tramping along with a steady gait, in the opposite direction. Carrie turned in her seat and looked back at the receding figure. "Barkow!"

DAY OF RECKONING

July 1, 2012, Sunday, 10:55 a.m.

THE GRAY VAN roared past Barkow, as he walked in the opposite direction. *Could that vehicle be from the Retreat? It passed me twice this morning.* He reached the driveway with its covering of crushed seashells and followed it to a clearing where a small red Toyota was parked before a stucco building. A sign nailed on a beam above the entrance read *Axelwood Retreat.*

Barkow stopped at the front door and listened. He tried the knob, found it unlocked, turned it and pushed the door open. The silence was broken by a muted shriek of terror in the depths of the building. Three sharp notes of caution burst in his brain.

Barkow heard distant, demented laughing as he entered a living room. A low, sorrowful theme in his mind began to rise in volume. He crossed a damp carpet where a pot lay on its side among the splintered remains of a pool cue. A mournful wail of despair resonated in the stillness, then a gasping intake of breath. Barkow followed the sound through the den and passage into the room of monitors.

From the base of a short stairway, indecent, psychotic chuckles drifted up. Barkow descended and peered into a room illuminated only with subdued red light. He slipped in like a jungle cat stalking its prey.

A gigantic shadow on a wall indicated movement. A hulking man-shape was bent over a long, low table. His hands roamed over the body of a naked woman confined to the apparatus. One hand caressed a breast. She was stretched full length from wrists to ankles.

As Barkow watched, the brute kneaded the soft, white breast, then squeezed. A dark nipple centered in its areola bulged out between his thumb and forefinger. He lowered his face, open-mouthed and closed his lips over the nipple.

Barkow crouched, muscles tense, on the verge of catapulting his body forward, but checked his leap, fearing the creature might bite and tear away flesh as he slammed into its body. A short whimper of despair erupted from the woman, joined by maniacal giggles gushing from the creature's slobbering lips. The huge man threw his head back and emitted a long, insane howl.

All caution vanished from Barkow's mind. He took three running steps and dove over the table, taking the burly man down. As they crashed to the floor, he rolled away, kicking his opponent in the head. He sprang to his feet and kicked three more times, delivering two broken ribs, a crushed knee and a dislocated jaw. A solid punch to the throat stopped the big man cold, and slamming his head against the floor put him to sleep.

Barkow loosened the straps holding the woman to the rack, then picked her up and carried her up the stairs. He slipped through the secret opening and out of the den to a sofa. Not until that moment did he realize she was Mary.

"My God, Mary! I'll *kill* that son of a bitch!" He covered her naked body with a sofa-throw lying nearby and held her.

After a long moment, she opened her eyes and started. "Where am I? What happened?"

In a soothing voice, he said, "Shh... you're all right now, Mary. Everything is okay now. You're safe and no one is going to hurt you."

Close to panic, she stared at him. "Who are you? Where am I? Oh, my God!" She exclaimed as her voice began to rise and words ran together. "That horrible black man! He... he...."

Barkow cradled her and quietly said, "Mary, listen to me. Everything's all right now. It's me, Barkow. You're safe now." As she burst into unreserved crying, he held her close and rocked back and forth, whispering words of comfort. Thinking to let her rest, he stood and carried her into Carrie's bedroom.

11:19 A.M.

Kojo came out of his unconscious state with a single thought. *I must get away from the demon that attacked me. It is God's punishment. God has sent a demon to kill me. God or Madam?* He could not utter a sound. The evil spirit had paralyzed his throat. His jaw hurt so much he was afraid to move it. He began to drag himself across the floor. At the stairs, he pulled his huge body upwards one step at a time, careful not to bend his damaged knee. Fear was his confederate. He watched for the demon through the eye that still functioned. He wormed himself with care, out of the stairway. His heart pounded hard as he dragged his massive body across the floor through the monitor room. *The demon might be lurking anywhere.* He forced his way through the secret passage and moved his body over the floor using one forearm to pull forward a few inches at a time. Kojo crossed the threshold into the central room. A low mumbling from the bedroom caused his bladder to release as fear paralyzed him. *The fiend is casting a spell on me! Is that why I am still alive?*

He cautiously began to inch out of the living room and across the tile floor of the kitchen, leaving a trail of urine and blood. He made his painful way out the open door onto a graveled walk. There he vomited bloody chunks. *The devil must have entered my body. Can this be the demon forcing its way out?*

He strained to pull his body across the gravel to the safety of the jungle. When he reached it, he continued to drag his useless leg and wriggle through the sour slime of the tropical forest floor until he finally passed out face-down in the marshy soil beneath a tree fern.

11:35 A.M.

Mary's crying slowly subsided as Barkow spoke quiet, gentle, calming words. Eventually she became quiet, enjoying the safety of Barkow's arms. Her senses returned and with them came the awareness that nothing was physically wrong with her. *I have been stripped naked and scared out of my wits, but not physically harmed. My joints ache, but otherwise I'm all right.*

Barkow used the comforter on the bed to cover her. "Are you all right, Mary?"

"I…. I think so," she murmured. "Are you really here? How did you find me? And where are we?"

"I found out they kidnapped you and I traced you to this place. I came to take you back to the States with me."

"You mean we're not in the United States? Where are we?"

Barkow looked about the room, noting the closet doors were open. "We're on the Caribbean island of Saint Lucia at a place called Axelwood Retreat. I'm sure this is Carrie Axelwood's bedroom. We have to get out of here right away."

"Yes, of course," Mary said. "But I need clothing before I leave."

"Do you think you can walk?"

"I think so."

"Okay. I need to check things out while you find something to wear. There are plenty of clothes in the closet. I'll be back in a short while. Don't leave this room."

The first thing he noted after leaving the room was the telltale signs of Kojo dragging his body through the room and across the kitchen. He found the vomit outside and followed the bloody trail across the gravel to the jungles edge. *Good riddance,* he thought as he walked back toward the Toyota. *Maybe I can hot wire this thing and use it to get out of here.* He yanked the driver side door open and looked inside. The keys were in the ignition. Barkow started the engine. The gas gauge indicated empty. He searched the garage and found three five-gallon cans of gasoline. One of them went into the gas tank of the car, and he carried the other two down to that strange room where he had rescued Mary.

Back in the bedroom, he found her sitting on the edge of the bed wearing a pair of jeans and a red shirt. She still looked a little stunned.

"Come on, Mary." He led her to the Toyota and helped her in. After buckling her shoulder strap, he said, "I'll be just a few minutes. Try to relax."

He closed the car door and returned to the house. Quickly and efficiently, he cased the building, room by room. When he came upon the set of rooms where Mary had been held prisoner, he knew what he wanted. He spied her purse on a coffee table. A quick check showed her passport, driver's-license and credit cards were there. He went into the bedroom and shoved a pair of sandals into the purse. In the living room, he took one of the candles from the chandelier that lay on the floor.

He broke the candle in half, pulled the wick out of the bottom section and discarded the wax. He made his way downstairs to the torture room. Five minutes later, he was back at the Toyota jamming his body behind the steering wheel as he tossed the purse in the back seat. The little red Toyota spun its wheels, kicking crushed seashells, dirt and dust behind as it rolled out of the yard, down the twisting driveway.

⊙ THE RED TOYOTA was three miles away when the burning wick melted the wax and burned its way into the pouring spout of the full can of gasoline. The explosion blew the basement to smithereens and when the floor burned through, the structure fell into the fiery pit to become more fuel for the flames. Within a few hours, the building ceased to exist. In the smoldering ashes laid charred metal frames of odd devices and kitchen appliances, all that was left of Axelwood Retreat.

Barkow's initial plan was to drive to Castries City and catch a plane back to NYC. The Toyota's engine sputtered and coughed its way to the village. They covered the nine miles into Dennery and drove straight to the baker's building where Barkow had eaten breakfast. The Toyota skidded to a stop as the baker came out of his door. He walked over to the car's open window and said, "Good afternoon, Mon. I see you were successful in rescuing the woman as you planned."

Barkow allowed a tight smile of satisfaction to draw across his lips as he acknowledged the baker. "Yes, my visit had a favorable outcome, but this car is about finished. Can you tell me the quickest way to get to Castries City?"

"Well, the Island Transport System is the only way, but the bus trip will not be available until tomorrow morning."

Barkow slapped the steering wheel. "Damn! There must be another way."

"There is. I know of a helicopter that has sometimes been used in cases of emergency for medical evacuation. The copter is privately owned and perhaps could be hired."

"That would be perfect. How can I contact them?"

The baker produced an Island phonebook. Barkow got the owner's number from a hospital in Castries and made arrangements. Within the hour, they were aboard the small helicopter, bound for the Castries City Airport.

By 6:15 p.m., Jacques and Carrie were onboard a flight destined for San Juan, Puerto Rico, to begin their cruise; Delsie, with five thousand American dollars, was at her parents' home at the southern end of Saint Lucia; Barkow and Mary were well into their flight to New York City; Kojo was curled in a fetal position deep in the jungles of Saint Lucia; and someone was making an anonymous phone call to tip off the Castries City Police that a body was located high on a ridge above a deserted cove near Dennery.

Part Three

TERMINATION

HOMEWARD BOUND

Aboard a plane bound for New York City, Mary was curled up with her head on Barkow's shoulder. They were hours into the flight and she was beginning to cast off the fear that had gripped her since Kojo had forcefully taken her from the rooms where she had been held prisoner.

Barkow looked at her. "How are you feeling?"

"Thank God you got there in time," she whispered. "That brute was going to kill me."

"All is well. We can buy clothes in New York and whatever else you need for the trip."

"Trip? What trip? I have everything I need in my apartment."

"You're going with me back to Phoenix, aren't you? So I can take care of you," Barkow said. "We'll rest a while, then take a long trip wherever you want. Paris, Tahiti, Florence, anyplace in the world."

"But my career," she said, confused. "I have to go back to my job."

"I have all the money we need. You'll never work again." He squeezed her tighter. "I love you Mary. I've loved you from the day we started that story." His voice dropped to a callous whisper. "I knew you'd come to your senses. That's why you searched for me."

Mary turned to look at him. "But Barkow, it's been over four years since that time. You know I've—"

"Hush," Barkow said. "Don't say it." His features and man-

255

nerism indicated her future had been agreed upon between them. "We are meant for each other. I know you had to wait until you were sure."

Mary pressed her face on Barkow's shirt as her mind began to consider what he was saying. *What is he thinking? He's a killer. I saw him try to kick that black man to death.* She began to understand. *I cannot live in Arizona.* She pushed away from him and sat up. She dared not look him in the face. "I need to go to my place and pick up some clothing and things. We should stay in New York a few days so I can straighten out some personal matters. That would be all right, wouldn't it?"

"Of course," Barkow said.

The speakers came to life. "This is the captain speaking. We are making our final descent into La Guardia. Flight Crew, prepare the cabin for landing."

They were the last ones to deplane following the other passengers up the enclosed ramp into the airport. Having no luggage, they caught a cab at curbside and taxied to her apartment.

"Please, sit down and relax," she said in a noncommittal voice. "I'm going to shower and put on some clean clothes." Barkow watched her walk out of the room.

"No problem, take your time," he said as he looked around the living room. Tasteful carpets covered hardwood flooring and costly furniture filled the area, lending a cozy, warm ambiance. A row of framed photos lined the mantel of the fireplace, side by side with some knick-knacks.

He wandered over and studied the pictures. One was of Mary wearing a black suit, sitting behind a polished desk. *Probably in her office*, Barkow thought as he picked it up. Next was a photo of Mary and another girl on the boardwalk. They were laughing and hugging. In yet another print, the same two were standing with an elderly man in front of a brass sign: *The New York Socialites Magazine.*

Mary went into the attached bathroom of her bedroom, turned on the shower and called Rusty on her cell phone.

"Hi, I'm back," she said as soon as Rusty answered the phone.

"Hi yourself, Honey. It is good to hear your voice. I missed you so much."

"Listen, Rusty, I really need you to come over," Mary said in a low voice. "First, let me explain quickly what has happened." As she began reciting all that transpired, her words came faster and faster until Rusty broke in.

"Hey girl, slow down. You're talking so fast I can't keep up."

Mary took a deep breath and forced herself to speak more slowly. When she came to the part of being in St. Lucia and held in a locked apartment, her words began to pile up one on another as she babbled with tears streaming down her face. Her voice rose amid the sobs until it became a near screech as she relived the episode with Kojo and Barkow, who had arrived just in time.

"I'm coming over right now," Rusty said.

"No! There is more." Mary almost shouted. "Barkow insists he is in love with me and plans to take me to Arizona," Mary said. "He's here in my apartment right now. Come over as quick as you can. I need you."

"I'll be there in twenty minutes," Rusty said and hung up.

Barkow waited on a leather couch, still holding the framed picture of Mary. He heard the sound of her voice once in the other room and knew she must have called someone. *She has been through a lot these past few days, h*e thought. *She's still in a state of shock. As soon as I get her back to Phoenix I'll hire the best therapist money can buy.*

Fifteen minutes later Mary came out of the bedroom, dressed in dark slacks and white blouse. She looked younger, fresh from a shower. She had brushed and pinned her hair back but applied no makeup. "I called Rusty, my best friend in the world to come over," she said.

"That's fine!" Barkow said evenly. "I'll be glad to meet your best friend. Come sit with me, please." He patted the cushion. Mary crossed the room and sat beside the man who had rescued her, knowing she owed her life to him. At that moment, a sharp rap sounded at the entrance and before anyone could move, the lock clicked and the door swung inward. Rusty stepped into the room.

REVELATION

MARY JUMPED UP. "Rusty!"

Surprised, Barkow also stood up and gazed at the striking redhead who stopped in the center of the room. High-heel cowboy boots, tight blue jeans and a tailored western shirt that threatened to erupt at the unbuttoned top. Long, dark red hair covered her shoulders in waves of shining luster.

Mary ran to the open arms of Rusty where they hugged and engaged in an extensive kiss. Barkow watched as they broke, but remained locked in a hug; Mary's back was to him, with Rusty looking over her shoulder. His expression of surprise faded as his eyes registered the determined stare from Rusty. Optimism deflated like a balloon with a slow leak.

A change in persona transformed Barkow's features into shadowed angles. Still holding her picture, he said, "Mary?"

She turned in the embrace to face Barkow, with Rusty standing behind her.

Barkow's eyes turned cold, lifeless, as the hurt of understanding transformed his features.

Seeing the change take place, Mary sagged against Rusty. Visions swirled through her mind: Barkow kicking Kojo as he writhed on the floor in hazy red light; Barkow slashing the throat of a sentry with a razor sharp trench knife.

Three sharp notes detonated in Barkow's brain, followed by total silence. In that infinite stillness, a distant drone approaching from far away merged into a vague rhythm. Growing more pronounced, the sound swelled into a cadence as it increased in volume and built to a roar, blocking all thought. Then the noise abruptly stopped and the world stopped turning. There was no echo, no emotion and no life. He was standing before a chasm, an endless drop into eternity, and teetering on a razor edge between stability and chaos as his world fell apart.

"I'm sorry," Mary said quietly.

Barkow glared as tears spilled over and coursed down his cheeks. Rusty stared at Barkow over Mary's shoulder. Her lips parted as she mimed, *She's mine.* Barkow staggered back from the brink as the picture fell from his hand. A sharp crack destroyed the silence when the glass shattered as it struck the floor. His eyes turned flat, cold, defeated. In the most difficult moment of his life, Barkow stumbled past the two women and out of their lives forever.

The only love he had ever experienced exploded like crystal on concrete. Sparkling shards flew in a thousand directions as his heart broke with the knowledge that Mary was forever gone from a secret place in his soul, where he had nourished and maintained his love. Mary—perfect, sweet Mary—no longer dwelled in that kernel of blind devotion.

Barkow lurched from the apartment building , stopped at the curb and dumbly waited for a cab, flagging down the first one.

"Nearest bar," he mumbled.

"Jackie's is a quiet place and it's only a few blocks, but I think they close at nine on Sunday," the driver said as he expertly swung into traffic and gunned the engine.

Distraught, Barkow stared out the side window. "It's okay." His brain sorted and cataloged each instant of time he'd spent with Mary Cruthers. He analyzed every thought pattern involving his mind-set for her and searched every possible avenue for a solution, a way to bring her to accept his desire and love him—and he found none. "Change of plans. Take me to the Ritz Carlton on 46th."

The driver swerved over to the inside lane and charged

through a green light then whipped back to the outside. Two blocks farther, he took a corner, tires squealing and roared up a ramp to the expressway. The taxi braked to a stop in the covered entry to the hotel nine minutes later. Barkow handed the cabbie a fifty-dollar bill and said, "Thanks for the ride." He opened the door and left before the driver answered.

Barkow's room was on the 28th floor and overlooked Central Park. He showered and shaved.

Afterwards in the dark hotel room, he let his mind wander. *She turned out to be so opposite from what I remembered. Has my love always been a one-sided affair that existed only in my mind?* "Apparently so," he said aloud as the next reflection came. *I can erase her from my world but not my memory.* He consciously examined every detail of his lost love, and eventually resolve arrived and with it came enlightenment. His inner compass had settled on a new heading and he recognized the course.

The next morning, he took a cab to a clothier's store and purchased a black suit along with enough accessories for a complete ensemble. He dressed in the fitting room and told the clerk to discard his boots and clothing, symbolic to him of discarding some of his past. From the store, he went to a coffee shop for food and the morning paper. Afterwards, he called Harold Goodfellow.

"Good morning. Great Metro Executive Offices. May I help you?"

"Good morning. G. B. Barkow calling for Mr. Goodfellow."

"One moment, please." He was put on hold.

"Good morning. This is Mr. Goodfellow's office. How may I help you?"

"Hello. G. B. Barkow calling for Mr. Harold Goodfellow."

"Thank you, Mr. Barkow. One moment, please."

When he had made the decision to leave Mary in the past, a substantial weight lifted from his soul. *That's the difference. I feel as if I've lost a hundred pounds.*

"Hello Barkow," Goodfellow said. "Are you in Phoenix?"

"Hi, Harry. Do you remember I said when things were wrapped up, we'd have lunch together?"

"That's right. Don't tell me you're in New York."

"Yes I am. Lunch is on me and I don't want to hear another word about it. This is your town, so you can select the spot."

"How about Delmonico's? It's trendy and pricey, but the food is good."

"Sounds perfect. What time?"

"I'll pick you up at one. Where are you staying?"

"I'm at the Ritz on 46th. I'll be in the lobby."

They rode in a chauffeured limousine, chatting of mundane sports items and business news. The driver pulled over and stopped at the entrance to Delmonico's. "Pick us up at three, Clarence," Goodfellow said to the driver as he got out. After being seated in subdued lighting with chamber music, they ordered lunch.

"I thought you would prefer this to the usual lunch crowd," Goodfellow said.

"Good plan."

"So what's new with you these days?"

"A number of things happened recently that started me thinking about a life-style change," Barkow said.

"Are you thinking of resigning?" Goodfellow said.

"Not entirely," Barkow said. "I wanted to run something by you. You know, Harry, I've always enjoyed working for you and your company. I have an excellent position, good pay and benefits. The problem is, many of the claims lack challenge. Any agent can handle them. A few are mysterious, with hidden facts that must be uncovered and information ferreted out. Often that involves matching wits with, shall we say, interesting people. Those are the claims that I enjoy working on."

"I see," murmured Goodfellow.

"I'm quite sure I will soon be the owner of a nightclub in Phoenix, which will take up some of my time. What would you think of me dropping my regular duties and only being called in on difficult cases? You can pay me on a case by case basis, say expenses covered and a fixed wage for time used." Barkow leaned back in his chair. "It would be less expensive for Great Metro and would free me up for some personal matters."

The waiter arrived with their lunch, placing plates of food before them. "I see no reason why it cannot be worked out," Goodfellow admitted as he snapped his napkin open. "The company and I are highly appreciative of the work you do for us on those cases that require a person of your abilities. I'll have a contract drawn up and sent for approval."

They fell to eating the exquisite food and drinking expensive wine as they discussed the key facts of employment conditions and delved into different situations that might come up.

ATTAINMENT

JULY 2, 2012, TUESDAY, 5:15 P.M.

AFTER LUNCH, BARKOW left New York for Phoenix and arrived that evening. After deplaning, he retrieved his car from the parking lot and drove directly to his penthouse. When he stepped from the elevator into the lobby, the door attendant, absorbed in his paperback novel, was behind the counter.

"Hello, Hank," he said.

"Hey, Barkow," the former cop exclaimed. "How ya been? What's new?"

"Not a lot, but I'm back in Arizona for a while." Barkow smiled. "Anything new happened or have any suspicious characters stopped by lately?"

"Only one guy was looking for you," Hank said. "Some kid named Larry Fitzsimmons, who claimed he wanted to thank you for your help. Said to tell you he received his payment and had a new gig at the Royal Playhouse, over in Tempe."

"Great," Barkow said. "I'm tired, so I guess I'll turn in. See you later, Hank." Barkow turned and started for the elevator.

"I'll be here," Hank said as he returned to his paperback.

Barkow arrived at his door and checked the toothpick. It was still pushed, broken end first, between the jam and door at the correct height, so he unlocked and stepped inside. A quick walk through the rooms showed nothing out of place. After a shave and shower, he relaxed in the den. A glass of ice with Blanton's mellow refinement took away the stress of the day and he was soon in bed for a night of uninterrupted sleep.

The next day was Tuesday, the third of July. Barkow had slept late, read the morning paper and watched the local news. *Tomorrow, the Metro office will be closed for the Fourth of July.* He thought and decided to call and ask Judy to lunch.

"Good Morning, Great Metro."

"Hi, Judy, Barkow here. How about a date for lunch today if you're not busy?"

"Sounds good. Where you want to meet?"

"I'll pick you up," he answered. "Twelve noon."

The black Mercedes sped through the midday traffic, eventually arriving at Van Dyke's Restaurant valet parking. They walked into the restaurant and were seated at a quiet corner table. A waiter took their order. While waiting for the food to arrive, Barkow said, "So how are things going with you?"

"Same ol', same ol'," She said. "It appears you're making some changes."

Barkow looked concerned. "Changes?"

Judy smiled. "I had a fax come through yesterday that said you are now a Great Metro Special Investigator and that you would only handle cases referred directly by the New York Executive Office but that you'll maintain an office here."

"Well now," Barkow said with a grin. "Harry got the ball rolling right away."

"So will you be coming into the office every day or what?"

"Actually, I only need to use the office on a very limited basis. I'll just keep the same one," Barkow declared. "About the only thing that will change is if they need something that cannot be handled by a regular claims adjuster. Then they'll call me."

"Good! I thought you were maybe moving to New York."

"Nope, you can't get rid of me that easily."

The waiter brought their meal on a cart and set their plates before them. "Will there be anything else?"

"Coffee later, thank you," Barkow said.

"Your face has healed nicely," Judy said as she looked closely at Barkow.

"Thank you, Ma'am."

"You seem in a pleasant mood," Judy said. "How did things turn out with Mary?"

"I found her. She chose to stay in New York at her job."

"That's odd," exclaimed Judy, sensing the implied reference that Mary had been asked to leave New York. "She seemed bent on finding you. What did she want?"

"She never told me," Barkow said as he became interested in his lunch.

Wisely, Judy did not press the matter. "Well it's good to see you back. I missed you."

⊙ THE NEXT DAY on the Fourth of July, Barkow drove to the Blue Note. It was 2:55 p.m. when he pushed through the blue beads into the lounge. Bobby was behind the bar and there were no other customers in the room. "Hi, Bobby," Barkow greeted. "How are things going since Bert quit the position?"

"Hey, Barkow. Been going good. I sold a few drinks I was not familiar with and had to look them up in a textbook."

"Textbook? Something you picked up someplace?" Barkow said as he took a bar stool.

"Oh no, not at all. I majored in Mixology in college and earned a degree as a mixologist," Bobby said with a laugh. "I have one of my text books here for reference."

Barkow grinned at him. "I didn't know you were college trained."

"Well," Bobby admitted. "It was an easy course with a degree. Now it's paying off. I hope I can work here as a regular bartender."

"I'm sure things will pan out for you," Barkow said. "Is Laura coming in for work today? I need to talk to her."

"Nope," Bobby answered. "I am only down here doing a little

cleaning up and just opened the place in case someone wanted a drink."

"I see," Barkow said as the beaded curtain into the lounge parted and Terry stepped in. "Hi Terry." He waved to her. "Good to see you again."

"Hey, Barkow. You look like your old self," Terry said as she went around to the back of the bar. Bobby met her and they hugged and kissed. "I'm just about ready to go, Honey."

"Well, well." Barkow grinned. "Looks like a couple of love-birds here."

Terry winked and Bobby hunched his shoulders. "We're going over to the fair grounds to watch the fireworks after dinner," Terry said. "You want to come with us?"

Barkow shook his head. "No can do. I have something else planned, but thanks for the invitation. I'll be on my way," he said as he slipped off the stool. "You two have fun tonight."

Barkow pulled the Mercedes out of the parking lot and as he drove he called Laura's home number. Her voice came mellow and soft over the speaker. "Hello?"

"Hello, Laura. Barkow here. I know it's a holiday and I don't want to butt into your plans."

"Not a problem," she answered quickly. "I don't have any plans."

Barkow smiled. "How about I buy you dinner?"

"That would be particularly friendly of you," she said. "And I have some information for you. You want to meet somewhere?"

"No. I want to pick you up at your place. What time?"

"Seven sharp. I'll be waiting."

"Until seven," he answered and hung up, feeling like a high school kid on a first date. He could not believe how utterly weightless he felt.

The black Mercedes rolled up to The Palms apartment complex at 6:55 p.m. Barkow parked and walked through the iron-gated arched entry into the foyer, then scanned the rows of name-buttons surrounding the single main speaker. He found Laura L. Logan's name and pushed her call button.

"Hello?"

"Hi. It's me," Barkow said, holding down the speaker button. "You ready?"

"I am. Would you like to come in for a few minutes? Perhaps a glass of wine?"

"That would be pleasant," he replied. "Which apartment is yours?"

"I'm in 246. Take the stairs from the foyer and turn left at the top."

"Be right up." He released the speaker button and in less than two minutes rapped on her door. It opened and there stood a vision of desire swathed in a pale jade cocktail dress.

"Please come in." She stepped back to hold the door open. The silken folds of lime pastel brought out the jeweled green coyness in her eyes.

Barkow stepped into the room and greeted her with a friendly embrace, then took a step back and gazed at her. The fragrance of gardenia hung in the air. "You look stunning," he said with a smile tugging at the corner of his mouth. "I should have brought flowers."

"You look especially handsome yourself," she said, looking directly at him as her lips formed the precisely pronounced words. "May I offer you a glass of wine? I have Merlot, Pinot Noir and Chardonnay."

"Merlot, please," he said with a slight nod.

Laura walked over to a highly polished roll-top desk. She slid the top upwards, over its curved track to conceal itself somewhere in the back. Barkow observed it was not a desk at all, but a truly clever reproduction piece that was, in fact, a liquor cabinet. She removed a bottle. As she walked from the room, she said, "I'll be right back. Make yourself at home."

Barkow gazed around the tastefully furnished room. It had a high ceiling, twelve feet above the floor with arched doorways leading off in several directions. Wall to wall tile covered the floor and formed baseboards. Leather furniture, a large screen TV, the liquor cabinet and a piano were arranged tastefully about the room. The desk cabinet had a built in stereo system. A beehive fireplace with a carved mantle of mesquite was set in one corner. He sat on a loveseat, sinking into the leather cushions. End tables stood at each side.

Laura returned with two goblets of dark red wine. Handing one to Barkow she sat down beside him and lifted her glass. "Salute," She said. They touched glasses with a clink and both took a sip. "So where are we going for dinner?" she asked. She had a way of slightly tilting her head, looking at him askance from pupils in the corners of her eyes.

"A place called Valentino's," he said. "Have you heard of it?"

"Oh yes, although I've never been inside."

"I'm sure you'll enjoy it. We have reservations for eight-thirty and the food is excellent." He took a sip from his goblet. "This merlot is first rate."

"I am glad you like it," she said. "By the way, I talked with the owner of the Blue Note. He is anxious to sell. Are you interested?"

"I'm definitely interested."

"When I asked his price, he suggested we have it appraised, split the cost and agree to the price being whatever the appraisal happens to be."

"That sounds reasonable," Barkow said. "Who picks the appraisal company?"

"The same thought occurred to me. He said it didn't matter to him, provided it was listed by the Better Business Bureau or a similar type of company that had a good reputation and references." Then she chuckled. "He's a very nice old man. He said we could work out payment arrangements if I didn't have the cash or wasn't able to finance it."

"You have been doing the books for the place. Does it turn a profit?"

"Yes, but a modest one. I believe with a little fixing up and advertising, it could double its income," Laura said.

"If I buy it, will you stay on?"

"I'd love to. Thanks!"

"What do you think of Bobby as a bartender?"

"He's young, but very personable and he has a pleasing way with the customers. I believe he's honest and wouldn't tap the till. One thing you should know is that Bobby and Terry have a thing for each other. Some owners don't want their employees having personal relationships on the side. Other than that, I think they're good people and I consider them both friends."

"Good. Your thoughts mirror my own. Thank you for being frank about it."

"Drink up," she exclaimed. "We have time for one more glass before dinner." Reaching for his wine glass she stood and went to the kitchen for refills. "There are some CDs by the stereo if you want to put on some music."

He went to the parlor grand in the corner. Touching the partially raised top, he ran a finger along its highly polished surface. Without turning, he was aware she had returned. The clean scent of gardenias had become noticeable.

"Did you find the CDs?" she asked, handing him a wineglass.

"I have a better idea," he spoke around a smile. "Why don't you play a song?"

She swept around him to the piano and, holding her glass out for him to take, sat down to the keyboard. Barkow turned, picked up a coaster from an end table and placed it on the ledge above the keys. He put her glass on it, as the simple melody of the introduction to "The Chains of Love" softly tinkled in the room. When the prelude faded to a slow, soft melody with a blue sound, it was soon accompanied by Laura's breathtaking rendition of the beguiling lyrics:

My chains of love are shackled to your heart.
Together we are bound eternally.

Your fate to pay the toll,
I own your heart and soul,
These chains of love will never set you free.
Each link within the chain is forged with love
And through the ages you belong to me.
My wish is your command,
And you must understand,
These chains of love will never set you free.

Barkow was transfixed, eyes closed, with a distant look about his features as he remembered his mother singing the same words. When the second verse ended, silence filled the room. In the stillness his eyes opened and settled on Laura at the keyboard, her eyes brimming with tears.

"My God, Laura! You sing like an angel. Where did you learn to put so much emotion in your voice?"

"I get choked up singing that song." She brushed away a tear. Barkow quickly handed her his handkerchief. She blotted away the tears as she tried to pull back from that emotional state, picked up her glass and drank deeply of the dark red wine. "I know all eight verses but sometimes I can't get through them without breaking down."

"I've never heard a better version than the one you just sang," Barkow said, still fascinated. "It's my favorite song and has been all my life." He sat down on the bench and put his arm around her, pulling her to him. "God, Laura, you sing beautifully."

"Oh come on, Barkow, it's time to go to dinner," she murmured against his shoulder.

On the way to Valentino's he asked her to find an appraisal company and have the owner approve it, then have them write up a joint agreement between himself and the owner. "By the way, what's the owner's name?"

From her tiny clutch bag, she produced a business card. "His name is Gary Noteaboone. He is eighty-six years old and looks like a wizened elf."

Barkow and Laura dined in a section of the restaurant raised higher than the dance floor. A three-piece band with the melancholy whine of a lone trumpet moaned a bluesy sound only that instrument can give.

"May I have this dance?" Barkow asked.

She smiled, nodded and rose from the table.

He led her to the dance floor and, hand in hand, they walked across to the musicians. Barkow held up a fifty-dollar bill to the bandleader and requested "The Chains of Love" by solo trumpet. As they slow-danced around the darkened floor, both realized something was beginning, yet neither spoke of it.

During dinner Barkow assured her, he would purchase the Blue Note.

"I will rename it *Barkow's Blue Note,*" he said. "Laura, I very much want you to stay on and both play the piano and sing. I would also like you to take the position of General Manager of the club. You'll have total control. A major increase in salary will begin with the job," he assured her. As they spoke about the business, he mentioned remodeling the building to add new restrooms, a storage room and two offices, one for each of them.

"I absolutely hate those little chairs," he said with a grimace. "We'll hire a decorator to come in and suggest furniture and decor. You will be in charge."

Small lines of concern appeared as her features became businesslike. "In charge of what?"

"Everything," he said with a sly smile.

AN EVENTFUL FOUNTAINHEAD

July 10, 2012, Tuesday, 10:30 a.m.

THE MONTH OF July sped past in a blur as events piled one upon the other. Barkow and Noteaboone struck a deal on July 10th. The building, land and business, after being purchased, officially became *Barkow's Blue Note Nightclub* on July 16, 2012. The nightclub was remodeled to specifications and completed on September 17, 2012. Barkow, Laura, Bobby and Terry were sitting at the bar having a celebratory drink at the end of that day.

"Everyone is invited to dinner tonight, on me," Barkow announced. "We've been closed down for two months and the new furnishings will arrive on Monday, October 20th. That will give us almost two weeks to prepare for a grand opening on November 1st." A cheer went up as they lifted their glasses to Barkow.

September in Phoenix is a beautiful month. Warm pleasant days in the valley of the sun and cool nights filled with blazing stars that seemed so close you could pick them like apples from a tree. The dinner took place at a Four Seasons Hotel. As dessert was being served, Barkow tapped his wine glass for attention.

"I want each of you to know how grateful I am to have such dedicated people working for me. If for any reason you wish to talk with me about anything, please consider me a friend as well as your employer. My door is always open to those I call friend." He smiled. "I believe you know Laura is the General Manager of Barkow's Blue Note. She is your first choice in discussing matters concerning the business. She has full control of hiring and firing. I consider the three of you to be friends. I look upon you as family. Now, I hear the band playing in the ballroom, so let's finish dessert and then go relax for a while."

After dancing with Laura and Terry a few times, Barkow sat with Laura, as Bobby and Terry were dancing on the shadowed floor.

"I've been thinking," Laura said. "You've shelled out a lot of cash since purchasing the club and remodeling it. You even bought all new club furniture and office equipment."

"What about it?" Barkow answered with a smile, noting Laura had a concerned look on her face.

"I know you want a grand opening. Will you give me a budget amount to arrange it?"

"Use your own judgment, Laura. I want it to be special, but not gaudy."

"Special, but not gaudy, eh?"

"Yeah. I trust your judgment. Please do whatever you think works."

"What makes you think I know anything about special and gaudy?"

"Because, Laura," he said, looking directly into her eyes. "You are special… but not gaudy."

For Barkow, the following two weeks went by in a blur. Laura seemed to be everywhere at once. In her office on the phone, then huddled behind the bar discussing bar stock with Bobby, later talking in low voices with Terry that was quickly hushed when Barkow came by.

The back bar was set up in concave tiers of steep steps built completely from mirrored glass. It filled an arched area that covered half of the north wall. A series of directional lights recessed in the curve of the arch, cast a warm, golden glow down on the mirrored steps and the huge assortment of bottled alcoholic beverages. As a centerpiece, a recessed box lined in light-blue tinted mirror, held an oversized bottle of **Blanton's Single Barrel Bourbon**, one of the world's best bourbon whiskeys: a gift from the **Blanton's Distilling Company** in Frankfort, Kentucky.

Thick, lush carpet covered the seating area where small tables with comfortable upholstered chairs awaited customers. A small polished wood dance floor curved around a raised concert grand piano centered in the northwest corner and again around a table for two, also raised and separated from the others. That table displayed a bronze *Reserved for Management* plaque. A dim glow of soft blue light filled the entire room with only the back bar area in mellow white light. They all agreed everything was finished; Barkow's Blue Note Nightclub was ready to go into business.

"I need to make a few notes in my office and then I'm heading home," Laura said.

Bobby took a final look across his well-stocked bar. "Come on Terry, let's cut out," he said as he shut down the bar and turned off the lights. Bobby and Terry came over to Barkow and said they were ready to leave. Putting an arm over the shoulder of each, he walked them out, thanking them for their help. Barkow said goodnight to both, locking the back door after them. Like magic, he transformed from being a man in control of his life and everything in it, to one of wavering indecision. The lights were all out except for a lone night-light at the bar and the outside lights over the parking lot. In the silence of the empty club, Barkow suddenly felt nervous and alone. He took a bottle of Blanton's Single Barrel Bourbon and a glass from the back bar, placed them on the bar and sat on one of the barstools. Somehow, he felt defeated and deflated at the same time. Realizations of truth began to pound in his brain. He poured the glass half-full and took a long swallow. His past boiled up around him like a cloud of thick smoke, drawing, pulling and trying to drag him into the dark clutches of depression. His business with Carrie, still on her cruise, was not settled and hovered in the back of his mind. Mary was forever gone into his past. He drank the remaining bourbon without tasting it. Using iron will, he forced his mind to reject the magnetic pull of taking action. He could have easily thrown a chair through a window or smashed his fist into a wall.

Something he had been putting off until now had to be

done. Without knowing why he suddenly stood up and grabbed the bottle in one hand and the glass in the other. Behind the bar, he washed the glass and replaced the opened bottle of Blanton's in the rack with other opened bottles. He walked slowly through the darkened club, making his way between tables to the single door marked *Private*. He entered the tiny hall, but didn't stop at his office door. He knocked on her door.

"Yes?" she called. "Come in."

"Hi," he said from the open doorway. "Are you about done for the day?"

"I'm out of here in two minutes."

"If you have a minute, I'd like to talk."

"Sure. What's up?"

He stepped inside and took the chair in front of her desk. "I've been thinking."

"About what?" she said, seeing the concerned set of his features.

"Us."

"I see," she said. "And what about us?"

"I want to tell you some things about me," he said. "I want you to know where I'm from. I have a feeling I've known you for years and realistically that just can't be—"

"You have, Barkow. You have known me for years, ever since you were discharged from the Army, and I love you, Barkow. I think I've loved you from the time I first met you and took you to my apartment."

"Your apartment?" he said, confused by the softness of her voice and the retreating volume of music in his brain.

"When you were discharged from the Army, you almost killed yourself drinking rot-gut bourbon in that LA dive where I was a barmaid, learning to play the piano for a bar crowd. I know most of your story, and together we can work through anything."

He stood up and pulled her from the chair. Holding her close, he said, "My God, Laura, you really love me?"

"Of course I love you. I have been so afraid you might not be able to love me," she sighed.

His eyes had returned to their familiar, soft gray steel. "Maybe, Laura, just maybe I *could* love again.

The music had dwindled away. It no longer played in his mind.

EPILOGUE

A WRIT WAS ISSUED from the Maricopa County Coroner's Office, regarding an official inquiry into the murders of Ronald Livingston, alias Rollo and Brandon Mitchell, alias Butch.

Barkow was summoned to give his deposition to a Maricopa County ADA prior to appearing before the Coroner's Jury at 9:00 a.m., December 3, 2012. Identical summons had been sent to everyone having a connection with the happenings at Axelwood Laboratories.

⊘ JACQUES AND CARRIE departed Puerto Rico aboard a cruise ship in a first-class four-room suite on the penthouse deck. They dined at the captain's table or in privately catered dining rooms. They cruised the Caribbean Sea to Rio and then south around Cape Horn to Easter Island, French Polynesia, Fiji, New Zealand and Australia. Carrie and her companion lived a life of luxury. From time to time, she made contact with a private personal computer. It was located in a London security vault, guarded by three heavily secured firewalls with various passwords required. She knew the outcome of the coroner's jury before the summons reached the ship in Sydney, Australia. On arrival in Christchurch, South Island of New Zealand they had taken a flight to Rome. Their plan was to rejoin the ship at some future port-of-call on the cruise.

Occasionally, Carrie's thoughts returned to Barkow. *We are not finished yet, Cheri. I almost killed you with drugs and perhaps I should have, but I do love you, Barkow and I will have you... one day, one way, or another.*

⊘ A HUGE HAITIAN refugee stumbled into *The Home Port* bar in Castries, St. Lucia. He spoke incoherently because his lips had been badly smashed; in the process of healing they were covered with scabs. He had a dirty rag tied around his head, covering one eye. He staggered with legs held apart and torso bent sideways, because of the great pain in his side.

"Elly Kusso," he mumbled.

A person at the bar spun his stool around and faced the battered man.

"Man, you one sorry looking dude," he said as he slid off the stool to stand in front of Kojo. "With a face like that you ain't going to find no Elly in here." He laughed.

"Elly Kusso," Kojo said.

"Go on, Fatso." The customer gave him a shove. "Get the hell out of here before I throw you out."

Kojo slapped the side of the man's face so hard he stumbled sideways and fell down. "Elly Kusso!"

The bartender came out from behind the bar and said. "Speak slowly, who are you looking for?"

"Kusso," Kojo said very slowly.

"Oh, I got it," the barkeep said. "You want Caruso... Billy Caruso. Right?"

Kojo slowly nodded. "Elle Kusso."

When Billy realized he was Kojo, he was taken by ambulance to an emergency ward and treated for his wounds. He was later admitted to a hospital for further treatment. Billy made a call to a private number and left a message: *Kojo arrived Home Port 8-27-2012 in bad shape. Now in hospital. When able, will send him on as ordered. Billy.* The message went to a private computer in London which recorded date and time and then archived into a database.

Approximately two months later, a second message arrived at the same computer. *Kojo arrived Bahamas Beauty 10-30-2012. All orders completed, Benito.*

CHAINS OF LOVE

Song Lyrics by A. J. Hoagland

My chains of love are shackled to your heart.
Together we are bound eternally.
Your fate to pay the toll,
I own your heart and soul,
these chains of love will never set you free.

Each link within the chain is forged with love
and through the ages you belong to me.
My wish is your command,
and you must understand,
these chains of love will never set you free.

An ancient heartbeat rhythm in your breast,
like jungle drums across a purple sea.
Resistance now will fall,
answer you will my call,
these chains of love will never set you free.

When e'er your heart is screaming to be held
and love is just an aching agony.
My arms will open wide
and hold you safe inside,
These chains of love will never set you free.

When e'er you see life through a veil of tears
and need a place of refuge come to me.
I'll drive away your fears
and kiss away your tears,
these chains of love will never set you free.

When bound in love and begging for the pain,
your torment stretched unto the last degree.
I'll soothe away your fears
and kiss away your tears,
these chains of love will never set you free.

Sometime within the future when we part
and thinking then you've seen no more of me,
into your thoughts I'll creep,
in dreams when you're asleep,
these chains of love will never set you free.

A time will come when you are gray and bent
and I am but a faded memory.
I'll call from outer space,
a smile will cross your face,
these chains of love will never set you free.

Chains of Love

Music & lyrics by A. J. Hoagland

My   chains of love are   shack-led to your   heart.

To-geth-er   we   are   bound   e--ter----nal---ly.

Your fate to   pay   the   toll;   I   own your heart and soul

(1)These chains of love   will   ne-ver set you   free.
(2)These chains of love will (rit) Ne--ver set you   free.
(ritard & slow to end)

ACKNOWLEDGMENTS

WITH HEARTFELT THANKS to my publisher, Sam Henrie, president of Wheatmark, and all the team members involved who were both friendly and helpful. Special thanks to Grael Norton, Wheatmark's acquisitions manager and a senior faculty member of the Authors Academy, Atilla Vekrony who redesigned my website and Lori Leavitt my account manager. It would be remiss not to mention the Green Valley Writers Forum, a critique group who gave sage and thoughtful advice.

CPSIA information can be obtained at www.ICGtesting.com
Printed in the USA
LVOW08s0136060214

372442LV00004B/288/P